# Death and Daffodils

# Death and Daffodils

LM Terry

## Dedication

To my gentle giant. You carried me high for the first years of my life so it's no surprise I've had my head in the clouds ever since. You never gave up on me, even when you should have. Thank you for that. I wish I had an ounce of the strength you had. I'm trying…and right now that's all I can promise.

# Table of Contents

# Native American Prayer

*I give you this, one thought to keep.*

*I am with you still, I do not sleep.*

*I am a thousand winds that blow,*

*I am the diamond glints on snow,*

*I am the sunlight on the ripened grain.*

*I am the gentle autumn rain.*

*When you awaken in the morning's hush,*

*I am the swift uplifting rush...*

*of quiet birds in circled flight.*

*I am the soft stars that shine at night.*

*Do not think of me as gone ~*

*I am with you still, in each new dawn.*

# Prologue

Death is knocking at my door. Not figuratively. Death is literally standing on my porch patiently waiting for me to open the door for him. I peek out the curtains, shivering at the site of the man who is here to end my miserable existence.

My story is about to end. So, I guess I should go back to the beginning. Back to a time when my life was seemingly perfect. Now it's nothing.

### Two Years Earlier

### Mia

"Hey, Mia, do you work Thursday?" my colleague, Chelsea, yells out to me as I head to my car.

"Yep, see you then." I pick my way through the parking lot, trying to remember where I parked. These twelve-hour shifts are killing me.

"Make sure to soak your feet when you get home and make that hubby of yours rub your back." She waves one last time before ducking into her car.

I roll my eyes. Yeah, Darrin rub my back? Fat chance. I'm sure his nose is buried in a case. Not that I'm complaining. This is what we came to the big city to do. We came here to make all our dreams come true and part of that is excelling in our chosen professions. He as a big city lawyer and me as a nurse. Everything is going according to plan. So, while he may not give me the attention I'm currently craving, he is doing exactly what we came here for.

I squeeze into my car pulling the seatbelt over my swollen belly. The tiny baby growing inside kicks. "I know, I know, we need to eat don't we, baby?" I whisper, giving my tummy a quick rub. As I'm backing out I notice a man slumped over his steering wheel near the back of the lot. "Hold on, sweet baby, we better go make sure everything is okay. Then it's cheeseburger time, I promise."

I drive over to park in the empty spot near the man's car. As I'm dragging myself out I see he's noticed me. When I approach his window, I see blood. A lot of blood. "Shit!" I rip open the door. "Sir, it's okay. Everything is going to be okay." As my phone rings 911, I grab my first aid kit and wrap a tourniquet around each arm to help stop the bleeding.

"Stop! What are you doing?" the man moans, doing his best to prevent me from applying pressure to his wounds. "Don't you get it? I want to die."

"Today you want to die, tomorrow might be a different story. Please let me help you. I'm a nurse. Help is on the way," I say in my calm, soothing professional voice. The man has lost a lot of blood and is no match for me at this point, so I continue my ministrations to save his life.

His head lolls to the side. "Let me go. I want to go."

"I'm sorry I can't do that. Everything will be okay, sir. Nothing is bad enough to take your own life," I tell him as I keep pressure on his wounds. The emergency staff is headed out now. Hopefully he makes it. Thank god I noticed him.

He leans forward in his seat so that his face is inches from mine. "If I live because of you, I will hunt you down and rest assured my next attempt at this will be successful and you will be coming along with me."

I back away as the staff loads him on a stretcher, hauling him inside. I follow them but turn once inside to head to my locker for a change of clothes. I don't have one ounce of energy left. I haven't eaten since eleven this morning and now it's well past eight in the evening. I should call Darrin to come get me. As I shed my bloody scrubs I think about what that man said to me. Most of the time people want to be saved. This was my first encounter where someone begged me to let them die.

After dressing I call Darrin. When he picks up it's all I can do to speak, I'm so tired. "Hey, can you please come get me. It's been a rough day and I'm beat."

"Really, Mia? I'm in the middle of putting my closing argument together. It's only a thirty-minute drive, babe."

I sigh. "Okay, I guess I can make it. See you soon."

"Hey, can you pick up some milk on your way home? Oh, and coffee. Got to go, this is some of my best work yet!" he says excitedly and then click…dead air.

Great.

I love his enthusiasm over cases, really I do. But, I would be lying if I said I wasn't disappointed. I'm dog tired. Oh well, just a little longer. Soon my head will hit the pillow and I can sleep all the way till Thursday. I make a quick stop by the ER to check on the man who attempted suicide in the parking lot. Looks like he's going to be okay. If I hadn't gotten to him when I did he would have been a goner.

I get back to my car as it starts to downpour. I look up and yell at the sky, "Really! You've got to be kidding me!" Darrin will have to go without milk and coffee. I'm pooped. I just need to get my butt home. The rain continues to come down hard, making it hard to see the lines on the road.

So, tired.

My eyes blink and I smack myself a few times to stay awake.

Two more miles, just two....

more....

miles....

# Chapter One

**Mia**

"You ready?" the guard asks holding the door to my cell open.

"Yeah, I guess." After folding my orange jumpsuit, I set it on the cot that has been my bed for the past year. I take one last look at the tiny space. I can't help but be disappointed. This was supposed to have been a punishment. It didn't feel like one.

"We're going to miss you around here," the guard says. "You are the only one who doesn't give us any gruff."

My only reply is the shrug my shoulders.

"Seriously, Mia, I hope you find yourself again. Life does exist after this you know?"

"Sure." I follow him through the building until he we reach the officer who will give me my papers and belongings. The outside world lying just beyond the door.

He pats me on the back without another word as I sign my release papers and then the lady officer hands me a bag. "You're free to go. Good luck, Mia."

"Thanks," I mumble and then stumble out into the bright sunlight. As soon as I'm outside I slide down the brick wall. I don't want to be out here. Here in a world where everyone I care about no longer resides.

I look in the bag and just like Darrin promised I find a plane ticket, a change of clothes, and an envelope with enough money to get home. Nothing else. I guess I don't know what I was expecting. This was our arrangement. Exactly what I asked for in the divorce. It's all I need.

A cab pulls up and I drag myself off the ground. Time to go home. I'm so tired. A tired that never goes away. It never will…until I get home. *Once I'm home I can end it.* It's this thought that makes me keep moving forward. Soon, soon I can sleep.

On the flight home I allow my mind to wander through the events of the past two years. The wreck, the trial, the divorce, the deaths. My hand subconsciously roams over my empty womb. No tears come anymore. I'm bone dry. I'm nothing. A walking zombie. There's nothing left. Only my beating heart, scattered thoughts, and nothing else.

It's almost over I remind myself. In the beginning I'd hoped that the punishment I received, my sentence, would somehow reset me. It didn't. A year in a cell was nothing. I suffered more in my head than in reality. Everyone was nice to me, including the other inmates. They all felt sorry for me.

# Death and Daffodils

Even the judge who sentenced me. He called me into his chambers and all but begged me to take the deal the prosecution was offering. Plead to lesser charges and get six months' probation. I told him I wanted the maximum punishment. "Mia, you were pregnant and overworked. You're not a bad person. Please take the deal," he had said to me. In the end I was charged with misdemeanor vehicular homicide and only given one year in county. Not enough. Nothing would have been enough.

I'm sure you have guessed what happened the night I drove home from the hospital. I fell asleep and woke up in a nightmare. One that hasn't ended. I was placed in an induced coma for many weeks to let my body heal from the trauma. The physical trauma would be nothing compared to the mental anguish I would suffer. I woke up to death, death and more death.

Only one person came to visit me, my dad's best friend, Thomas. He came once. He told me about my parent's accident. Told me he would look after things and that he had hired an attorney to represent me. It was the only time I saw him. He wrote to me many times over the past year, but I never opened any of the letters. I refused to even touch the envelopes and had them all returned to sender. Why? Because, nothing matters.

My attorney set Thomas up as my power of attorney which officially ends today. My attorney visited me once a month after Thomas realized I wasn't going to read any of his correspondence. He rattled on about leasing out my parent's land, fixing a well, replacing the roof due to a bad hailstorm. Things that really didn't matter to me. And, I guess the land isn't my parent's anymore…it's mine…for now. I should have asked the attorney to write out my will. Shit, why didn't I think of that? Will a handwritten one be enough? It doesn't matter. It's what I'll do. I'm leaving everything to Thomas.

I wait until everyone exits the plane before I leave my seat. I watch as a young couple struggle with their carry-on luggage and the toddler who has been crying for the last thirty minutes of the flight. I wonder what the family I killed would be doing right now if I hadn't fallen asleep behind the wheel. Would they be taking their little girl on vacation? Would they be home snuggled up watching Disney movies? If I hadn't fallen asleep what would I be doing with my own little girl? My angel baby, Erelah. Would Darrin and I be watching her toddle around our townhome?

"Miss? Is everything okay?" a stewardess asks, ripping me from my fantasy.

"Yeah, sorry," I answer, grabbing my plastic bag from the compartment above me.

I'm headed to get a rental car when I spot my dad's old blue Chevy pickup outside the glass windows in the pickup line.

"You didn't think I'd come to welcome you home?" a gruff voice rumbles behind me. I slowly turn to see Thomas, hands in his pockets and trademark smirk on his face.

"Hey," I whisper.

"Come here, darlin," he says.

Reluctantly I take a few steps towards him. He reaches out, pulling me into his arms. This is awkward. It's been so long since someone hugged me. He doesn't seem to care I'm uncomfortable. "Welcome home." He kisses the top of my head and then leans back, trying to get me to make eye contact with him.

I avoid his gaze, dropping my eyes to the ground. "You didn't have to come. I was going to rent a car," I tell him sullenly.

# Death and Daffodils

He chuckles and steers me out the door, pointing us in the direction of my dad's truck. "I thought you might like to take a ride in ole' blue. I'll give you the scenic tour. I warn you though, not much has changed."

What's he talking about? Everything has changed. He opens the passenger side door for me. As I climb in I notice my dad's work gloves. They are still on the dashboard where he used to toss them after a long day working on the farm. I swallow the lump that is slowly forming in my throat.

We drive in silence, well except for the old-time country music playing on the radio. My eyes are glued to the window. It's early spring and everything is just starting to turn green. Spring, a time for new beginnings. Not for me though, this is the season for my end. Evidently I sigh out loud because Thomas reaches over and takes my hand in his.

"I know this isn't easy, darlin, but you'll get through it." He shakes my hand, trying to get a response out of me.

"Sure," I say, focusing my attention back to the window.

After several hours on the road I notice we missed our turn to the farm. "Where are we going?" I ask.

"There's no food at the house. You need to eat, and I need to check on things at the bar. Two birds one stone."

"I'm not hungry. Could you drop me off before you head to town?"

"No," he says.

"No?"

"No," he answers adamantly.

"I'm not hungry and I want to go home."

"Eat and then I'll take you."

I thump my head back against the seat. Great, just what I wanted to do. I want to be home. I don't want to eat and I sure as hell don't want to see anyone. It's a Monday evening so I'm praying for the bar to be empty. The town has exactly four businesses. The bar, store, gas station and post office. That's it. There aren't even any traffic lights here.

When we get to the Tipsy Cow…yes that's the name of his bar. Anyhow, when we get inside he points to a stool at the far end of the bar. Hesitantly I glance around. All eyes are on me. I'm sure I've been the talk of the town. Homecoming Queen turned murderer. All in the blink of an eye. I take the seat and let my hair fall over the side of my face, shielding me from the stares.

"Want a beer?" Thomas asks, taking the seat beside me.

"No, thank you."

"Dina, two beers, burgers and fries," he yells down to the lady tending the bar.

"Sure, thing boss," she replies, winking at him.

He chuckles and leans over to tuck my hair behind my ear so that he can see my face. "We've got a lot to talk about, seeing as you haven't been accepting any of my letters."

"What's there to talk about. Mom and Dad are dead. My baby is dead. I killed a family of three and Darrin divorced me. End of story."

"That's the past. Let's talk about the future."

10

I grimace. The future? There is no future but, he can't know that. "Do we have to talk about it right now?"

"No, but I want you to be thinking about where you go from here," he says as Dina shoves two bottles in front of us.

"Sure," I whisper, taking a sip of the beer I didn't want.

"You could continue to lease out the land or you could think about hiring a few hands and farming it yourself, unless you don't have any intention of sticking around here. I'll help in any way I can, darlin. I just need to know what you're thinkin." He tosses back half his beer in one swallow.

The answer to that question is easy, it's the latter. I have no plans on sticking around. "I don't know," I simply answer.

"No hurry, hon. The leases don't expire for a few months. I'm just going to need you to start talking to me."

"Thomas, I appreciate all your help. Really I do. But, I'm not your problem. You have your own life. You shouldn't waste it worrying about me."

"Waste it?" He laughs and continues, "Haven't I always been there for you? Why would I stop now?"

"Because dad is gone and I'm not worth it."

He looks up at the ceiling for a minute like he's asking the heavens for an answer on what to do with me. When his gaze returns to me he just shakes his head. He turns as Dina brings out the burgers. "Change of plans, sweetheart. We're going to need those to go. I need to get this girl home."

Dina winks at him again before turning to swing her ass for his viewing pleasure. When she returns with our supper Thomas tosses the rest of his beer back instructing me to do the same. Yuck, I've never been much of a beer drinker, but I do as he asks and then he ushers me from the bar.

We make the trip out to the farm in complete silence. I'm feeling slightly buzzed from the beer. It's been a long time since I've had any alcohol in my system. He pulls up in front of the house, shutting off the engine. The house is dark, everything is dark. This is the first time I've been home since I left for college. That was ten years ago. Thomas takes my hand and drops the keys to the truck in my palm. "Ready, to go in?" he asks.

I nod, having to swallow that damn lump down again. He goes in ahead of me to turn on the lights. The minute I step inside the kitchen I sense the loss of my parents. My head knows they're gone but my heart was expecting to see them here. My mom at the stove and my dad sitting at the table reading to her. My eyes roam, stopping at the empty dog dish. "Where's Timber?"

Thomas sets our burgers on the table, avoiding my gaze. "I wrote to you," he pauses, gathering the courage to look me in the eye. "I had to put him down. He was old, Mia. He couldn't walk anymore. He went peacefully."

"I see," I say, lowering myself into the chair he pulls out for me.

"I'm sorry."

"No, no, don't be sorry. I'm sorry you've been left to deal with everything." I thought my tears had dried up, but I feel them now. One leaks out, slowly rolling down my cheek.

He sits down next to me and reaches over to wipe my tear away with his thumb. "Listen, I want to talk to you about what you said at the bar. I'm not here because your dad was my friend. I'm here because of you, Mia. You're like a daughter to me. I would've liked to have had kids of my own but there is no woman on this planet who could put up with my shit long enough to produce a child. You, you are my only family now."

I chew on my lip. Don't listen. Don't listen to him. Don't let him guilt you into staying. I can't stay. Not for him. Not for anyone. "You have Dina," I offer.

He laughs loudly and slaps the table. "Dina is a tease, darlin. God, I've missed you, kid. It's good to have you home. Now eat." He points to my burger. I manage to get half of it down. After he is satisfied that I've eaten enough he helps me clean up.

"Maybe I should stay with you tonight being it's your first night back." He rubs the back of his neck, looking a little unsure of what to do next.

"No, I'll be fine. I'm tired. I'm just going to go straight to bed anyhow."

"You sure? I need to go lock up the bar, but I can come right back."

"No, you've done enough for me." I push him towards the door.

He spins around before I can close it on him. "Mia, you call me if you need anything, you hear?"

"Yes, I hear."

I watch as he heads to his truck. He stops in the driveway and glances back at me. I offer him a small smile and wave. He sighs but gets in and fires it up. My eyes follow his taillights, clouded by dust, all the way down the road until I can't see them any longer.

Finally, the moment I've been waiting for…time for me to go.

# Chapter Two

## Mia

Twenty different pill bottles. Let's see which ones will kill me. Nope, not this one. What about the little blue ones? Um, no, definitely not these. Christ, there are certain things you should never know about your parents. Some of these might do the trick but, I don't know if there are enough of any of them. I look at the bottles, a few used for patients with cancer. Most of them are prescribed to my dad. I wonder why he had them.

Shit, I didn't want to leave a mess but maybe shooting myself would be easier. I could lay out a tarp or something. I know, I'll do it outside, yeah, that sounds like a good plan. I turn the light on to the basement and head down to my dad's office. His gun cabinet is empty. What the fuck? I search around and come up with nothing. Ugh. Thomas must have taken them.

# Death and Daffodils

*Think Mia. A million people a year do this successfully. It can't be that hard.*

I'll hang myself. That's it. I wander around the barn finding everything I need. I drag the ladder out to a tree I think will work best. I'm standing on the ladder tying the rope to a sturdy branch when I glance over at the tree across from me. My eyes land on the treehouse my dad built for me when I was five. Perching on the step of the ladder I reminisce over the words he said to me when he finished it. *Mia, this is your space. Your little haven. But, never forget that mom and I are always here for you. You're never alone.* But, I am alone. I don't want to be alone anymore. I want to be with them, and I want to see my sweet baby, Erelah. There's nothing for me here. With determination I finish tying the rope and wrap it around my neck.

*Jump, Mia.*

*On the count of three then.*

*One, two, three…jump.*

*For Christ's sake just jump!*

*Goddammit do it!*

I pull the rope off my head and climb down the ladder kicking it over once my feet hit the ground. It clatters loudly in the cool night air, scaring a stray cat in the brush pile behind the barn.

I can't even do this right. I managed to kill my parents, my baby, my marriage, my career…a family I didn't even know but I can't fucking kill myself!

The sun is starting to cast a pink glow on the horizon. I wanted to be gone by now. The thought of seeing the sun rise to signal another day makes my heart sink. I can't do another day.

Maybe, I'm just afraid of the jumping part. Okay, different plan. I'm a nurse, I mean I used to be one. Anyway, I know how to end this quickly. Let's get it done.

Before I crawl into the bathtub I scribble a note stating Thomas is to get all of my possessions. I can't believe I almost forgot to do that. Maybe that was what was holding me up. Okay, now I'm ready. I hold the shiny razor over my arm lowering the blade until it touches my skin. I push slightly and watch as a small bead of blood pools. *Push then pull back, you can do this.*

Minutes become hours and before I know it the sun is completely up and pouring through the bathroom window. A beam of sunlight catches the blade and then I remember…. the man I saved in the parking lot. He must have cursed me. That has to be it. That is why I can't do it. That motherfucker cursed me! I was so sure he would be thankful someday that I saved him. I even told him nothing could be so bad to take your own life.

I was wrong.

So very wrong.

And, now cursed.

I'm stuck here.

# Chapter Three

**Mia**

"Just leave the bottle," I tell Dina, throwing back another shot of tequila.

"Sweetheart, did you drive here? Maybe, we should call the boss man to give you a ride home. You've had a lot to drink."

"Nah, I'm fine. I'm here to party. Where is everyone? Party poopers." I lay my arm across the bar, resting my cheek on it. "I want to drink and drink and drink and drink the day away. Yeah, the day away." I drag my head off the bar and fill the shot glass, knocking another one back.

"Honey, it's the middle of the afternoon. That's why you're the only one here," she frets.

"Party for one. One…only one," I say sadly. I get up from the bar and stumble to the bathroom. When I come back the tequila bottle is gone and in its place is a tall glass of water.

"Nooo," I whine and stomp my foot. "I'm not done. One more, just one more, Dina." I pout.

"One more but don't tell the boss man, he is on the way to get you and he doesn't sound happy," she says as she pours me one last shot.

"Oh, he's not happy. Pooh, on him. I'm a big girl. I can drink alllll day and alllll night," I sing, drooling down my shirt.

She pats my hand then backs away to the far end of the bar. I slam the shot down. Not enough. I'll just help myself if she won't pour me another. I slide off the barstool just as the door slams opens, the hinges rattling from the force. "Mia," Thomas bellows.

"Thomas! Yay! Dina, party for two," I cheer as I fall…flat…on…my…face.

"Goddammit, Mia," Thomas gripes above me.

I don't remember much after that. Actually, I don't remember anything after that. Until, I wake up in my bed. My bed at the farm. With a monster of a headache. Fuck. I'm still here. Still alive. Still nothing.

I make my way downstairs, shielding my eyes from the daylight pouring in through every goddamn window in the house. Fuck. Why are these all open? I start pulling shades down as I make my way through the house. "Leave them open," Thomas yells from the kitchen. I roll my eyes and continue to pull them down until I reach the kitchen. "Sit," he orders.

# Death and Daffodils

I plop down in a chair, dropping my forehead to the table. He taps my shoulder and when I look at him he sets a glass of water and two pain relievers in front of me. "Drink the whole glass, Mia." The only reason I listen is because I need to quiet the parade currently stomping around in my skull.

When he returns he sets a plate in front of me with bacon, eggs and toast. "Eat." He takes the seat beside me as I poke around the plate with my fork. He slides the note I scribbled indicating that I was leaving everything to him across the table. Did I write that today? Or was that yesterday? What day is it? "Care to explain?" he asks.

"Just a precaution," I whisper, not taking my eyes off my plate.

"Just a precaution," he repeats. "A precaution in case you actually kill yourself?" he pauses, trying to speak without his voice cracking. "I found the rope hanging from the tree, Mia. The razor, the open gun cabinet, the pills! What are you thinking?" he yells, unable to contain the terror in his voice.

I don't say anything. There's nothing I can say to make him feel better. If I could do it...I would. But, I can't. So, I'm stuck.

He stands abruptly. "Finish everything on your plate then get your ass outside and pull the weeds in your mom's flower garden."

"What?" I say, dumbfounded by the sudden switch in his mood.

"You heard me." He turns the water on in the sink, not even turning to look at me.

"But, I...I don't feel good. I have a hangover."

"Tough shit, kid."

"I'm not a kid."

"Then quit acting like one. Eat then weeds. End of discussion," he says and then walks away.

I listen as the shades snap open in the living room. Fuck, he is mad.

I wonder if I could do something to get myself arrested. Jail was better than this. I could do nothing there. Be nothing. Something that wouldn't hurt anyone. Rob a bank, something like that.

Snap goes another shade making me jump.

No way can I finish all this. I manage to shove half of it down then stand to scrape the scraps into Timber's dish.

Wait…he's gone.

Gone.

Just simply…gone.

The plate in my hand drops, crashing to the ground. Thomas comes running out. "What the…" he stops when he sees me. The look on his face says it all…pity. He pities me.

I rush for the broom closet to clean up my mess, but he stops me. He gathers me in his arms, and I lose it. "I don't want to be here," I cry.

"I know, darlin. I know." He rubs the back of my head, keeping me tucked tightly in his embrace. "I'm a poor replacement for your parents but, I'm here, Mia. I'm here for you and you are going to get through this."

I shake my head back and forth. "I don't want to get *through* it. I want it to end."

"No." He pushes me back slightly, forcing me to look at him. "You don't get to decide when to check out of this place. You're young. You have a whole life ahead of you. Promise me you won't do anything like that again. Promise me," he says, shaking me in his arms.

"Obviously something's wrong with me. I can't do it. It's a curse," I tell him.

"It's not a curse. Your mind is telling you it's time to go but, your heart knows it's not. You have something left here to do." He kisses me on the forehead then releases me to get the broom. "I'll clean this up. Go tend to the weeds."

I sigh. "Still with the weeds? What's so important about pulling the damn weeds?"

He crouches down to scoop up the broken plate. He pauses to look up at me. "Well, for one you could use some fresh air, two it needs done and three I told you to. Now get out there."

I stomp off like a teenager. Fine I'll pull weeds. Not because he told me to but because I want to be alone. After stopping by the garden shed for gloves and a spade I glance around the yard. She has several beds. Where to start?

Daffodils, her favorite.

As I'm yanking weeds I think about how my mom always had fresh cut flowers on the kitchen table. Daffodils were her favorite. I remember her telling me that you had to be careful not to put them in a vase with other flowers. "The daffodil will wilt all the other flowers in the water very quickly," she told me. So, when daffodils adorned our table they were always alone. They were pretty but, alone. Like me. I'm like the flower. I wilt everyone around me. I guess I'm supposed to be alone.

A bead of sweat rolls down my temple as I continue to work. I sit back on my haunches to take off my gloves and wipe my brow. I stab the spade in the dirt. Thunk. What the fuck? The spade hit something. I take off one of my gloves and rub the back of my hand over my forehead. Man, it's warm today. I pick up the spade and tap it down in the dirt again. There is something there. I tug my glove back on and start digging. Hmm, just an old coffee can. Weird, this has been a flower bed ever since I can remember. I toss it aside and continue working.

Before I know it all the flower beds are weed free and the sun is setting. Where did the day go? I'm going to be stiff tomorrow. Thomas comes outside as I'm putting everything away. "I need to go to the bar. I'll wait while you shower but be quick so we can get to town."

"Go, I'm fine."

"I'm not leaving you here. Not after what you pulled." He puts his hands on his hips waiting for me to continue my argument.

"Thomas, I promised you I wouldn't do it and I won't. Okay? I'm fucking tired from pulling weeds all day. With a hangover I might add." I put my hands on my hips, mimicking him.

He chuckles. "Okay, but by god, so help me if you do anything stupid…" he pulls me into his arms hugging me tight. "Seriously, Mia. I can't handle losing you too."

"I know," I whisper into his shirt. He smells like cigarettes and beer, but I love it. I love him. I didn't realize how much I missed him until now.

Death and Daffodils

"I am coming back to stay tonight. No arguments. You might have won this battle, but you won't win that one." He releases me and backs away, winking.

I stick my tongue out at him.

"Just for that you get to help me till the garden tomorrow."

"Great, can't wait."

He starts his truck and pulls up in front of me rolling his window down. "I'll bring something back for supper. We'll get groceries in the morning, okay?" He spits out the window waiting for my response.

"Okay, sure," I shrug.

He smiles and then takes off down the road. The wind picks up and I shiver as it blows across my skin. The numbness returns. I should go in and shower but why? Who cares? I walk towards the shed to lock it up for the evening and then turn to go back towards the house. Sleep. I need sleep. Never enough sleep to shake the tiredness I've felt for so long. I trip over something, sending me stumbling to the ground. Fuck. I roll over to see what I tripped on. It's that damn coffee can I found in the daffodils. I kick it with my foot and the lip pops off, papers spilling out.

Quickly I crawl to it and shove everything back inside putting the lid back on. I don't know why but, I'm not sure I want to know what's in there. My mom didn't have secrets. Nothing that would need to be buried in the yard. I grab the can and head inside not even stopping to turn the lights on until I get to my room.

I flip the light on and set the can in front of me on the bed. My heart is beating fast. *Calm down, Mia.* It's just a fucking coffee can with a few papers inside. It could be a time capsule. Yeah, that's what it is. I crack open the lid and peer inside. A time capsule would have more than papers inside it. Scratching my head, I consider my options. What if they say something I would be better off not knowing? I should just torch it all now.

I lean over to grab my old lighter out of my bedside table. I feel around in the drawer afraid to take my eyes off the can, because well you know, it might vanish. Score! I rip my eyes away from the can to look at the bag of weed I just pulled out. Yes! I can't believe my parents didn't go through my room after I left for college. I shove the baggy under my leg and lean over searching again until I find the lighter.

Tugging the papers out of the can, I put the flame next to them. *Do it, Mia. Light 'em up!* I let the flame go out, unable to do it and drop the papers back inside. Flopping back on the bed I release a sigh of defeat. I'm tired. Just so damn tired. Who cares what the fuck is in the can? My mind drifts to Erelah, my little angel. It's no different from any other night. The dark always brings her to me, no matter how hard I try to stop it. I guess I don't want it to stop. I want to hold on to the pain. I deserve it. Every. Damn. Bit of it.

# Chapter Four

**Mia**

I wake to a light creeping across my wall. Shit, Thomas. Quickly I shove the weed and lighter into the coffee can and shove it under my bed just as he walks into my room. "Mia, are you okay?" He asks, sitting down next to me.

"Yeah," I rub my eyes. "I came in after you left and must have fallen asleep."

He pats my knee. "Go shower and then come down to eat."

After he walks out I grab the can and pull the papers out. I shove them in with my change of clothes and head down to the bathroom. I need to know what they say. They could simply be secret recipes for all I know. My mom was one hell of a good cook.

The hot water starts to steam up the bathroom as I take a seat on the counter, tugging the papers out from my clothes. They are papers that appear to have been ripped out of my mother's journal. I recognize the little flower on the corner of each page.

Oh no. No. My dad had cancer. I keep reading. An uneasy feeling creeps into every cell in body. They weren't going to tell me. They felt things were going well in my life and they didn't want me to suffer unnecessarily. But, I would have found out eventually, you can't hide something like that from someone for very long.

My eyes scan the pages and then my heart sinks. They weren't going to tell me because they planned on taking their own lives. They were going to do it before it got to the point of my dad's cancer becoming recognizable. I shove my fist in my mouth to contain the sob threating to escape. My heart aches for them. I just can't see them doing it. My mind flits to their accident.

They were headed to me when they lost control of their car and crashed. On the way to see me at the hospital after I fell asleep at the wheel. Thomas told me they left the minute they received the call. Both were pronounced dead on the scene.

Wait, she is referring to death as if it were a real person.

*Death emailed today. He received the transfer, so I guess that's it. I can't even explain the weight that Death has lifted off my shoulders. Everything will be okay. Death will make sure I don't have to go one day without John. And, John won't have to suffer a long drawn out illness. My only regret is that we will never get to meet our grandchild. Mia, please forgive me. I can't live without your father. I can't.*

 I drop the papers in the sink and quickly hop in the shower. What the fuck did I just read? This can't be. No way did I read that my parents committed suicide. All this time I blamed myself. I thought it was because of me they died. Did this Death person do it? Did he cut the brake lines on the car? Did he poison them?

My brain refuses to wrap around all of this. This is something out of a horror movie. What the fuck?

"Mia, you okay in there?" Thomas asks from the other side of the door.

"Yeah, almost done."

When I get downstairs Thomas is elbow deep in the ribs he brought home. I throw the papers on the table. His eyes scan the words as he wipes his hands off on a napkin. He tosses it on his plate and then raises his eyes to meet mine. Between his sorrow and grief, I see the truth.

"You knew?" I ask, my voice shaking.

"I'm sorry, Mia."

"Stop. Just go. Just go," I say turning away from him.

"Mia, please let me try to explain for them," he begs.

"They left me when I needed them the most."

"If they had known what was going to happen to you, I truly believe they wouldn't have gone through with it. But…"

"Shut. Up! I said get out."

He doesn't say anything else. Only when I hear the screen door open and close do I dare turn around. It all makes sense now. How Thomas had everything set up so quickly. It was all already in place. Why? Why didn't they tell me?

Oh, maybe because I had been so busy pretending my life was perfect that everyone believed it, including my parent's. And, they didn't want to pop that perfect bubble. That makes me sad. Didn't they know how much I loved them? No, how would they? Not once did Darrin and I come back home after we left for college. We went right from high school, to college, to married life all at breakneck speed. Staying busy, giving one hundred percent. That's what we did. We did everything perfect. We were the perfect storybook couple.

They thought I had everything figured out, so they left. They left me.

Well, they don't get to have the last say. If they can leave so can I. My mom didn't want to live without my dad, and I don't want to live without them. Without, Erelah.

The sun rises yet again as I sit out on the front porch staring at the daffodils. The spot where my mom buried her secret. Maybe this was the plan all along. This is how it was supposed to be. It's time. My mom left the can for me to find. It's the key. The key to going home.

The search on my mom's computer begins. Please, please let this work. I spend a few minutes going through a list of passwords I found in her billfold and I'm in. I log into her email scanning for any emails that mention death. Nothing. I open a new email and start typing in the word death. Three letters in it brings up her history, a list of possible emails. Right there on top *death01@ gmail.com*. Really? How original.

I roll my eyes.

Well, here goes nothing.

*Dear Mr. Death,*

*I recently learned my parents hired you for your "services". Imagine my surprise. Anyhow, you owe me one, well actually two but, I only require your services for one. Then we will be even.*

*Sincerely,*

*Daffodil*

Send.

Now to wait. But, not for long. Seconds to be exact.

*Ms. Daffodil,*

*I'm not sure you know of what you speak. I require proof that my services are needed.*

*Death*

My heart pounds in my head. He is there. He answered. I type quickly.

*I do know of what I speak. Google my parents for my story and you will surely find the answer as to why I require your services.*

*Daffodil*

I don't get a response the rest of the day, or the next. Two days later I receive the message I've been waiting for.

*Dear Ms. Daffodil,*

*I see your needs do meet my guidelines. Please respond at your earliest convenience if my services are still requested. Please be certain this is what you desire. Once I receive your response the terms will be irrevocable. This will be my final correspondence.*

*Oh, and Ms. Daffodil...you did not wilt the rest of the flowers in your vase.*

*At your service,*

*Death*

He understood the connection to my alias and more importantly, he agreed to accept me as a client. Is this what I want? I think so.

*Dear Mr. Death,*

*Thank you for your timely response. I do still require your services.*

*Eternally thankful,*

*Daffodil*

*P.S. I did wilt them. I was never meant to share a vase with so many other beautiful flowers.*

I delete everything from the computer. All of it. Something my mother should have done, but she was just leaving me the key. After I finish, I call Thomas and invite him to supper. None of this is his fault. None of it and I have been nothing but a brat to him. I'll make it up to him. Make amends before I go.

I burn my mother's journal notes and set to work on cleaning the house. Will it be days, weeks, or months before Death comes? Shit, why didn't I ask for more details? Shouldn't this kind of thing be given a little more discussion? He should have asked more questions, shouldn't he? *How would you like to die Ms. Daffodil? When would be a good time for you?* Things like that.

Grabbing the computer again, I send him a quick email. He probably won't answer, he said he wouldn't respond again. Something makes me want to test him. No, not that. I need answers. Just answers. I'm not testing him.

**Dear Mr. Death,**

**I'm sorry to bother you again. Shouldn't this be something we schedule?**

**Just curious,**

**Daffodil**

I tap my fingers on the table, listening to the dryer rumble in the background.

**Dearest Daffodil,**

**My policy is to keep the process as natural as possible. You knowing when my services will be rendered would be unnatural don't you think?**

**Also, curious,**

**Death**

\*\*\*

*Mr. Death,*

*No disrespect but is any of this natural? I thought if I knew when to expect you I could be ready.*

*Daffodil*

\*\*\*

*Are you telling me that you are not ready? Because if that is the case then I will have to retract the offer of my services.*

*My apologies,*

*Death*

\*\*\*

Shit, no! What have I done? I pull at my hair. Dammit!

*No, please no. I'm sorry. I don't know why I emailed again. Please. Please come. I'm ready.*

*Desperately needing you,*

*Daffodil*

A few minutes go by and then he responds.

*I'll be seeing you soon Ms. Daffodil.*

*No worries,*

*Death*

No worries. I let the breath out I had been holding. No worries. Death will take care of it now.

# Chapter Five

### Death

Her mother loved daffodils. When I was eight she came for the summer and brought my mother a bouquet of the bright yellow flowers. They had been college roommates. She visited that summer to take some of the burden off my father. Give him a break if only for a week or two. I remember her stomach swollen with child. A child who now calls herself Daffodil.

I shouldn't have answered the first email let alone the several that followed. She wants to die. I should deny her. I lied to her and to myself. Her circumstances do not meet my guidelines. Has she had it rough? No doubt. But, she's young. Things could get better for her. But, that's not my business. My business is only to decide whether someone meets my requirements and then take them out.

# Death and Daffodils

Even though she is not someone I should do business with the fact remains that I do owe her. I never killed her parent's. Fate took over before I was able to render services. I should have returned the money her mother paid but how? She was gone. Her husband gone. I couldn't very well come forward and say, "*Here is the money Mrs. Tanner gave me to kill her and her husband.*" No, that couldn't have happened. So, I guess this is how I will repay them. Right or wrong.

It's sad Mia refers to herself as a Daffodil. I knew the minute I saw her signature where she was coming from. You may think that you understand the reason for mine. Death. It's not because I kill people. Well it is. But, not in the way you think. I am dead. I am death. The day my mother asked me to pull the plug on her ventilator was the day I died. Nothing else has existed for me since. Death became my everything. My purpose. The irrevocable link to my mother. Hence the name I'm entrapped in. I acquired it at eight years of age, during the very summer that Mia's mother was visiting.

Mia's mother knew it was me, the one who had done the dirty deed. She begged me to confess to her. She even admitted my mother had asked her to do it. I'm pretty sure my mom had asked everyone. Including my dad. But, I was the only one with the balls to actually go through with it. I set her free. I gave her peace. Me. I did that.

And, now I do it for a lot of people. Mia's mother also did not fit my guidelines. Her husband fit them to a tee being as he was already a stage four at his initial cancer diagnosis. But, she kept my secret for years, so I agreed to take them both. When I learned of their accident I smiled. He finally beat me to the punch. I believe God has too many sheep to look over. He will eventually get to you but how long will you suffer before he makes an appearance? That is where I come in. My job is to expedite the situation. Bring you to his doorstep so to speak, so he doesn't have to waste time looking for you. Speedy delivery. I make a mental note, that would make a fine tagline.

My eyes wander to the daffodils on my hotel table. I don't know why I thought to bring her flowers. I've never taken flowers to any of my other clients. The cheerful yellow flowers stand out in the drab, dark room. What will run through her mind when she sees me standing on her doorstep, flowers in hand. *Will she be frightened?* No one is ever frightened when I arrive. They are always ready. Always. She will be too.

I did my research on her. Yes, just normal research. Not because I thought she was pretty or anything. It was because I wanted to see how she fell into my guidelines. Anyhow, I don't think I would like her. Too perfect. I bet she has a pretty big hate club. Girls had to be jealous of her. Perfect family, grades, good at sports, football player boyfriend. And don't get me started on the fact that they started dating in elementary school. What kind of boy or girl for that matter even likes the opposite sex at that age? Yep, she has had to have had her share of haters over the years.

Sad to say but I bet people were actually happy to see her take a misstep. I'm not one of those types but, plenty of people are. In a small town I'm sure there are plenty of them residing there. I'm doing her a favor. Saving her from the humiliation I'm sure she is suffering.

I have a secret to admit. I am looking forward to this one. I'm not certain why. The lie I tell myself is because this one I'm leaving the city for. I've never left the city. Never. No need until her. I wasn't even going to leave for her mother. They were going to come here. In fact, I'm still living in the same house that mother died in. No reason to leave. None. Until now.

I thought about demanding Daffodil come here but something pushed me to go to her and that excites me. It's something new. Something different. When I read the word daffodil in her very first email it lit a spark in my dark. So, here I am. Guidelines be damned, I want to give her what she desires. Even at the risk of leaving my haven.

I haven't decided how to do it which is also new for me. You see I'm a planner. Everything organized and thought out down to the last detail. But, this time I have an urge to wing it. I know it's not wise. I should have a plan. I'll see how she takes me showing up first. Like I said she doesn't fall into my guidelines. So, I'm proceeding with caution. This is simply repayment for the unused funds her mother gave me but, if I don't think she really wants it perhaps I shouldn't do it.

Death is permanent after all.

# Chapter Six

**Mia**

I've given up. He's not coming. I quit showering two weeks ago. Would have quit eating too if Thomas wasn't here shoveling food down my throat.

"Mia, I don't want to do this but, maybe we should think about sending you to a treatment facility. Just for a little while."

"Fine, give me the sandwich. I'll eat."

"I'm serious here, darlin. You're scaring me," he says, handing it over.

I prop myself up on the couch and take a bite. "I'm fine," I grumble with a full mouth.

"You're not." He hangs his head and rests his elbows on his knees. "If things don't get better I'm going to have to intervene, Mia. You can't keep living like this."

I know I can't keep living like this. I'm not supposed to be living at all. I must have spooked Mr. Death. Now I'm back to just being stuck.

"What changed the last few weeks? You had been doing so good."

"I'm tired, Thomas. I just need to sleep it off."

"That's all you do is sleep. No, this is something more."

"I'm not going to a mental facility. No. No fucking way."

"The town is celebrating one hundred and fifty years this weekend. Parade, carnival and a street dance. You should go. You need to get out of this house. See your friends. You can't hide out here forever."

Sure I can. But, that's not what he wants to hear, and I want him to leave so I will entertain him for the moment. "I'll think about it. Okay?"

"Okay." He slaps his hands on his knees and stands. "I won't be back until Friday. I've got to run into Davenport. I stocked your fridge but, how bout you ride along with me?"

"No thanks," I tell him.

"Yeah, I didn't think you'd come. At least get in the damn shower. You stink."

As soon as I hear his truck start I drop the sandwich on the coffee table and roll over to go back to sleep. Just as I start to doze I hear a knock. I sigh. Is he seriously going to make me answer the door? What the fuck does he want to ride me about now?

When I step into the kitchen I see a man standing on my porch. I peek through the curtains. It's him. Death. My eyes drop to the vase of daffodils he is holding. He knocks again lightly. Death is literally knocking on my door. Am I ready? Yes, I'm so ready.

I rush for the door, holding it open for him. "Please come in," I say as he scoots past me. I look around the yard. No car. How did he get here? After the door closes I slowly turn around to face him. He sets the vase of flowers in the center of the table.

"You seem surprised to see me," his voice glides like velvet across the room.

"I…um…I didn't think you were coming." I drag my eyes away from him. He was not what I was expecting. What was I expecting?

"Were you hoping I wouldn't?" he asks, taking one step towards me.

I struggle to keep my feet planted. Do not back away from him. You want this. You need this. "No, I wanted you to come." When he doesn't say anything, I dare to look at him. His eyes are scanning the room. They stop on mine and he smiles.

"Don't be nervous," he says as he moves towards me and I can't help but backup against the door. My hand snakes down in search of the handle. His hand reaches my throat before I get the door open. "Shhh, easy now," he whispers.

Fuck, this is it.

# Death and Daffodils

As his big hand tightens over my throat I brave to meet his eyes. They are dark as night. It's happening. He's unlocking the gate. I fall into the depths of his gaze. A wave of euphoria rushes my system as my eyes flutter closed and I moan out loud at the intensity of the moment. He pauses, holding me there, on the brink of the black abyss. His breath whispers over my cheek and I shiver.

Abruptly, he releases me. I lean over sucking in oxygen as my lungs burn. He grabs my hand and drags me to the broom closet. He shoves me inside and slams the door shut in my face. What the fuck? I shake the handle. He locked me in the closet. Oh fuck. No! I bang on the door. "Let me out!" I scream, but he doesn't open the door.

I wait quietly, my breath coming out in pants as I try to figure out what just happened. Why did he stop? After a few minutes of silence, I decide to knock on the door. "Mr. Death?" No answer. I press my ear to the door, but I can't hear anything. Shit, did he leave? I shake the door handle again hoping it will magically open.

Slumping down to the floor I consider my options. What options? I'm at his mercy. He has either left me in here to starve to death or he is out there setting the scene. I sniff my armpit. Maybe my body odor offended him. That or my unbrushed hair. I sigh. He's not here for a date. He's here to kill me. There was a time I would never have let someone see me in such a state. Now, I simply don't care. I straighten my leg out and kick the door. "Fuck you," I yell.

Still the only response from the other side is silence. Sitting in the dark, small space should frighten me but it doesn't. Actually, having his hand wrapped around my throat didn't scare me either. I'm sure the excitement, the strange feelings I'm having are all in anticipation for what is to come. My death. That has to be it. Oh god, I moaned out loud when he had me pinned against the door. Maybe he thinks I'm weird. Am I weird? None of that felt right. That's a lie, it did feel right… it shouldn't have felt right should it?

I'm losing my mind. Waiting. Waiting. He had to have left. That or he is the stealthiest death dealer on the planet. No, he is definitely not stealthy. He knocked on my door for Christ's sake. I really don't know how to explain him. He is scary. Sexy scary. Like, you wouldn't be scared of him if you saw him in a dark alley. But, more a someone who can see right through you type scary. Someone who takes what he wants, when he wants.

He is dark. Dark hair, dark eyes. Those eyes. Eyes I had to tilt my head to look into he is so tall. Tall and lean. Well from what I could see. He was wearing a black suit. A black suit with a silver tie. And a five o' clock shadow that shows off his chiseled good looks. I slam the back of my head into the wall. What the fuck am I doing? Swooning over the man who is here to end my life. I guess this could be a normal reaction. Yes, it would be normal to feel a connection to someone who is going to end your life.

My hand roams over my belly. It feels so empty. One day it was full of life and then I woke up to nothing. For months I fought phantom kicks only to remember she was gone. Soon, I will be able to be with her again. I curl up in the corner and close my eyes. Patience. I have confidence Death will take care of everything. He looks like someone who wouldn't leave me hanging. No, he will accomplish what he came here to do. I have no doubt.

Hours pass as I doze off and on. When I wake I notice a light peeking in under the door from the kitchen. It must be night. Wait, is he searching the cupboards? I crawl to the door and peek under. He is still here, but all I can see are his shiny black shoes. I watch as he walks towards the door and I hear the screen door slam behind him.

# Death and Daffodils

I sit back against the wall. What is he waiting for? Maybe he only kills at night. Any minute it will be time. He doesn't make it very easy. I thought this would be quick. This is anything but quick. The door creaks open and I hear his footsteps move close. His shadow blocks the light bleeding into the broom closet from beneath the door. Oh, shit. He is coming for me.

Just then the door opens. I cover my eyes with my arm as he reaches inside pulling me out. He quickly drags me outside. He stops in the middle of the yard and releases me. "What is that noise?" he asks, finally turning to look at me.

"W-what noise?" I ask confused. Maybe this guy is a nut job. Great, I instigated this whole thing with a crazy.

"Don't tell me you can't hear that." He tries to mimic the noise he is hearing, and I laugh. I cover my mouth with my hand. What was that? I haven't laughed in…well, I can't remember. He looks at me clearly irritated.

"I'm, I'm sorry. Are you talking about the nature sounds of the night?"

"Nature sounds of the night?" he shakes his head not understanding.

"Like, the crickets, bugs, frogs." I shrug my shoulders like it should be obvious.

He spins in a circle, his gaze trying to permeate through the dark. "Those are bugs and animals?"

"Yes. You've never heard them before?" I wrap my arms around myself, suddenly insecure about being alone with a strange man. Oh, what am I worried about? That he will kill me? That's the whole point isn't it?

"No, I haven't. It's so strange. Like a familiar song, or the sound of rain pattering on the roof. I like it." He turns to look at me but then notices the sky above us and his mouth drops open. "Are those stars? Real stars?"

I follow his gaze, tipping my head towards the heavens. I let out a long drawn out sigh. "Yeah, real life stars," I answer. Where is this guy from? I watch as he paces, taking in what is evidently his first night in the country. "I take it you're not from around here?"

"No. This is my first time out of the city. The only nighttime sounds I hear is the noise of sirens, dogs barking, or kids crying. Nothing as beautiful as your nature sounds."

I guess I'd tuned out the sound. Now that I'm listening I realize how much I've missed it. I look back up to the stars. Death is right. There are no stars in the city. I wanted Erelah to see the stars, so Darrin and I spent an entire afternoon one day sticking little glow in the dark stickers all over the nursery walls and ceiling. I wonder if they are still there. The urge to go to her hits me. "I don't mean to be a pest, but could we get on with it?"

"On with what?" he asks tipping his head, an inquisitive look on his face.

"You know. Can you just do it already?"

"Are you sure you're ready to leave all of this behind?" He waves his arm out.

"Yes, I don't have anyone to enjoy it with anymore." I rub my foot over the grass, the cool dew wetting the tips of my toes.

"And you need someone to share it with? That seems silly. Why?"

"It's always better to share something with someone than to experience it alone."

"Hmm, interesting concept." He notices the dew getting his shoes wet and tries to wipe it off on the grass which only gets them wetter. Finally, he gives up and his eyes meet mine. "Are you enjoying it now?"

What?

"I…I don't know."

"You're not alone. I'm here with you."

"Yeah, but I don't know you."

"So, you can't enjoy the stars or night sounds with me but, you can enjoy the thought of me ending your life?"

"I don't *enjoy* the thought of you ending my life."

"It didn't sound that way when it was happening."

That's it. I'm done. I turn toward the house stomping all the way. Just as I'm about to lock him out he sticks his foot in the doorway preventing me from doing so.

"Did I embarrass you?" he asks with no emotion whatsoever on his face.

"No. You didn't." He did but I'm not going to tell him that. "You were supposed to come here and kill me. I don't have time for all this…this, whatever this is." I let go of my hold on the door and throw my hands up in defeat.

"Do you have something better to do? Perhaps shower, locate a brush?" he taunts.

My blood boils. Again, he has managed to embarrass me. I storm off, headed to my bedroom. He follows, hot on my heels. "Just go," I yell over my shoulder.

"You passed the bathroom," he tells me.

"Fuck. You." I grit out.

He grabs me from behind, wrapping his arms tightly around my waist and hauls me towards the bathroom. I try to grab onto anything I can, knocking a few pictures from the wall. He pries my fingers off the doorframe in my last attempt to keep him from hauling me in there. Once inside he kicks the door shut behind us. My eyes meet his in the mirror. "Are you going to drown me?"

"No, you are going to shower."

"No. Fuck no."

"I believe everyone should die with dignity. You definitely don't smell dignified." He nods his head towards the shower.

"What do I need to smell good for? For you?" I laugh and renew my struggle in his arms.

He reaches down to crank the water on.

"Okay, if I shower will you just do it?" I ask, wanting nothing more than for this to be over.

"Maybe."

"Tell me you will do it and I will shower."

"That's not how this works, Daffodil." He picks me up off my feet as he steps inside the shower, clothes and all. He sets me down and I immediately back up under the spray to get away from him.

"You are crazy," I spit.

He runs his hand over his face to clear the droplets of water landing there. "Me? You are the one who hasn't showered for…I don't know. How long has it been?"

Now I'm just mad. "What. Don't you have the balls to do it?"

He stills. I made him angry. "Oh, Daffodil. You have no idea how big my balls are."

I spin around to avoid the furry in his eye, shaking in fear. This isn't a game anymore. I'm not sure what is happening. This is not what I signed up for. "Get out and I will shower."

"Hm, aren't we in a predicament? I'm all wet now." I hear him move behind me and then he reaches around to throw his wet jacket out onto the floor, his shirt and pants following. I stand frozen, my eyes glued to the shower wall.

"Your turn."

I start to cry. "Please don't do this," I beg.

"This is what happens when you don't listen, Daffodil." He touches my shoulder and I jump. He sighs. "Listen, I will turn around. You undress, shower, then wait for me right outside the curtain until I finish. Understand?"

"Yes," I say shakily.

47

"Okay. Get busy," he orders.

I glance over my shoulder to see that he has turned around. Quickly I undress, shampoo my hair, and wash myself. I do my best not to look at his naked backside. I ignore the fact that my fear has sparked something new inside me. It created a burn similar to what I felt when his hand was around my throat. Within minutes I'm wrapped in a towel waiting for him outside the tub.

"Now, that wasn't so hard was it?" he mumbles from the other side of the curtain. I don't answer and he pokes his head out to give me a warning glare. I watch as water drips from his hair cascading down his face. His handsome face.

Stop.

"No," I answer gruffly.

He only takes a few minutes and then steps out. Steps out in nothing but his birthday suit. My eyes have a mind of their own and peruse over his body once, only once, before I shove a towel at him. I somehow manage to keep my eyes locked on his as he dries off. Once he has wrapped the towel around his waist he reaches around me to open the door bringing our faces inches apart. "Please do it now," I whisper.

He opens the door and pushes me towards my room. "We will talk about that tomorrow after a good night's rest."

Gently he pushes me onto my bed. "I'm going to sleep in your parent's room if you need me," he says as he turns to walk out.

I scramble to sit up on the bed. "Wait!" I get on my knees on the mattress and place my hands together in prayer. "Please, please do it now. I can't face another day."

He pauses before shutting off my light. "Tomorrow we will talk. Goodnight, Daffodil."

*Please god, please just take me. Take me. Take me. I don't want to be here anymore.* I recite these words over and over in my head. Praying, begging as tears soak my pillow. *Please don't let me wake up tomorrow.*

# Chapter Seven

### Death

*I*nteresting. My reaction to her is indescribable. I've never reacted to another person like this before. She intrigues me. Excites me even. She activated a side of me I thought didn't exist. I shouldn't have done that in the shower. But, she pushed me. I like that she pushes me. I like it a lot. Which is odd.

One time. One time I would like to help someone live instead of die. This is the first one that hasn't wanted to die. She thinks she does. I could be wrong but I rarely am. There is so much life in her. She is spunky, flawed, cute and broken. Unfortunately, the broken part is overriding everything else at the moment. She is nothing like her social media shows her to be. I really didn't think I would like her. But, I think I do.

# Death and Daffodils

I stretch out on her parent's bed staring at the ceiling. Her sobs are beginning to ebb. I'm sure she is terribly disappointed in my services. Oh well, she can add it to her list of displeasures. I like it here. It's so different from the city. I think I'll stay awhile.

Another wail comes from her room. This is something else that is new. Hearing her cry, makes me want to do things. Things I've never done but, perhaps should explore.

I sit up and listen. Her tears make me want to touch her. I should go to her. Yes, I should go to her.

"Daffodil," I whisper in the dark and her sobs come to an abrupt halt. She stills beneath the covers. "Are you okay?"

"Go away unless you are here to finally do what you came to do."

"You mean coming here to your home to kill you or coming here to your room to comfort you?"

She sits up quickly. "You could comfort me by ending my suffering."

I move towards her and she scoots back a few inches. The body naturally will try to protect itself even if the mind knows what it wants. No matter how much someone wants to die, their body usually puts up a little fight at the end. I slide under her covers, laying back against the pillow soaked in her tears.

"Come here," I demand. Hesitantly, she crawls to me. This. This is…nothing short of amazing. These feelings I'm having are delightful. She pauses when she is next to me. "Lay down." She listens laying quietly next to me. The heat radiating off her comforts me like a warm summer breeze. I prop myself up on my elbow and lean in to smell her.

"Wh-what are you doing?"

"Just getting to know you."

She wants to run. I sense it in the tautness of her muscles. I place my hand over her throat and just like before she moans, and I notice the slight hitch of her hips. *Interesting.* I squeeze lightly then release my grip. Her skin is soft like the petals on a flower. My fingertips brush over her collarbone and her breath catches in her throat.

"Who are you?" she asks her voice quivering.

"I'm Death and you are my Daffodil," I reply leaning in to taste her lips.

She tries to push me away, but I roll my body on top of hers trapping her. This invokes a struggle. She shoves with all her might trying to get me to move. "What the fuck is wrong with you?" she screams.

"Six months," I whisper over her lips.

"What?" she says breathlessly, her chest heaving with her efforts.

"Six months. I stay for six months and if you still want to die then I will do it."

"This isn't how it's supposed to work."

"How is it supposed to work? Have you done this sort of thing before?"

"You kill me. That's how. You do it now. You don't make me wait."

"That's how it usually works, when you meet the guidelines."

"You said I met them. Remember? In your email."

"I lied," I say rolling off of her and sitting on the edge of the bed.

"What do you mean you lied?"

"You didn't meet my requirements. I lied. I was only trying to repay your parents."

"For what?"

"I didn't kill them. God got to them before I did. I didn't know how to return the money. You know?" When she doesn't say anything, I turn around to look at her.

"They died because of me," she whispers.

"No, they died because their time was up."

She shakes her head furiously back and forth. "No, I killed them and that family and…"

"Stop." I lay back down and pull her in close to me. She doesn't fight this time. She is too busy grieving. Once I have us settled I continue, "Tell me about her."

"My mom?" she hiccups.

"No. Erelah."

She lifts her head to meet my eyes. "You know her name?"

"Yes. It means angel." I read everything I could find about her. To see if she met my guidelines. Not because she is cute. She tucks her face back into my chest and I squeeze her tight. This feels nice.

53

"Nobody's ever asked me about her. I don't know what to say. I never got to meet her. She was just gone when I woke up."

"Tell me what she was like when you carried her inside you. What your hopes and dreams were for her. The things you bought her. Whatever you want to tell me."

"I don't know. This is weird. I don't even know you. I hired you to kill me not listen to me ramble on about the baby I lost."

"I truly want to hear you talk about her. That is if you want to. We don't have to know each other to speak to one another. We've been doing a bang-up job of it all evening." I feel her smile against my skin. Oh, yes. This is really nice. I like this.

She sits up and reaches under the bed for something. "Have you ever smoked pot before?" she asks.

"No. This is a drug free zone." I flip the light on and gesture towards my physique. Subtly she licks her lips.

"I see that," she chides. "Grab the papers out of the drawer. It's better to have deep conversation when you're high."

"Oh, is that so?" I hand her the papers and she begins to roll herself a joint.

"I don't know. Just something I heard. I haven't smoked since high school. Nobody knows that I did. It was my little secret. You know to take the stress off." She lights it up and hands it to me as she lets smoke billow out of her mouth.

# Death and Daffodils

"I wouldn't take you for the stoner type?" I take the joint from her. This is all about new experiences. Right? I take a hit and then make a complete fool of myself as I cough up one, if not both, my lungs.

"Yeah, there is a lot people don't know about me," she replies sadly. She pats me on the back which does nothing to help.

"Why do you hide things about yourself," I say once I quit hacking.

She takes another hit, knocking the ashes off in an old coffee can. "I don't know."

She hands the joint to me. "No, thank you. I like my lungs just fine the way they are."

Shrugging she brings it back to her lips taking another long draw. Beautiful, she is beautiful. "I was so excited when I found out I was pregnant. I didn't care if I had a boy or a girl. I wanted it to be a surprise, but Darrin wanted to know the sex of the baby. He seemed a bit disappointed when we found out she was a girl. He wanted our first child to be a boy."

She pauses waiting for a response from me. I just want to listen. I want to know her thoughts, her disappointments. Plus, I love the sound of her voice.

"I think she would have been a gymnast or a ballerina. She would do complete somersaults in my stomach. You should have seen it. It looked like there was an alien in my belly." She rubs her stomach for a moment before continuing. "Tonight, when you were looking at the stars it reminded me how Darrin and I put little glow in the dark stars all over her nursery. I missed being able to see the stars. I wanted her to see them every night."

"The stars are beautiful here. I didn't realize how much the city lights prevented us from seeing them."

She half smiles. "It is one of the nice things about living in the country. I think Erelah would have liked visiting here." Her smile fades. "My due date was only a month away when I had the accident."

"They didn't let you see her?"

"No. I was in an induced coma for several weeks. My dad's friend took care of everything. There was a service for her and my parent's here. She was already in the ground by the time I woke up."

"Is she nearby?"

She chews on her bottom lip snuffing the joint out. "Yeah," she says quietly.

"You haven't been to visit?"

"No." She hugs her knees curling up in a ball. Oh, no she doesn't. She is closing herself off again.

"We will go tomorrow."

She raises her eyes to mine. "No. I don't want to visit her at the cemetery. I want to see her in heaven."

I sigh and drop my head. "Six months."

"Why six months?" she asks calmer than I'd expected.

"I don't know. There is something about you. I need to be sure this is the right thing. I'm not a monster you know?"

56

She laughs lightly. "No, I don't know but, I'll have to take your word for it now won't I?"

"I guess you will," I tell her as I stand up to go back to her parent's room. She seems calmer now. "Maybe tonight you will see Erelah in your dreams. Good night, Daffodil." I shut the light off and then make my way out the door.

"Mr. Death."

I pause in the doorway not looking back. If I look back I'll want to stay.

"Thank you for listening to me talk about her. Everyone else avoids the subject. Talking about her somehow made her real and not just some figment of my imagination."

"You can talk about her with me anytime you like. It makes her real to me too. I'm sure she is a sweet soul. Just like her mother."

# Chapter Eight

**Mia**

I wake to the sound of the vacuum cleaner. I pull the blanket up over my head. No. Not another day. I'm slightly less tired than I have been though. I don't think I woke up once in the night.

Evidently, Death is still here. Unless I've been gifted cleaning fairies.

The vacuum makes a horrendous noise and I hear Death, curse. "God dammit," he yells. I shove the blankets down. I suppose I better go see what the fuck he's doing. I change and then head to the bathroom. My reflection scares me. Oh god, is this how I looked last night. Maybe I will just brush my hair.

# Death and Daffodils

When I get downstairs, I see Death fighting with the vacuum. He doesn't even look at me when I enter the room. "I'm sorry I think I broke it," he mumbles. "I was trying to clean up your little death nest. It's disgusting."

I walk over, switch it from the hose setting to floor. "There, I'm glad to see your personality didn't change overnight," I say with a scowl on my face.

He hesitantly starts it up and then gives me a thumbs up when it works. I roll my eyes and head to the kitchen. I guess I could do a little cleaning in here. I would hate for my mess to offend the dark one.

The bread is about to expire, I should use it up. Maybe some French toast? I'm not doing this for him. I'm doing it because I hate to waste the bread.

Soon the vacuum shuts off and he comes out with a bag of trash. "Do you always live like this or is this just a way to make life even more miserable?"

I crack another egg harshly against the bowl. "Garbage can is out by the barn." I choose to ignore his comment. When the door closes behind him. I rush to lock it. I'm not going to sit here and listen to him criticize me all day. When he comes back and realizes the door is locked he knocks. I know he can see me but guess what? I don't care. I smile and continue whipping up breakfast.

He leaves. Good. Maybe he left forever. I stop stirring. I still need him. I don't even know how the man got here. Surely he didn't have a cab drop him off. Fine, I'll unlock the door. Only because I want him to finish what he initially came here to do. As I turn to go unlock it. Smack! Right across my ass. "Ouch!" I turn around to see Death staring me right in the face. "What the fuck?" I rub my bottom.

59

"Don't do that again," he says as he takes a seat at the table. "What's for breakfast?"

I'm stunned stupid. He just hit me. He hit me. How did he get in and how did I not hear him come up behind me? I stand there like an idiot with the whisk in my hand.

"Hello?" he says stretching his long legs out in front of him. I notice then that he has a pair of my dad's jeans on with his white dress shirt that he evidently laundered this morning. I blink at him. "Cat got your tongue?" he asks.

"Six months you said. You don't plan on staying here for six months do you?" I rub my backside again, the sting still burning my ass.

"Yes. Why?"

I chuckle in an evil witch sort of way as I go back to work on breakfast. "This isn't going to work."

"It has to." He locks his hands behind his head.

"No. You go home and in six months I'll email to let you know I'm still interested in your services."

"You have my services now. They are just different than you originally thought."

"I don't want your services if they involve constantly criticizing me, attempts at kissing me and HITTING me."

"Is that how you see it?" he asks.

"How else should I see it?"

# Death and Daffodils

"I'm trying to help."

"Help?" I pull the French toast off the skillet and drop a few on a plate for him, with eggs and sausage. I set it down in front of him and take the seat on the opposite side of the table.

"This looks good," he fills his mouth with food. I watch him eat. A sense of satisfaction comes over me. My cooking seems to be one thing he doesn't find fault with. I tap my fingers impatiently on the table however, because this conversation is not over. When he finishes he pushes the plate back and wipes his mouth on a napkin finally raising his eyes to meet mine. His dark, mysterious eyes.

"Let's talk. Shall we?" he asks.

I nod my head.

"Eat and then we will talk." Then he gets up, puts his plate in the sink and walks outside.

"What the fuck?" I yell out in frustration. This guy is a prick. Thomas is going to be home in a few days. I need to get a handle on this before he shows up. Death needs to be on his merry way by then. I angrily scarf down some breakfast and clean up the mess. When I realize he isn't coming back inside I head outdoors to find the pain in the ass.

I find him standing below my treehouse staring up at it. "Did you eat?" he asks not even turning around.

"Yeah."

"Did your dad build this for you?"

"Yes, when I was five."

"I like it, but it doesn't look very safe." I watch as he climbs up the steps, his head disappearing inside the opening.

"Yeah, well it could use some work." I'm growing impatient. The longer he is here the more at home he makes himself. "I thought we were going to talk?"

He climbs back down and plops himself on the ground a few feet in front of me. "Do you really think I'm criticizing you? Because, I'm not. Well, I am but it's all in good faith. I want you to see the obvious. You need to shower. You need to clean up your mess and you need to eat. Oh, and your hair looks much better brushed. I mean the whole cave girl look is sexy as hell on you but…"

I sit down beside him and smack him on the arm.

"Oh, so you can hit me, but I can't hit you?" He laughs and when he does it…it does something to me. He has a nice smile. He should use it more.

"I didn't hit you, hit you. I tapped your arm in jest," I say laying back to look up at the clouds.

"I didn't hit you, hit you either. I spanked your ass because you asked for it by locking me out."

Something stirs in me and I sit up. "Well, you can't do that."

"Why, did I injure you?"

"No, but it isn't right."

"It felt right to me."

"Whatever." I wiggle around a bit. "You can't stay here. My friend Thomas will be home in a few days, and he will not like you being here. How would I even explain it?"

"You tell him I'm a friend from the city who came out to keep you company." He lays back on the ground to look up at the sky, like I had been doing. "This is nice. I like it here, Daffodil. I really would like to stay here with you."

"Ughh, fine you can stay for a few weeks. A trial run but we need to set a few ground rules."

He sits up excited. "Okay, you go first with your rules and then I'll tell you mine."

I hug my legs to my chest. "Why do you get rules? This is my place."

"It's only fair." He winks at me and a tiny, tiny barely noticeable little flutter erupts inside me.

"Okay, for one I shower *alone*."

"But, you at least shower right?"

"Yes," I scowl at him. "Another thing, you can't touch or kiss me without permission."

"Sorry, I just wanted to see what it felt like to kiss. I'd never had the urge before." He sits up brushing grass off him.

There's something about the way he said that. "To kiss me you mean?"

"Yeah, I had an urge to kiss you. I've never had that urge before."

I sit up straighter my brows furrowing. "So, you've never…" I let my words trail off. No, surely I'm misunderstanding. He has to be older than me.

"You are correct. I've never kissed anyone before."

"Anyone?"

"Is this something I should be ashamed of?" He rests his arms on his knees dropping his head.

"No. No. That's not what I'm getting at. It's just unusual, that's all. How old are you?"

"Thirty-six." He looks up at me. "See you do think it is something to be ashamed of. I can tell by your expression."

"No, I think it's. I think it's admirable. You didn't do it because society made you believe you should. You waited until you felt you wanted to."

"Well, actually we didn't kiss. If I ask now would you let me kiss you?"

I blush the same color as my mother's roses. "I…I don't know. I've only kissed one person my whole life."

"So, we aren't much different. We both keep our kisses to ourselves unless we mean them."

"Okay, so why do you want to kiss me?" I ask, patting the heat in my cheeks.

"Why do you want to kiss me?" he counters.

"I never said I wanted to kiss you."

"You must, you said I just needed to ask permission. And I did and then you got nervous because you've only ever kissed one person. It's understandable. You are anxious to kiss someone new."

"Are you anxious?"

"No."

I chew on my bottom lip. Can I trust him? This is the most bizarre interaction I have ever had with anyone. Ever! "Maybe you should wait. I might not be the right person to give your first kiss to. It should be special. Actually, I envy you."

"You do?"

"Yeah, I mean you're older. You know who you are, you know your body, what you like, what you don't. Your first time is going to be special. Mine was just a fumbling around pre-teen mess. Nothing special...comical but not special."

"I think giving you my first kiss will be special. So, I'll wait until you give it to me. Something to look forward to," he says with a wink before laying back down to stare at the clouds.

I lay back down and watch the big puffy clouds float by. Soon, I'm daydreaming of what it would be like to kiss him. I've only kissed Darrin. I wasn't his first though. He kissed Rebecca Lynd before he kissed me. Rebecca and I have been rivals ever since. We bumped into her a few times in the city. Needless to say, she isn't my favorite person nor am I hers.

I've never been someone's first kiss. It's funny to be thinking about being someone's first at twenty-eight years of age. It makes me feel a little giddy knowing he wants to kiss me.

"That one looks like a hippopotamus," he points to the sky.

"No, it doesn't. It looks like a train with smoke coming out the engine."

He laughs. "You aren't very good at this because it looks exactly like a hippopotamus, Mia."

I roll my head to look at him. "You called me by my name."

He continues to gaze at the sky. "Is that okay? Or is that another one of your rules?"

"No, it's okay. Are you going to tell me your real name?"

"Maybe," he rolls to his side and props himself up on an elbow. "After you kiss me."

"I can't call you Death when Thomas shows up. He might think that's a bit strange." I smile, just a little smile at him.

"Well I guess you better give up a kiss before then." He flops back over and continues to stare at the sky. I do the same. An easy silence settles over us and this is how we spend the rest of the day. Lying on our backs letting the clouds pass us by.

# Chapter Nine

## Mia

Now that the night is settling I find myself repeating my chant. *Please don't let me wake up tomorrow. Please.* I don't know why the night is always the worst. Death and I had sandwiches for supper, we ate in amenable silence. Today was a little easier. I let my mind reminisce over my childhood. That and the kiss. I doubt I ever kiss him. I have to keep reminding myself why he is here. Not for kisses, even though he thinks he wants one.

The screen door creeks open and Death stops the porch swing I've been swinging on with his leg. The abrupt halt of movement almost tips me out but he catches me and then hands me a joint. "What's this?" I ask.

He sits down next to me and begins to push us both on the swing. Slowly he rocks us back and forth. "I thought you might want to talk. This seemed to help last night so I thought we could give it another try."

"Are you going to smoke it with me?" He hands me the lighter and I fire it up.

"No, thank you."

I shake my head and take a deep drag off it. It did help me sleep last night. Might as well not let that bag go to waste. "What do you want to talk about?"

"Oh, I don't know. We don't have to talk. I like the sounds at night here. It's so peaceful."

"Yeah, I guess I'd tuned it out. I've kinda tuned everything out since my accident."

"You fell asleep at the wheel?"

"Yep."

"So, you blame yourself?"

"Who else would I blame?"

"Circumstance."

I cock an eyebrow at him. "I knew I was tired. It was my fault. I shouldn't have drove home." I tuck my legs under me and take another hit letting the smoke blow out as I continue to speak. "I accept that it was my fault. I wanted the maximum punishment but, it wasn't enough. Not nearly enough."

"So, are you wanting to die as a punishment? Because you don't feel your sentence was enough?"

"Yes and no. I mean how much should one suffer for taking six lives."

"Six?"

"I include my parents. They would be here if it wasn't for my accident."

"I think we've already established that they wouldn't be. I'm very good at my job." He stops the swing temporarily to listen to something he hears before resuming.

"That's to be seen. So far I'm not impressed."

He laughs and his white teeth flash in the dark. "Question. Were you suicidal before the accident?"

"What? No." I scowl at him.

"Before you found out you were pregnant? In high school?"

I snuff the joint out on the arm of the swing and stand up. How dare he? He grabs me from behind before I can stomp off. He whispers into my ear, "Think about, Mia."

"I...I had bad days, but I never tried to kill myself," I say irritated, trying to peel his hands off my waist.

"Shh, I'm just trying to figure out if you've been unhappy for a while or if it is strictly because of the accident."

"My life was perfect. Everything was going according to plan."

"Whose plan?"

"Mine and Darrin's. It's was what everyone expected from us."

"So, you were living everyone else's expectations?"

"Yes, I mean no. Let go of me." I wiggle in his arms.

He releases me and just as I'm about to retreat inside the house he says something that makes me pause mid-step.

"Do you want me to punish you, Daffodil?"

"No," I whisper. "I just want you to kill me."

## Death

Mia hasn't been happy for a long time. You can't be happy pretending to be something you're not. Today we spent the day, the *entire* day, just staring at the clouds. It was amazing. To do nothing. Watching clouds, absorbing sun, fresh air, and nothing else. I get the impression that she was on the go for most of her life. If I'm honest with myself we're alike. I'd never taken the time to stare at the sky before. That and the fact that I haven't been true to myself either.

I wonder who I would've been if my mother hadn't asked me to help her end her life. Would I have had a normal life? A brighter one? This is the first time I've pondered the question. Being here is making me question a lot of things. Life is slower here. It allows the space and freedom to explore your thoughts and feelings.

Last night I made her angry. I'm good at that it seems. I thought maybe I could offer her something that she was needing. To feel adequately punished for what she believes are her transgressions. I guess I was wrong. Anyhow, today is a new day.

I've always been an early riser and let me tell you something, waking up in the country is nothing short of wonderful. I've been out exploring the property and ran across the graves of Mia's family. They were just a short walk from the house. I came back to the house and cut her mother a few daffodils and these cute, tiny pink roses for Erelah.

I've asked her twice now if she wants to visit her daughter's grave but both times I got a resolute no. It is beautiful here. The graves are on a little hill overlooking a creek. I think Mia would like it. I'm not sure she even knows where the graves lie.

When I get back to the house I see she is still in bed. I push her door open being anything but quiet. She covers her head with a blanket. "I need you take me to the library?" I tell her plopping myself down beside her.

"Go. Away," she mumbles beneath her shield.

"Come on. I need to go to the library." I nudge her gently.

"Take ole' blue. But, I warn you there isn't a library in town you will need to drive on to the next one."

"Ole' blue?" I question, tugging the blanket down so I can see her eyeballs.

"The pickup." She pulls at the blanket until we are in a tug of war.

"I can't drive."

She lets go abruptly causing me to tumble off the bed. The most beautiful sound comes from above me. She is laughing. She peeks over the edge. "What do you mean you can't drive?"

I prop myself up on my elbows. "I mean exactly what I said. No need for a license when there are bus lines, cabs, the subway, uber…"

"Okay, okay I get it. What do you need to go to the library for? A how-to manual on how to apologize."

"What am I apologizing for?"

"For being an asshole. We were having a fine time yesterday and you had to go and ruin it by being Mr. Know It All."

"Is that what I was doing?" I try to sit up, but she nudges my forehead making fall back over. She lays back on the bed so I can't see her.

"I honestly don't know what you are trying to do," she says, sighing.

I climb up beside her. "I do need a how-to manual."

She huffs, blowing hair out of her eyes. "Go on," she says impatiently.

"On how to plant a garden." Her eyes meet mine and she stares for a moment before responding.

"You just put the shit in the ground," she says with more hostility than necessary.

"Well, I've been looking at the stuff out by that dirt space, which I assume is a garden spot. There are some plants in little containers and a few seed packets. I don't know how it works so I need to read up on it."

"You're going to plant my garden?" She rolls her eyes.

"Yes, the stuff looks like it's about to die and since you don't seem to have the motivation to do it. I thought I would give it a go."

"Farmer Death," she says. "It just gets better and better." She rolls to the side of the bed and sits up. "I'll teach you."

My eyebrows shoot up in surprise. "You will?"

"Sure, I'll supervise, and you'll do all the work. That way when Thomas returns he will get off my case about it." She walks over to the window, pulling the curtains back to look down at the very spot we are talking about. "I know he thinks if I work outside it will cure me of my melancholy. He is wrong. Nothing can cure it. Only death."

"Well right now *Death* wants to learn about gardening. I'm so excited," I tell her.

She shakes her head and grabs a pair of jeans off the floor. "Whatever, Death. I'll meet you outside."

# Chapter Ten

**Mia**

I wake with a start. Shit, Thomas is here! Shit, shit, shit. I jog to the stairs while pulling a shirt over my head, at the same time tugging a pair of leggings over my hips. "Mia," he yells from the kitchen.

"Hey," I say running my fingers through my hair. "I thought you said you wouldn't be back till Friday?"

"It is Friday." He smirks and leans against the counter pouring himself a cup of coffee that evidently Death made.

"Oh, yeah right. The week must have gotten away from me." I sit down, tucking my legs underneath me.

# Death and Daffodils

"The place looks good, Mia. You even got the garden in." He quirks an eyebrow before taking the seat next to me at the table. "I must say I'm a little surprised."

"Yeah, well I had help." As if on cue Death walks into the kitchen. Thomas looks at him and then back at me. "Thomas this is a friend of my mine from the city." I give Death a death glare. I told him this would be awkward. I still don't know his name.

Death takes a step towards Thomas holding his hand out to him. "Nice, to meet you Thomas. I'm Azrael."

I want to smack myself in the face. Azrael? Really? The angel of death? Are you kidding me?

Thomas shakes his hand and then glances at me again. "It looks like you have been helping Mia get a few things done around here."

Death, or Azrael as he is calling himself now pours a cup of coffee. "Mia, would you like some coffee?"

"No," I reply curtly. Thomas gives me a look. "I mean no thank you, *Azrael*." I accentuate his newest alias.

He sits down across from Thomas and I. "Mia, has been teaching me all about country life and I have been keeping her company."

Thomas nods his head taking us both in. "So, are you both going to come into town for the big doins tomorrow?" he asks while eyeing us both suspiciously. I feel like a teenager getting caught with a boy in my room.

"Yes," Death says at the same time I reply no.

"I know Mia isn't much of a morning person but maybe you can convince her to at least come to the street dance in the evening. I'm sure a lot of her old high school friends will be there."

The last thing I want is to see my old friends.

"We will be there," Death affirms.

"Uh, no. There is no *we*. He might be there, but I won't be." I nod towards Death.

"I'd like to take a look at the garden. Azrael, care to join me?" Thomas asks.

I stand to walk out with them, not at all comfortable with them being alone. Thomas turns to block my way. "Azrael, I'll meet you out there." Death pauses but then walks out closing the door behind him.

"What? I can't look at the garden with you?" I cross my arms in front of myself ready to challenge him if need be.

He just stares into my eyes and cups my cheek. "I'm glad you're still here, Mia."

"I..." I stutter, "where else would I be?" He doesn't know. Surely, he doesn't know who Death is.

"I was terrified to see what I would find here today." He runs his fingers through the bottom of my locks. "You brushed your hair and showered." He tips his head and smiles at me.

"Yeah, well my house guest wasn't too fond of my stench," I say dryly.

He nods and then turns to leave.

76

I sigh. Great, now I have two assholes to deal with.

## Death

I wonder if this is what it's like to meet a girl's parents. I wipe my palms on my jeans. Well, not my jeans but you know. Fuck I'm nervous. I'm never anxious. What if he asks me to leave?

I squat to study a tomato plant. It looks better than it did in that little plastic thing it came in. I can't help but feeling like I rescued it. Thomas's shadow passes over the plant and I look up at him.

"Care to tell me your real name, boy?" he asks. No beating around the bush. Before I answer he holds up his hand. "Wait, never mind. You don't need to tell me you need to tell her. Got it?"

"Yes, sir," I say somewhat befuddled.

"I know who you are, and why you're here." He lights up a cigarette. "Question is why is she still here?"

He fucking knows. "Her mother told you about me?"

"We were real good friends. I knew everything about them."

I shake my head and stand. "Mia doesn't meet my guidelines."

"No, I'm sure she doesn't and even if she did she is quite unique isn't she?" He strolls around the garden inspecting it.

"She is."

"This is the most life I've seen in her since the accident. But, I'm sure you understand my concern with you being here."

I nod. "Yes, it's understandable. I made a deal with her. Six months. In six months, my hope is that she will remember what it is like to live and she will choose it."

"And if she doesn't?" he asks, finally meeting my eye.

My heart constricts at the thought she won't choose to live. I drop my head. I don't want to think about that right now.

"I see," he says. "Right now, we are on the same page. If that should change…" he trails off.

"I won't be able to do it," I blurt out quickly.

"Well, Azrael, I wish you the best of luck then. Mia's mother told me you were a good man. Because I thought the world of her, I will trust her instincts. But, know this, I will have my eye on you."

"Of course, I only want to help her," I tell him.

"Okay then." He looks me up and down. "Maybe I should take you to town. Mia, could use a new dress for the dance and…" he points at my attire, "you could use some jeans that fit."

"Yeah, I hadn't planned on staying." I dust my borrowed pants off.

"I'll deal with the one inside while you get ready. Should only take a couple of hours. It'll give us a chance to talk some more. Mia's got a lot to deal with and if the two of us work together maybe we can get her through it."

"Sounds like a plan," I hold my hand out to him to shake on it. He takes my hand but doesn't release it right away.

"She's all I got, kid. We can't fail her. Do you understand?"

"Yeah, I think I do." He lets go of my hand and releases a long drawn out sigh. If we are going to be allies I should probably give him a heads up on my ignorance to all this. "I should tell you that this country stuff is all new to me. That and people in general. I'm a bit of a loner."

"I know. Mia's mom talked a lot about you and your mother. I think this will be good for both of you. You must be thinking the same thing. Otherwise you wouldn't be here." He drops his cigarette stomping it out.

My eyes wander over the garden Mia and I planted. Well I planted and she supervised but without her I wouldn't have had a clue on what to do. "I like it here. Mia said I could stay a few weeks. A trial run of sorts. I'm worried I'll mess it up."

He laughs. "She doesn't want you here because you are making her actively participate in life. It's easier for her to hide when she is alone. Go get ready, kid." He points to the house and follows me in. Mia jumps up from the table when we enter clearly nervous about what we've been talking about. I smile as I walk past her to clean up. This is good. This is really good.

While I'm in the bathroom I hear raised voices. Okay, scratch that. I hear Mia's raised voice and Thomas's calm cool one.

"What do you mean you are taking him shopping?" she yells.

"He needs some things. You want him wearing your dad's pants to the street dance tomorrow. They are two inches too short on him, Mia. What's the big deal? You said he was a friend. Isn't this how we treat friends around here. It's called hospitality."

"He…he doesn't need them. I'm not going to that dance."

79

"Well, maybe he wants to go the dance. He is a nice-looking man. I'm sure the local bachelorettes will eat him up," Thomas says with a chuckle.

A cupboard door slams shut. "Whatever, Thomas," she says testily.

I smile at my reflection. Did I detect a hint of jealousy there? This Thomas guy is smart. He knows how to handle Mia. I could learn a lot from him I have a feeling.

When I enter the kitchen, she is leaning against the counter with a grumpy look on her face and her arms crossed over her chest. Thomas is leisurely sipping another cup of coffee. I changed into my suit and I notice Mia's eyes roam over me. When her eyes meet mine she quickly masks her appraisal and rolls her eyes. She turns her back to us, banging dishes in the sink. "Have fun," she snips.

"Oh, we will," Thomas chides. He stands up and takes his mug over to set it on the counter beside her. He grabs her waist and pulls her into him giving her a kiss on the cheek. "Be good while we are out." He shakes her slightly as she rubs her cheek huffily to let him know she is unhappy. I think he knows. "Ready, kid?"

"Yep, let's do this. Mia do you need anything from town?" I ask politely.

She pauses and then continues washing the dishes. "Yeah, how about a jar of fucks." She swivels around giving us both a death glare. "You know so that I have some to give." And…back to the dishes. Wow, she is in prime form with Thomas's arrival. Thomas shakes his head and opens the door for me. Before he closes it I hear him tell her one last time to be good.

Thomas looks at me over the hood of his truck. "I hope you're ready for this. She can be a handful."

"Her anger is good. It's an emotion. She has every right to be angry. What happened to her sucks. If she has to take it out on me so be it. I can handle it."

He nods and gets in the truck lighting up another cigarette before starting it up. "As long as you know what you're up against."

"I do. What was she like before?"

"An all-American sweetheart. But, I got to see a different side of her. I'm probably one of the few who has. She used to worry a lot about what other people thought of her. She strived for perfection."

"I know what she showed the world from her social media. I guess I'm curious to learn about the real Mia. Not the one she put out to the rest of the population."

"When she would tag along with her dad and I, she was more of a tomboy. She wasn't afraid to get dirty. She loved to go fishing with us down at the creek. Well, she didn't fish. She would wander downstream and swim. She loved it there. I think it was one place she could be herself."

"Is that why you had her family buried on the hill overlooking the creek?"

He looks at me and then back at the road. "Did she take you there?"

"No, I stumbled across it while I was out exploring. It's beautiful. I've asked her everyday if she would like to visit them. The answer is always the same."

"Like I said, she has a lot of things she needs to work on. She's going to have bad days ahead but, I hope she can find some good ones too. Hopefully soon." He flicks his cigarette out the window and drums his fingers on the steering wheel. "I'm going to swing by the bar when we're done. I have something that I would like you to give to her. When you think the time is right. I tried to send it to her when she was in jail but, she refused her mail and it all came back to me."

"Why don't you give it to her? Especially if it is something special."

"I'm not good at that type of stuff, kid. I don't like seeing her cry."

"So, you're going to make me give her something that will make her cry? Don't you have something that will make her happy?"

He laughs. "She'll be happy she has it someday. She needs to face the fact that her parents and baby are gone. She wants an easy way out of the pain and there isn't one. The only way is straight through it."

"Besides death," I say grimly.

"Yeah, well that ain't happening on my watch." He gives me a sidelong look. "We're both in agreement on that right?"

I nod my head. "I want her to live."

"Me too, kid. Me too."

We spend the afternoon at the mall. I bet we look comical. Two men, one in a suit and the other in ripped jeans and a Tipsy Cow t-shirt. But, unlike Mia, I don't care what anyone thinks of me and neither does Thomas.

Before heading back to the farm, we stop at the Tipsy Cow for a couple of beers. Thomas brings out an envelope and hands it to me. I slide the contents out on the bar as he takes the seat beside me. One of the items is a photo of Mia. Mia is unconscious and in her arms is a beautiful baby. She looks like a porcelain doll. She is perfect...a perfect little angel. I sit up straighter on my bar stool. An unfamiliar feeling creeps up my spine.

Thomas puts his hand on my shoulder. "You see what I mean now?"

"Yeah," I whisper. Hearing Mia talking about Erelah is one thing. Seeing them together is quite another. I pick up the other item. It's a tiny jewelry box. When I crack it open I see a silver heart charm on a chain.

"Open it. It's a locket," Thomas says. He stares at the beer in his hands, tapping it lightly on the counter. This is hard for him.

When I open the locket there is a tiny image of the picture of Mia and Erelah on one side and a lock of fine hair on the other. I nod my head. This is something she will cherish…someday.

"I should have gone to see her when she was in jail," Thomas says guilty. When his gaze locks with mine I see tears pooling in the bottom of his eyes.

"Something tells me she would've refused to see anyone."

"Yeah, you're probably right. Anyhow, I can't bring myself to give it to her. Will you?"

I close the box and put everything back in the envelope. "That depends?"

"On what?"

"Has she been known to bite?" I ask with a smile on my face.

He laughs and slams his palm down on the bar. "I like you, kid," he says before finishing off his beer.

"I'm far from being a kid. I'm thirty-six. But, this is the first time I've had a beer in a bar like a man, so I guess if the shoe fits I'll wear it."

"I call anyone younger than me kid. Plus, I still don't know your name."

"Touché," I say tipping my beer to him.

"We should get back so you can see what she's up to." He rises from his stool stretching.

"You're not coming in?"

"Hell no, boy! She's been stewin all day. You're on your own."

"Gee, thanks," I reply dryly.

"I think you can handle her," he chuckles, patting me on the back.

I sure hope so. Now that she knows I have an ally she might not be so willing to open up to me. She needs to start facing things. If she doesn't she'll never be able to move forward.

# Chapter Eleven

## Mia

I spent the whole afternoon alone yesterday. Like what is going on? Thomas and Death shopping? Are you kidding me? Anyhow, I found myself pacing the house. Waiting, waiting for Death's return. It was dark by the time I heard Thomas's truck pull in last night. So, I hastily made my way to my bed and pretended to be asleep.

Death stood in my doorway for a long time watching me. He probably knew I was awake, but he didn't say anything. I really wanted to know what they talked about all damn day and into the evening, but I wasn't going to give him the satisfaction of seeing me up waiting for him. I'm not waiting on Death. Well, technically I am waiting for death, just not on Death. Anyway, you know what I mean.

Every morning this week he has gotten up early and left. Today I'm going to find out just where in the fuck he goes. Once I hear the front door close I quickly toss back the covers. I dressed before dawn and have been lying here waiting for him to leave. He poked his head in once. I think he was satisfied I was asleep. At least he didn't watch me forever like he did last night.

As I walk through the kitchen I grab a piece of burnt bacon he left lying out. He should leave the cooking to me. I peek out the door, my eyes follow him to the back of the house. As quiet as a mouse I shadow him. He stops briefly to take a pocket knife out of his jeans. Carefully he picks through my mom's flowers making his selections. Is he cutting them for the table?

Once he has a handful he continues through the yard pausing only briefly to look up at my treehouse. He winds his way through the yard down to the dirt path that leads to the creek. I stop at the fence. Do I want to follow? I haven't been back here for many years. My heart aches but my curiosity wins out and I creep along the tree line staying hidden a few yards behind him.

The breeze blows the leaves on the trees, hopefully masking any noise I may be making. He doesn't stop so he must not sense that I am being a creeper behind him. He turns off the path to climb the little hill that my parent's and I used to picnic on. And then he crouches down and lays the flowers on the ground…

No.

No.

I back up tripping on a branch. The noise draws Death's attention and his eyes snap to mine.

# Death and Daffodils

I turn to run but Death calls my name. His voice floats down the hill reaching out and snagging me like a bear caught in a trap around the ankle. I can't move. *Come on Mia, run.* I'm frozen. My mind races. I want to stay...I want to go...I don't...I don't know what I want.

Death walks up behind me slowly. "It's okay, Daffodil. Come with me," he encourages gently.

"I thought they were buried at the cemetery. Thomas didn't tell me they were here," I say, my voice cracking slightly.

"It's beautiful and peaceful here."

"Yeah." I turn my head, hesitantly looking over my shoulder at him. He smiles and holds his hand out for me to take.

"Come with me, Mia. I promise I'll stay with you. We can stay for a few minutes or all day. Whatever you need." He wiggles his fingers encouraging me to reach out to him.

I watch in awe as my hand slowly moves towards his. Why does it seem like time is stuck in slow motion? His fingers wrap around mine gently as soon as they make contact. He is warm, comforting. My eyes roam upward to meet his and when they connect he smiles.

My stomach is churning as he pulls me up the hill. I don't know if I'm ready for this. He releases my hand when we get to the graves. I lower myself in front of Erelah's stone. Death sits beside me quietly. My fingers flit over the etching of her name. The cut is rough against my fingers. All of a sudden a group of starlings rush out of a tree. I watch as they fly up to the sky in sync, their patterns making waves against the blue sky.

I glance at Death. His eyes are on the little birds too. Eventually they take up residency back in the tree. He slowly turns his face towards me. "Is this where you have been coming every morning?" I ask.

"Yes."

"Why?"

"Your mother loved daffodils so I thought she would like them, and I guess it is somewhat routine for me. When I was in the city I visited my mother every day." His finger flits lightly over the yellow petals as he answers me.

"Your mother is gone too?"

He nods somberly.

"Wait, I never told you that my mother liked daffodils."

"I knew your mother. She was friends with mine. They were college roommates."

"Catherine?"

"Yep," he plucks some grass from the ground but, he doesn't look at me.

I'm stunned. My mother loved Catherine. She used to tell me all of the daring things they did in college. Mom thought I should be a little more like them. Let loose a little. "Have a little fun, Mia," she would encourage. But, I didn't listen. I didn't even live in the dorms. I moved in with Darrin. He insisted. Back then he was a bit of a control freak and wanted to know where I was at all times. Funny how things change. Now he could care less where I am.

"I'm sorry, I guess I don't remember my mom mentioning Catherine had children. She passed before I was born. I always wished I could've met her."

"She was amazing. Every weekend she took me somewhere in the city that I hadn't been. She loved to explore new things. The energy that woman had was crazy, until she got sick." He turns his head away from me.

"How old were you when she passed?" I ask, reaching over to place my hand on his shoulder. His muscles tense beneath my palm, so I pull away. "I'm sorry, you don't have to talk about it. I understand."

"I was eight," he whispers.

My heart constricts. That is sad. I had my parents for twenty-six years. He only had his mom for eight. I stare at Erelah's grave. I didn't even have her for a day. Life is so unfair. "I hate life," I cry.

He turns abruptly. "Don't say that," he growls.

"Why? It's true." I shrug my shoulders.

"Life is a gift." He grabs my chin and turns me to face him. "You will see, Mia. I will make you see."

I laugh at his seriousness. "Good luck, buddy." I jerk my head out of his grip. "Your mom died when you were eight how can you say it doesn't suck?"

"Because it doesn't. Sure, sometimes it hurts but my mom wanted more than anything to live and it killed her to ask me to help her end her life. I'm thankful every day I wake up to a new day. If for no other reason than to honor her memory."

He helped his mom die.

Oh, my god, he was eight! I don't think I could mask the horror on my face if I wanted to. "Oh…oh, shit. The other day in the shower when I said you didn't have balls…oh god, I'm so sorry. How horrible." Again, I reach out and place my hand on his shoulder.

He stares at my hand resting on his shoulder before lifting his gaze back to mine. "Yes, and I still find the courage to get up and live every single day."

My hand drops off his shoulder. I shake my head back and forth. "I'm not like you…I can't do it. I wake up every morning cursing that I'm still here. If that's being a coward then that's what I am."

"But, you do get up and live every single day. It's been two years, Mia, and you are still here."

"Not by choice."

"No?" he cocks his head.

I hug my knees to my chest. He is right. I have survived two years without them. My eyes drift over each of the three stones, lingering on Erelah's. "I wish I could have seen her," I whisper.

Death scoots close to me and puts his arm around my shoulder hugging me to him. "Did I ever tell you sometimes I moonlight as a genie?" I watch as he reaches into his shirt pocket and pulls out a photo. "Your wish is my command," he says, placing it in my hands.

When my eyes drop to the photo the scab that had formed over my grief rips open. The image is of my angel wrapped in my unaware arms. She is beautiful. Her hair is dark like mine. A sob escapes me, and Death squeezes me tight, pulling me closer to him. He whispers over my hair, "It's okay, I've got you, Daffodil."

She has a perfect little button nose. Tears cloud my eyes as I stare at the photo. "Is this supposed to make me want to live?"

"Live to keep her memory alive."

"I didn't even know her," I cry.

"You did…you *do*, and you are the only person on this earth who does. Live and share her. Share her with the world…with me."

# Chapter Twelve

**Mia**

I wake to Death stroking my hair. I push myself up off the ground. "Shit, did I fall asleep?"

"No, you didn't fall, you cried yourself to sleep." He helps me sit up. "Do you feel better?"

The sky is so pretty it is the same color of fuchsia as the flowers on Erelah's grave. The leaves bristle in the wind above me and suddenly I have an overwhelming sense of being home. "You stayed here all day with me? You could've left."

"I enjoyed watching you sleep." He smirks and rises holding his hand out for me.

I roll my eyes at him but take his hand and allow him to hoist my aching limbs off the ground. "It's going to be dark soon, I guess we should be going," I grumble.

"We can stay all night if you want. I'll run home and get the blankets and you can build a fire," he teases.

"Oh, I do know how to build a fire. Do you?" I dish back.

"I don't. You do know now you will have to teach me." He bumps his shoulder against mine. "But, seriously, if you want to stay, we stay."

I hug the photo to my chest. "No, I'm ready to go back."

He takes my hand and we walk down the hill. I pause at the bottom and look back at my family. I'm having a hard time walking away.

Death shakes my hand. "Hey, we can come back in the morning."

I focus my attention back to him. He has been coming here every morning. Not to impress me but because he wanted to. Death has a heart...who would have guessed? "That would be nice," I say giving him a shy smile.

When we get to the house I ask him what he would like for supper. "Thomas invited us for supper at the bar, his treat," he answers casually.

I laugh and begin to dig through the cupboards. "Seriously, what do you want?" He pushes me back and closes the cupboard.

"We are really going to the Tipsy Cow and then we are going to see what this street dance is all about. I'm curious."

"Oh, you're curious? Well, I'll tell you, it's a place for a bunch of assholes to hang out and get slopping drunk."

He shrugs his shoulder. "I want to see it for myself."

I open the cupboard, sticking my head inside so he can't close it again. "Have fun," I mumble from inside.

"I can't drive remember?" He peeks around the door at me.

"Call Thomas. You two seem to be buddy buddy." I ignore his hot breath on my neck.

"Are you jealous?"

I face him so that we are nose to nose. "No." I slam the cupboard door making him jerk his head back in surprise.

"Come on. I even bought you a new dress." He places his hands over his heart, begging me.

"You. You bought me a dress. This I have to see." I grab his shoulders and spin him to lead the way.

He jogs up the stairs and I trudge up slowly behind him. He is in and out of his room, I mean my parent's bedroom, before I even make it to the top. I stop halfway up to stare at the bright yellow sundress he is holding up.

I try to hide the smile that forms on my face with my hand. It's so bright. I love it. I never would have worn something so bright before. The me before would have worn something a bit more practical, more something that everyone else was wearing. The me now wants to wear black, like my heart. But, there is something about this dress that I do love.

"You don't like it?" He frowns, running his eyes up and down the thing.

"No, no I like it. I just don't know if it's me?"

"But, do you like it?" he asks, confused.

"Yes, I do."

"Then it is you. Wear what you like. Why would you like it but not wear it?" He shakes his head still dumbfounded.

"Because what would people think with me wearing something so bright so soon after…"

"Soon? Two years is too soon to wear yellow?"

I grimace but chuckle. He's right. It's just a color and it's just a dress. I walk up the steps to stand by him, taking the dress from his hands.

"So, that's a yes?" He dips his head to catch my eyes.

"I guess. I'll go for a little bit. Are you sure you want to be seen with me?" I stare at the floor waiting for his answer.

He tips my chin with his knuckle insisting I look at him. "I want everyone in the world to see me with you." He smiles widely and for the first time I notice the silver specks in his black eyes. God they are beautiful.

Heat creeps up the back of my neck as I blush. "Okay, I'm just warning you. I'm number one on the list of top ten things to gossip about."

"Ooh, then let's give them something to gossip about. You can tell them that I'm Boris, your Russian lover. Tell them I wrote to you while you were in jail and we fell madly in love. Tell them I have a criminal fetish."

"Or, I could just tell them the truth. That you are Death, I am Daffodil, and we are playing a deadly game of Russian Roulette. I've pulled the trigger several times only to be met with an empty chamber. And, you are the only one that can find the one containing the silver bullet," I say dryly.

"I like my version better," he states straight faced.

I roll my eyes and turn to go to my room to get ready to go out.

I can't believe I let him talk me into this. Why did I agree? I don't want to go. I'm only going for him. Not because of what Thomas said about the bachelorettes in town but because I just don't want him to have to go alone. Yeah, that's it. That has to be it because I definitely don't want to go. "I don't," I say adamantly to my reflection.

Death walks in without knocking. "Ready?" he asks excitedly.

"Um, no. Look at me I don't have my hair done nor do I have any makeup on."

He screws his face up. "Ewe, you don't need that crap. You're perfect as you are. Your hair is brushed, and it looks nice, shinny. Definite improvement from a few days ago. Let's go."

I just stare at him in the mirror and grab my black eyeliner bringing it up to my eye.

"If you put bat wings on your eyes I *will* be embarrassed to be seen with you."

"They aren't bat wings," I say angrily, dropping the eyeliner. Fine, if he doesn't give a fuck I really don't either. I don't care what the hell I look like. "Fine, I'm ready."

# Death and Daffodils

He smiles like he won and pushes the door open wide for me to exit before him. I narrow my eyes at him and slowly pick up my red lipstick and purse my lips, coating them with a thin layer of the shimmery stuff. I smack them loudly before letting my gaze meet his. I thought I would find a scowl but all I see is a man starved for my lips. I stand abruptly, knocking over my chair. "I'm ready," I say, hastily setting the chair upright.

I hustle past him and notice he hasn't taken his eyes off my lips. Great, Mia, just put a bullseye on the one thing Death is willing to do for you. He came here to kill me but now all he wants is to kiss me.

He reaches out and grabs me by the waist. "Wait, I have something for you." He pushes me back to my vanity and turns me to face the mirror. He leans around placing a silver heart locket around my neck. I watch as he clasps it, his hands hovering longer than necessary once it is fastened. "It's from Thomas." It rests just above the swell of my breasts. It's beautiful, the etched swirls in the silver reflect the light like little jewels. "Open it."

I try with shaky hands. Death reaches around me, stilling my hands. He opens it for me and rests it in his palm so that I can see the contents. My tear-filled eyes meet his. "I'm glad I let you talk me out of the eyeliner," I cry and laugh at the same time.

He closes it and drops it gently against my skin, his fingers brushing lightly over my breasts. "Let's go live a little for Erelah. Even if it's just for tonight," he whispers against my temple.

I nod once.

My head and my heart are confused as we head out into the night. Should I go? Just, tonight. One night. One night for Erelah. Death jogs out in front of me blocking me from getting in the driver's seat. "Teach me to drive."

"Ah, no." I stop holding my hands up.

"What? Are you afraid I'll kill us both?" he says with a smirk.

"Good point," I toss him the keys and head around the truck for the passenger side.

He fist pumps the air. Good god, little things make him happy. "I can't believe you've never drove." I slide into the middle of the seat so I can help him.

He hesitates a moment as he gets in, seeing me in the seat so close to him. "Oh, there is added benefits to this learning to drive thing." He wags his eyebrows up and down as he settles in the seat.

I shove him in the shoulder. "Stop, or this lesson will be over before it starts."

## Death

This is fun. Daffodil is a great teacher. I glance over at her. The windows are rolled down and the wind whips her hair. The smell of her shampoo wafts over me. She is like breath of fresh air, dressed in yellow with a hint of a smile on her face. Someday, someday I will see a genuine smile.

"You are doing good." She sounds surprised.

"I'm a quick learner." I wiggle my eyebrows at her.

She looks at me. "No."

# Death and Daffodils

"No, what?" I chuckle.

"No, I'm not going to teach you to kiss…or other things for that matter."

This makes me laugh hard. "I think you will find I won't need much help. I'm pretty sure I'll be a natural."

And just like that there it is…the world's most beautiful smile. "You're pretty sure of yourself," she says, blushing.

"You'll see." I take my eyes off the road to wink at her.

She rolls her eyes. Which, I must let you know only increases her level of cuteness. "Whatever, Death. Wait, you still haven't told me your name. What am I supposed to call you in public?"

"You know the deal." I shrug.

"Okay, Death it is." She slides over to the passenger side door as I carefully pull up in front of the Tipsy Cow.

"See, I knew I could get us here in one piece," I tell her, holding the door to the bar open for her.

She turns to me as she brushes past. "Aren't I lucky?" Again, rolling her eyes.

"You do know I think it's cute when you do that." I point to her eyes.

"Good to know. No more eye rolling maybe I switch to flipping you the bird," she says sarcastically. At least I think it was sarcasm.

"You guys made it," Thomas bellows, coming out from behind the bar. "Mia, you look beautiful." He goes to hug her but stops when he sees the locket around her neck. He reaches out and touches it with one finger.

"Thank you, Thomas," Mia says, a slight quiver in her voice.

He hugs her tight and mouths a "Thank you" to me over her shoulder. I nod.

"Come on I have the best brisket in the state and it's a damn proven fact." He rounds the bar and swats his bartender on the ass. She smiles at him and winks at Mia and I as she hustles to the kitchen to get our meal.

There are a few other patrons in the bar but it's not too crowded. Thomas has a beer tent set up at the street dance. Most of the townspeople are there celebrating the towns birthday. When Mia gets up to use the restroom Thomas immediately takes her seat.

"We got a problem, boy," he says quietly. He glances over his shoulder to make sure Mia isn't behind him. "Her damn ex is in town."

"And?"

"He brought his new wife with him." He pauses before continuing in hushed tones, "His very pregnant wife."

"Oh." I sit up straighter as his words start to make sense. "Oh. Oh, shit."

"Yeah, and that ain't the half of it..." he quits talking when he sees Mia round the corner.

"I think I'm ready. Thanks for supper, Thomas. Are you coming to the dance?" she asks.

"No, darlin. I got to stay here and tend bar. I got my young bucks working the tent over there. Why don't you both stay here and have a few more drinks. Keep me company for a while."

"Sorry, I promised this guy all the excitement of the drunks at the street dance."

"That's okay. Now that you say it again it doesn't sound like much fun."

"Oh, no. You made me put on this dress, we are going." She kisses Thomas on the cheek and grabs my hand pulling me out of the bar, giving Thomas and I no time to argue.

Crap, this isn't good. Not good. I guess she will hear about her ex eventually, if she hasn't already. I mean it's a small town. I just need to be ready to deal when shit hits the fan. Calm...I need to stay calm. I don't even know this guy and I already want to kick his ass.

No more than ten feet past the yellow tape blocking off the street for the dance does she spot him. I know the minute she does because all of the color drains from her face. He is standing by the beer tent surrounded by other couples. He spots her at the same time. I notice a blond woman beside him follow his gaze until it lands on Mia. She smiles nastily and sidles up to him taking his hand and placing it on her swollen belly.

Mia sucks in a breath doubling over as if someone punched her in the gut. I quickly pull her around the corner of the stage. "Daffodil, listen to me." I shake her by the shoulders urging her to take a breath. I cradle her face in my palms, leaning in close to her. "Don't let them get to you."

She shakes her head, the shock of what she just saw wearing off. "I...I want to go home."

101

I look around. I don't want these fuckers to win. "Hey, let's blow off the dance and go over to the carnival."

"The only people at the carnival at this time of night are teenagers," she says peeking around the corner to punish herself with another look.

"Please," I beg. "I never got to be a teenager. Please indulge me."

She looks at me shifting her sorrow from herself onto me. Thank god. "Oh, Death. You've never been to a carnival?"

"No," I say with a pout.

"O..okay. Let's go to the carnival." She runs her hands over her face preparing to step back out into view. Everyone knows she is here now.

"Listen, Daffodil. This is your chance."

"My chance at what?" She nervously smooths down her dress.

"Your chance to be you. You don't need to impress them anymore. You might be dead in six months, right?"

Her mouth opens like she is going to say something but then it snaps shut. She stares past my shoulder at the carnival behind me, thoughts swirling behind her eyes. "You know what. You are fucking right. Let's go stuff ourselves with greasy food and ride until we puke."

I pull my head back grimacing. "Let's not get carried away."

She laughs puts her arm through mine and walks out into the crowd. We walk right past her ex, and head for the flashing, bright lights of the midway.

# Chapter Thirteen

## Mia

I'm so hurt. Not for myself. For Erelah. Darrin fucking put a baby in Rebecca fucking Lynd! Are you kidding me? How could he? How could he forget our little girl? And, then to come back here. He never wanted to come back here. I all but begged him to come back and visit our families. He told me our life wasn't here anymore that it was there in the city. But, here he is with a very pregnant Rebecca by his side.

My eyes glide to Death as we stand in line for our carnival tickets. The smell of greasy food, loud music and bright lights calls to us just beyond the ticket booth. He looks nervous. He never looks nervous. His eyes dart to me, looking apprehensive. Then they flit to where the street dance is going on and his gaze turns almost murderous. Then he looks over his shoulder into the darkness towards the Tipsy Cow, wondering if he should take me there, to Thomas. And, again they are back on me only this time I'm staring him down, so he pauses, his manic eyes remain on mine.

"We don't have to do this," he says.

"We came out tonight for Erelah. I'm doing this," I tell him as I step up and ask the carnie for two armbands.

Death pulls out his wallet and pays for them. "He looks like a prick," he states as we walk hand in hand under the bright arches leading the way to the fun.

"Yeah, well the very pregnant lady to his left was my high school nemesis. Actually, since grade school. She was his first kiss." I glance at him and catch him wrinkle his nose which warms my heart a tiny bit and I giggle.

He looks down at me and smiles. "Where to first? The Ferris wheel is the only ride I've ever been on. Should we start there?"

"So, you weren't lying? You've never been to a carnival?"

"Nope, I'm a carnival virgin."

I blush at his reference. "Well, rule number one, the Ferris wheel is always the last ride of the night," I state matter of fact.

"Oh, so you are an expert?"

"I am, aren't you lucky?"

He stops and turns to look at me. "I am luckier than that bastard back there." He nods towards the dance. "I have a girl next to me, who is pure of heart *and* an expert at fun…so I'm hoping," he teases. He brushes a lock of hair behind my ear, then cups my cheek in his palm.

The lights, the music it all seems so far away in this moment. "I didn't say I was an expert at fun," I say trying my best to break this magical feeling in the air. I'm sad, I'm mad, I'm…. I'm not supposed to be having fun.

"Hmm," he shrugs dropping his hand. "I've had nothing but fun since meeting you, so I guess we'll just have to agree to disagree. He grabs my hand and pulls me towards the tilt-a-whirl. "Is this an acceptable ride to start the evening off?"

"Yeah, it's my favorite actually," I grumble still trying my best to be miserable. It's becoming increasingly hard to do around him.

When I slide into the seat beside him and the bar drops trapping us in, I let my gaze wander over him. He is excited, almost childlike in his enthusiasm. When the ride starts he locks eyes with mine and grins at me like an idiot. I roll my eyes, then remember his remark about liking my eye rolling. The ride picks up speed effectively sliding me right into him. His rich laugh wraps around me like a warm blanket and he places an arm firmly around my shoulder so that I don't slide all over the seat. And. Then. I. Laugh. I try to stop, really I do, but I can't. We spin and spin and it throws me out of my blues and right back to a teenager again. Back when life was much lighter. Only this feels better. Freer.

We are both wiping our eyes as the carnie comes around to release us. "God, that was a good time," he says laughing and crying. "What next?"

Death and I ride and ride and ride. All thoughts of Darrin and pregnant Rebecca put on the back burner for the time being. "This is so much more fun than a dance," I tell him as we share a funnel cake.

He reaches out brushing powdered sugar off my nose. "I don't have anything to compare it to but, this is the most fun I think I've ever had, Mia."

The way he says my name makes me almost choke on the overly large bite I just took. A group of teenagers take the table beside ours. Their laughter prompts him to look their way. I grab the lemonade we are sharing taking a big gulp to wash the cake down. I watch the way he stares at them. He really didn't have a childhood. He hasn't even kissed anyone. It makes my heart ache. And that surprises me. My heart hasn't ached for someone other than myself in a long time. It hasn't happened since the day I saved that man in the parking lot at the hospital.

He must sense my eyes on him. He slowly turns to me. "What are you thinking about," he asks.

"You."

"Me?" he looks surprised.

"Yep, I'm wondering if you've ever had a deep fat fried Oreo?"

"A what?"

"An Oreo cookie, a deep fat fried one." He stares at me like he has no idea what I'm talking about. "You know the cookies with the creamy middle and you dip them in your milk?" I shake my head at him.

"Oh, those. No, no I've never had one."

"A deep fried one or never had one period?"

"Never had one, they look hard."

"Well, that's why you dip them in milk." I hop up and order us some. When I come back he looks a bit sad. I shove the paper container in front of him. "These will turn that frown upside down," I tease.

He smiles and my heart blips. Just a small blip. No, maybe more like a drip. It's been frozen for so long, but Death seems to be melting it. This could be a problem. I want to die. I want him to be the one to take me there. But, for tonight maybe I can help him. Give him a glimpse of what it's like to have fun and be carefree. Yes, maybe I can help him and then he will help me. Help me get home to Erelah.

He hands me an Oreo. I bite into it and moan closing my eyes. Oh, god this cookie is delightful. It is nice to eat and not worry about my weight, to not worry about anything. Like Death said, I could be dead in six months. May as well enjoy while I'm still here.

When I open my eyes, his hand is paused in mid-air and his mouth is hanging open. "You," he clears his throat and shifts in his seat trying to compose himself. "You appear to enjoy junk food." Again, the loud sounds and bright lights of the midway dim and fade away. I shake my head to clear the air and laugh.

"I do love them," I admit.

He bites into his and when he groans it sparks me. It fucking sparks me where I haven't been sparked in a long, long time. An ember catches and a warm fire begins to brew low in the pit of my stomach. "These are fucking good." He groans again, surprised.

"Yeah, junk food ain't half bad is it?" He shakes his head in agreement and it's then I notice his eyes look like a starry night. Dark black pits that I first found so appropriate for someone who called themselves Death. But, now I see the light in them, and it's fucking beautiful. I bite the inside of my cheek hard. Stop, Mia. You're just caught up in the carnival and you're using him to distract yourself from seeing Darrin again. This is nothing. This is nothing. This *means* nothing.

107

After we drop our trash into the overflowing trash can Death checks his watch. "Looks like we have time for maybe one more. Ferris Wheel?" he questions tipping his head.

I nod once and he takes my hand leading the way. The midway is clearing out as the evening is winding down and when we get to our final ride of the night there is no line. "See," I tease.

He smirks at me as we approach the carnie. As he is locking us in the seat Death hands him a twenty. "Let's make it a worthwhile ride," he winks at the man. I jab him in the ribs.

The carnie laughs and backs up keeping his eyes on us. "Sure thing man."

When the ride starts all thoughts of the carnie disappear as we glide through the crisp night air, up into the stars. "I've always loved the Ferris wheel," I tell him.

"You can see a long-ways from up here." He looks up at the sky taking a deep breath. My vision doesn't scour the landscape or the stars above, they are locked on the ones that swim in his eyes. The ride jerks to a stop at the top. Death looks at me and the world drops away. It's like I'm floating in this magical space. When he looks at me, he sees me. Not the me I show the world. He sees me. He doesn't shy away from my quirky, from my dark, from the fact I want to die.

"This would make a great place for a first kiss," I whisper. His pupils dilate, nostril's flare and the burn in my belly rises another few degrees. I want to be his first. I have to be his first. I lean towards him, but he places his hands on my shoulders stopping me.

"Wait," he says breathlessly. "I don't want you to kiss me as him." I shake my head confused. Does he not want to kiss me? My head whispers, *who would want to kiss a piece of shit like you,* but my heart tells me he wants to, he really wants to. "I mean I don't want you to kiss me as Death. I...I want you to kiss me as myself." He swallows hard.

My head swims. Is he like me? Is he hiding? Pretending to be something he's not. No, that can't be. He is so damned confident in the role of Death. He just wants me to know his name. His name. Suddenly, I really want to know his name. I wait patiently as a breeze flits across my skin making me shiver. "Brentley," he whispers into the night.

Brentley. He looks like a Brentley. Stoic. Dark. Sexy. Mine.

He threads his fingers through the back of my hair and pulls my face close to his. His breath flits over my lips and the world around us dissolves. I close my eyes as his lips touch mine. Warm, warm, warm, my heart beats with each thought. And then he parts his lips and I follow right behind. His tongue seeks mine tentatively at first. Exploring, savoring and then he closes his fist in my hair and his mouth leaves mine making me gasp out loud like I've been drowning. He sucks and bites his way down my neck, pulling my head back to give him more access. I open my eyes seeing nothing but stars and feeling nothing but his hot mouth on me.

He works his way slowly back to my mouth. Taking, taking, taking. And oh god does it feel good. No way is this his first time. No way. But, it feels like mine. It's like he is infusing himself into my lungs. Crawling into me and settling down for a nice long stay. Oh god it's good. Really, really good. His smell surrounds me. He tastes like mint and powdered sugar. Like mine. Oh, god, so good.

And then the ride jerks to a start and he pulls away from me reluctantly. Our eyes don't leave each other. What the fuck is happening? I thought I was giving him a first kiss. A peck. Okay, maybe I planned on a little more than that but, this. Well this is a horse of a different color.

He has me locked in his sites. I see it now. Just like this morning when I felt like I had stepped into a bear trap. Except this time, he has my eyes. I can't look away. Even when the ride stops and the carnie pulls the bar up to let us off, I can't seem to look away.

Until…someone grabs my arm and jerks me angrily out of the seat and down the steps.

"Wait," I yell, glancing behind me as Death slowly gets out of the seat. I try digging my heels in, but Darrin is viciously, yanking me farther away. "Stop," I scream. He does which abruptly sends me right into his backside. He let's go of my wrist, spinning on a dime to face me. I stumble back a step. "What in the fuck, Darrin?" I spit.

"What in the fuck? What in the fuck?" he repeats, gripping his hair.

I feel Death, I mean Brentley, behind me. And I don't just feel him. I sense the darkness that Darrin has summoned in him at pulling me so harshly off the Ferris wheel, ruining our magic. *Our magic?* Fuck!

A few people have stopped to gawk at us. I notice a few of Darrin's friends standing off to the side. I turn my head to glare at them and they all drop their gaze to the ground. I place my hands on my knees trying to catch my breath. Brentley places his hand on my back.

Darrin noticeably bristles at the gesture. "Did you fucking come here to embarrass me?"

I stand up straight and frown at him. "Embarrass you?"

"Who the fuck is this, Mia?" He points to Death. I turn and look at Brentley. Nope, not Brentley. He's Death. Definitely Death. He wants to kill Darrin and for some reason that makes my heart drip a little more.

# Death and Daffodils

"Who this is, is none of *your* fucking business."

"You fucking come out here acting like a goddamn teenager! Kissing a man in the open like you don't have a fucking care in the world. So, yes, Mia. I want to know why the fuck you came here to embarrass me."

I laugh, an evil little laugh. For some reason having Death at my back has made me grow a pair. "First off, Darrin. I didn't fucking know you were in town. Second, you...you," I point my finger at him, my hand shaking.

Death pulls me close to him and whispers in my ear, "This piece of shit isn't worth it, Daffodil. Let's go home." My eyes stray from Darrin's angry ones to Brentley's starry night ones. And, I let go. I let go. Just like that. I nod once and allow Brentley to gently pull us away from the crowd that has now formed.

Until, Rebecca fucking Lynd opens her bitch ass, little mouth. "She has no shame. Darrin was lucky to get out when he did," she comments loudly enough for my benefit.

I pull away from Brentley and instead of going over and punching Rebecca in the mouth like I should. *I should but the bitch is pregnant and that's not who I am.* I march right up to Darrin so that we are toe to toe. "Did you ever love me? Love our daughter?" I whisper so only he can hear.

He doesn't answer. He just blinks at me, shocked at my close proximity. I back away when he doesn't answer. I know. He doesn't have to tell me. My heart breaks for Erelah. This man should have loved her. But, he has never loved anyone, other than himself. I see it now.

I back up until I bump into Death's hard chest. He grabs me around the waist, sensing my brief bought of strength is about to evaporate and he pulls us out of there. My dark angel of Death picks me up off my feet as soon as we are out of sight and carries me all the way to old blue. He sets me in the passenger seat gently and then hops in the other side and fires her up.

I stare at him as he drives in silence. He glances at me. "What are you thinking?" he asks, hesitantly.

I want to cry. I want to stomp around and throw a tizzy fit but instead I laugh. He keeps glancing from me to the road like I'm crazy and maybe I am. He is clearly nervous. "That was one hell of a first kiss," I say, laughing so hard I think I'm going to piss myself.

He relaxes and grins at me. "I told you I would be a natural."

"No way was that your first time."

"It was. I swear. I'm just that good," he teases.

"Thank you…for tonight. I had fun." I throw my head back into the seat. "Well, until…" I trail off, trying to swallow the lump in my throat.

"Want me to take him out?" Death asks matter of fact.

I roll my head to look at him. "No, I want you to take me out."

He sighs loudly. "Even after that epic kiss? Really?"

I nod sadly. "Even an epic kiss can't make me want to stay in this fucked up world." I turn away from him to stare out the window. I don't know if I'm being completely honest with him anymore. I don't know what I want. I just want the pain to end.

# Chapter Fourteen

### Mia

I wake up early and sit on the steps out front waiting for Death. I know his name is Brentley but, I need him to be Death. I'm feeling guilty about the fun I had last night. I shouldn't be having fun. I don't deserve fun.

I'm waiting for him to get up for his morning walk to visit my parents and Erelah. I have to go. I have to let her know she is loved. What if her spirit knows that Darrin never loved her? That breaks my heart. I'll let her know that I love her enough for both Darrin and I…when I get to her. But, for now I need to show her in the ways I can here on earth. For now.

"Mia, you're up early," Death says letting the porch door slam behind him.

"You said we would go back to the hill this morning. I didn't want you to leave without me."

He stands beside me and reaches down for my hand. "I wouldn't have left you."

I look up and see the sincerity in his dark eyes. I let him tug me off the ground then follow him over to one of the flower beds. As he is cutting the daffodils for my mom he asks me to select something for Erelah. It's nice being able to do something for her. It's all I can do right now. I pick these little blue flowers that remind me of tiny bells. Death kneels beside me, carefully cutting them at the stem. He places a handful in my palm.

Again, he takes my hand and we walk in silence all the way to hill. I like that it's so easy for us to be together and not talk. We place the flowers in front of the stones and then sit a while. I turn away from them after a time and stare down towards the creek. Death finally speaks.

"Thomas told me you used to like to swim down there."

I offer him a smile. "I did. I'm glad Thomas had them buried here. I should do something nice for him. I've been a brat ever since he picked me up from the airport."

"I think he's just happy having you here."

"Yeah, I'm here, for now." I pluck at the grass tying knots in the blades before dropping them back to the ground.

"He came over last night to check on you. Said he heard we had a run in with your ex."

"Aw, is that what it was? A run in?" I smirk.

"I told him we were minding our own business. It was the prick who started it." He lays back propping his head on one arm. "He had to talk me down. I wanted to go back into town and kick his ass. You know I could take him easily."

I laugh and toss one of my knotted pieces of grass at him. "I'm sure you could but, what would that do?"

"Thomas said the same thing." He pauses before continuing, "He was really worried about you."

"Darrin is the least of my worries. I don't care about him. I'm just hurt for Erelah." I'm ready for a change of subject. I'm sick of thinking about Darrin. Strangely, I find that I'm curious to learn more about Brentley. "Enough about me. Tell me about you. Do you have another job? Do you have family? What is your favorite food?"

"Eh, I'm boring," he says nonchalantly.

"Anyone who calls themselves Death is definitely not boring. Come on, I want to know more about you."

He cocks an eyebrow at me. "You do huh?"

"Yes, I do."

The brilliance of his smile makes my heart stop. "I'm flattered. That kiss must have knocked your socks off." I roll my eyes which only makes his smile bigger.

"Okay," he says. "Where to start? I have no family, only my father. We don't talk much. I don't have another job. This one keeps me busy. My favorite food? Hm, before last night I would have said cheesecake but now I'm going to have to go with the Oreo. It was life changing," he adds.

115

"Was that the only life changing thing about last night?" I say it before I think. It comes out of nowhere. Am I flirting with him? No. No. No. I'm just making conversation. See why silence is golden? For me, talking usually leads to foot in mouth, which is why I like to be quiet.

"No, it wasn't the only thing. But, to be certain it was a life changing kiss I think we should do it again. This time with no crazy ex watching us."

He wants to kiss me again. Again! My heart drums against my rib cage as he watches me closely. "Are you sure you don't want to kiss someone else. How do you know I'm not complete garbage at it? You should probably shop around."

His laugh rumbles low and seductive. I feel my heart continue to drip like it did last night. It had been incased in ice for the last two years and the spark he ignited has been burning steadily through my system since yesterday. Drip. Drip. Drip. He speaks pulling me from my own thoughts. "I never wanted to kiss anyone until I met you, Daffodil. And, now, I never want to kiss anyone other than you."

I blush and pull my knees up to my chest. "You can't mean that."

"Oh, but I do," he says and then he stands pulling me with him. He takes a look back at the graves behind us. "Do you want to stay longer?" he asks.

"No, I'm good." I glance over my shoulder, silently saying goodbye to my family and follow Death down the hill.

"Can I ask you something?"

"You can ask me anything." He stops and plucks a wildflower, tucking it behind my ear.

# Death and Daffodils

"What made you stop when you first came here? I mean, you know, you stopped, and you locked me in the closet. Why?"

He curls a lock of my hair around his finger, staring down at me. "You startled me. I wasn't sure what to do. I needed time to think."

"I…I startled you?" He releases my hair and continues to walk.

"You did. You have to understand. I help people who have already been handed a death sentence. When I arrive, they are ready. They aren't scared. They aren't surprised. You, you were different."

"How was I different?"

"Well the obvious is you aren't sick."

"I am though. My heart is sick."

He walks to the garden shed and digs out a couple of hoes, he hands me one. I take it and follow, still not understanding why he stopped.

"Your heart is sick, but it will heal." He holds up his hand before I can argue. "It will," he says sternly.

I lean on the hoe, watching him tiptoe through the garden. "You can't even tell a weed from a plant, can you?"

"No, I can't which is why you are here." He points to the empty spot beside him. I make my way and begin pointing out the carrots that have begun to sprout along with the cucumbers. He nods and starts tugging out weeds with enthusiasm.

"Okay," I concede, "I understand I'm not sick. I get it. But, what else was different?"

"You were excited and curious. I'd never seen that before."

"Maybe I was excited for my pain to finally be over."

"Or, maybe you were excited for something different. Something new. Something that you and you alone had orchestrated. It was the first time you did something outside the box that you and everyone else had put you in."

"It wasn't the first time out of the box," I say angrily. "Getting in an accident that killed a family and my baby was the first time out of the box. And you know what happened when I was tossed out of that fucking box? Nobody wanted me anymore."

"Not true."

I stomp out of the garden.

"Go ahead. Run. But if you think about it you'll realize I'm right."

I don't stop until I get to my room. I peek down at him. I try to focus on his good looks and not what he said. I don't want something new, something different. I don't want anything. He crouches down to inspect the row of corn we planted. I know he is trying to figure out the weeds from the plants and I should help him but, I can't. He will have to figure it out on his own. And…he does. Sighing I lay my head on the windowsill. The breeze tickles over my skin.

My eyes trail back to him. He is different from Darrin. He pushes me and not in the same way Darrin did. With Darrin it just was. What he decided was gospel. Death makes me question things. Things I don't really want to question but now thanks to him I do. Blah.

Thomas's truck rumbles outside. Great. Someone else pushing me. He walks around the side of the house smiling at Death like they are long lost friends. He lights up a cigarette and as he does his eyes flit up to my window. Busted. Great, just fucking great. I stomp downstairs and right out the front door. I need to get away from these two.

Thomas moseys around the house watching me get in my truck. He smirks, pointing his cigarette at me. "Where you headed, darlin?"

"Anywhere but here," I tell him but, then I feel bad for once again being a brat to him. Once I'm in ole' blue I roll my window down to let him know I'm only going to the grocery store and will be back in a bit.

"Okay, Mia. Be good."

Rolling my eyes, I back out and head into town.

I ignore the stares from the other shoppers as I make my way down each isle. I wonder if Death likes spaghetti. Wait, I don't care if he does. I. Don't. Care. I grab a package of Oreos before heading to the register.

I push the cart up and groan internally seeing who will be checking me out. Darrin's best friend Matt. Great. Great. Can this day get any worse? I keep my eyes lowered as he rings me up. When he starts picking up bags to help me out, I politely decline his help.

"Mia, let me help you," he insists.

Once we get everything in the back of the truck I tell him thank you and get in. He leans against my window. "Hey, I'm sorry about last night. That wasn't right. Darrin and Rebecca were both being dicks."

I let out a huff sending a chunk of my hair fluttering off my face. "It's okay. You have nothing to apologize for."

119

"I do. I should have come to see you the minute you were back, and I should have stopped Darrin last night." Why is he lingering at my window? I want to go home.

"I'm not very good company these days Matt. It's all good. It was nice seeing you, but I need to get back. Thomas is waiting for me."

"Speaking of Thomas. He mentioned that you might be hiring a few hands to help on the farm."

"Oh, I don't know. I haven't given it much thought."

"Well, I'm interested if you do. I got laid off from the mill a few months back. Things have been kinda rough. Tina can't work, she has to stay home to take care of our son. He has leukemia." Matt drops his head and swallows hard. I feel a tug at the thawed-out part of my heart. Like Matt is holding a string attached to it and yanking it towards him.

"Oh, Matt. I'm so sorry to hear that."

He runs his hand through his hair. "Yeah, it's tough. Tina is amazing with him though. I want her to be able to stay home with him. But, shit, everything's so damn expensive. This is the only job I could find." He sticks his thumb out towards the store. "It's not enough. We might have to move if I don't find anything, but we don't want to leave our families. You know?"

I sit back in the seat. I don't know. My family is gone and when they were here I didn't even come visit them. "Thomas is back at the house. Why don't you come to supper and we can talk? He…well he knows more about the farm than I do at this point. But, if I can help I sure will."

120

Matt smiles and his mood visibly lifts. "Oh god, Mia, if you help me I will be eternally grateful. I get off here in a few minutes. I'll be right behind you."

I nod and give him a smile before backing up. Matt needs help. I feel so bad for him. The worry lines are etched deeply in his face. Maybe Thomas can get him started on the farm and when I'm not here they can keep it going somehow.

On the drive home I wonder how Matt and his wife keep going each day. I wonder how I have managed to keep going for two years. *Please god, let Matt's little boy be okay.* I don't want anyone to suffer the pain of losing a child.

As tears threaten, I realize they aren't for me. They are for Matt and his family. And, last night when Death told me he had never been to a carnival, my heart ached for him too. Am I finally starting to worry about someone other than myself? Is that what I have been doing? Have I been selfish?

I notice something move through the grass in the ditch just ahead. Shit! I slam on the brakes as a deer bounds out right in front of me. Too late. The deer bounces off the hood of the truck, slamming into the windshield. I close my eyes and pray to god that I make it out of this. Finally, the truck comes to an abrupt stop slamming my head into the steering wheel.

Fuck.

The truck is tipped slightly in the ditch. All I can see are weeds and a cloud of dust around me. My heart races, oh my god. I pat myself down, I'm alive. Thank god, I'm alive. I touch my head where it hit the steering wheel, pulling it back to find blood on my fingertips. Quickly I take a peek in the mirror. I split it good, but nothing a few butterfly stiches can't fix.

Then. It. Hits. Me.

And, I start to cry. *Erelah, I'm so sorry.* I wanted to live. Why did I pray to make it out of that? A good mother would want to get to her child as fast as she could. Oh, god. I'm so torn. What is happening?

"Mia! Mia," Matt yells. The dust is settling, and I turn to see him struggling through the weeds and mud to get to me. The truck is sandwiched between the banks and he can only open the door an inch or two. "Are you okay?"

I nod but I can't stop crying. This was it. This was my pass in the road. My wakeup call. It was literally do or die. Do I want to live, or do I want to die?

"Shit, I'll be right back. I'm going to get Thomas. Hold on Mia. I'll be back!" I watch as he runs back to his truck and takes off down the road towards the farm. It's only a couple of miles. It won't take long. I feel guilty because I know Thomas is going to shit himself. He will be so scared.

And, Death? What will he think? Will he be scared too?

Or, will he just think that God almost got to another one before he did.

I shouldn't care what he thinks.

But, I do.

# Chapter Fifteen

### Death

Thomas and I are just getting ready to head inside when a pickup flies into the driveway, skidding to a stop. A man I recognize from the street dance hops out and yells, "Thomas, Mia had an accident. We need to get back to her."

Thomas and I run towards his truck and the man tells us to follow him. I barely get my foot in the door before Thomas floors it, spinning us around in the driveway. He looks at me. "If she did this on purpose that's it, I need to get her help."

"You think…" my words trail off. No. She wouldn't. Did I push her to hard? Shit. What was I thinking? This was out of my expertise. I should have left her alone.

We only go a few miles and I see the pickup wedged in the ditch. We pull up and get out running to the truck, but she isn't in it. My eyes wander over the blood on the steering wheel and my heart stops.

"She was just fucking here!" the man who brought us here shouts.

Thomas hits me in the arm and points. She is sitting on the ground, her back towards us on the edge of a freshly plowed field. Her head is lowered, and she is bowed over something. Shit, it looks like a deer. I let out the breath I'd been holding.

She didn't do it on purpose.

We all run over to her and Thomas crouches down beside her pulling her into his arms. "Mia, are you okay?" She nods but doesn't speak. I walk around so I can see her face. I drop to my knees beside her. She raises her head, locking eyes with me. Shit, her head is bleeding. Then she says five words that make my heart beat faster than any words I've ever heard.

"I don't want to die," she cries and buries herself into Thomas chest.

He hugs her tight. His eyes meet mine and then roam up to the man who brought us here. The guy takes a step back at her words, his eyes wide with surprise. Crap, I hope this guy is trustworthy. All Mia needs is for more rumors to swirl about her.

"Shh, it's okay, darlin. I got ya." He rocks her back and forth until she quiets down.

"Mia, are you sure you're okay? Does anything hurt?" I run my hands over her arms and legs, looking for anything that may be broken.

"Just where I hit my head."

I reach out to pull her off the ground. She accepts my hand, holding on tight. When she is upright I tug her tightly to me and she hugs me around the waist. I place a kiss on the top of her head. Is she finally choosing life? Thomas stands and walks around the dead carcass on the ground. "Damn, darlin. You tagged yourself a ten-point buck."

She giggles against my chest and the sound is a symphony that wraps around my heart. I think I'm falling in love with her. "Dad would be so jealous," she says and then pulls away from me to look back at the truck still in the ditch.

"Brentley, why don't you take my truck and get Mia back to the house," Thomas says, lighting a cigarette.

"I'll help you pull the truck out," the man with us adds, quickly averting his eyes from Mia and me.

"That would be great, kid," Thomas replies, giving him a curt nod.

Mia walks over to the man. "Thanks, Matt. You still plan on coming for supper?"

"Ah, are you sure?" He finally looks at her. "It can wait. You should probably rest." His gaze drops to the ground.

She invited him to supper? Why does this revelation claw at my insides?

"I'm fine. You need to figure out something for your son and I want to help." She smiles at him and he gives her one back. She slowly turns around to make her way back to me.

Once she is back by my side the clawing subsides a little. A little. I wrap my arm around her and lead her to Thomas's truck. We make the short trip home in silence.

125

Inside I follow her to bathroom where she pulls a first aid kit out from under the sink. "Are you sure you shouldn't go get checked out. I mean you could have a concussion or something," I say, pulling her hair away from her forehead so I can inspect her injury.

Her eyes meet mine in the mirror and she smiles sadly. "I used to be a nurse, remember?" She leans over the sink and takes a bottle pouring it over the open gash in her head, rinsing it thoroughly. I hand her a towel when she finishes. She pats around it carefully and then takes a few butterfly stiches out to close the wound.

I take them from her. "Let me." I set them down and spin her around to face me. My hands wrap around her waist and I lift her up onto the counter. She holds her hair back as I step between her legs. I carefully apply two of the butterfly stiches. She winces at the initial contact, making her knees clamp tightly against my thighs. A groan escapes me before I can stop it.

My eyes dart to hers looking for fear but that isn't what I see. She bites her lip and then she leans forward and presses her lips to mine. Oh, god her perfect lips are on mine again. I'm not sure why she's the only person I've ever met that makes me feel this way. Every nerve in my body is signing a happy little tune.

She bites my lip as she pulls away releasing it after all other contact is lost. She gives me a little, flirty smile and my heart soars. She lays her forehead on my shoulder and I place my hand on the back of head holding her there. "You scared me today, Daffodil."

"I know," she whispers.

"I'm glad you want to live, Mia."

# Death and Daffodils

She lifts her head and desperate eyes lock onto mine. Blue, glassy eyes filled with unshed tears. She is the most beautifully, broken thing I've ever looked upon. "I'm so torn, so scared," she whispers and then she scoots to the edge of the counter, wrapping her arms and legs around me. She clings to me for dear life.

I hold her. I hold her. I hold her.

But, a little niggle of self-doubt creeps into my head. She doesn't want to die. She doesn't want death. She doesn't need *Death*. She doesn't need me anymore. I didn't plan for this. My only plan when I came here was to deliver death. But, now what? She wants to live. That's good. It's what I wanted for her after I saw that spark of life in her.

But, what I didn't plan for was now I want to live too.

I found something here with her.

But, I'm going to have to leave and go back to a life filled with death. My soul cries right along with her.

Daffodil gave me a glimpse at the sun and now I'm not sure I want to crawl back into the darkness.

# Chapter Sixteen

**Mia**

I'm so confused, it's like waking up for the first time in years and I'm not sure where I am or what is happening. I'm clinging to Death. He holds me tight allowing me to absorb his strength. I don't know if I have ever had anyone hold me like this. He makes me feel like everything will be okay.

I thought I had given up, thrown in the towel. But, I realize I hadn't given up I'd just been fighting it. Life is a bitch. I can't fight anymore. I have to surrender and that scares the living shit out of me. A knock on the door interrupts our moment and Death reluctantly releases me, helping me to my feet. "It's open," he says. His eyes graze mine and there is a sadness amongst the stars.

Thomas slowly opens the door and peeks in. "How ya doin, darlin?" He steps in and inspects Death's work with the stiches.

"I'm okay," I assure him.

"I got the truck back."

I grimace.

He chuckles. "Don't worry, darlin, just a broken windshield and a dent on the hood. That cattle guard on the front did its job. That truck is just like the energizer bunny." He tips my chin with his knuckle. He smiles when I raise my eyes to his. "No worries."

Death starts to back out of the room. "I'm going for a walk, I'll be back," he says before ducking out quickly.

Something is off. Why did he look so sad? Is he thinking about leaving? I don't want him to leave. I rush to my room and watch as he walks across the yard. Maybe he is just going to creek. He pauses under my treehouse. His shoulders slump as he stares up at it. He climbs the ladder and disappears inside.

I bite my lip to stop tears from falling and turn to see Thomas standing in my doorway. "What's going on between you two?" he asks, sitting on the edge of my bed.

"I don't know," I whisper.

He pats the bed, and I plop down beside him. "I know who he is and why he is here. Or, maybe I should say *was* here."

"I'm sorry," I say quietly.

"You don't have to be sorry, Mia. I get it. I'm glad you're coming around. I'm not naive. I know you'll have bad days but, if I'm right I think you might be starting to see some good ones?"

"Yeah, I guess. Brentley likes it here. He's making me see how much I like it here too."

He smiles at that. "Your parents would be proud of you, Mia."

"Proud that I have been acting like a spoiled, selfish, brat?"

He chuckles and hugs me to his side. I lay my head on his shoulder. "Yes, because you're still going. Listen, Mia. I don't know why things happen the way they do. Why your little angel was taken from you and then your parents. It's not fair and it sure as hell makes no sense but, you need to focus on the fact that they are together. Your mom was so happy the day you called and told her you were pregnant."

I laugh and cry remembering that day.

"She bought everyone a round at the bar that night. She was beaming and so was your dad. Wherever they are I know they are snugglin that little girl of yours. They are lovin on her just like they did you. She is okay, Mia. They are okay. And, someday you will be with them but it's just not your time."

I shake in his arms as I cry. Tears, an endless supply of tears these days. Once, I thought they had dried up but, I guess I was wrong. Finally, able to speak again, I brush the tears away with both hands. "I feel guilty for living. It's hard for me to enjoy anything because it just makes me feel like shit."

"It will get easier. One day at a time, darlin." He squeezes me tight. I'm glad he is here. Why did I try so hard to push him away? I've always loved Thomas. Always.

"I suppose we should get downstairs. I promised Matt a meal."

"Matt and I decided tomorrow might be a better night." He stands and pulls me with him.

"But, I want to help him."

"And, we will. Tomorrow. I've got some ideas on how all this can work. I think Matt will do a great job. We probably need to think about hiring one more guy though." I follow him downstairs and into the kitchen. "I was thinking you could ask Brentley."

"Brentley?" I grab Thomas's shoulders and spin him to face me.

"That's what I said."

"He doesn't know the first thing about farming." I stare at the tile on the floor, I hadn't noticed till this moment that it's new. My parents must have put it in after I went away to college. I guess I missed a lot that was going on in their lives.

"Neither did your dad when he started but, he turned into one hell of a farmer."

"But, he has a job," I whisper looking over my shoulder like someone might overhear our conversation.

"You said yourself he likes it here. Maybe he's interested in a career change. Who knows but, it doesn't hurt to ask, right?" He pulls his smokes out of his pocket, anxious to get outside and have one. "Unless, you are ready for him to leave."

"I don't know. He is a pain in the ass sometimes."

He raises an eyebrow and tips his head. He laughs lightly. "Ain't we all, darlin." He turns to walk out the door but stops holding the screen door open. "See ya, tomorrow."

"Yeah, okay." He winks before letting the door shut behind him.

I slowly spin in the kitchen, looking around. So, much has happened in the past week. Everything is changing. Do I want Brentley to stay? He scares me. I mean I know I'm safe with him. It's a different sort of fear. He makes me feel things. He sees me, even when I do my damn best to hide.

I walk outside and head for the treehouse. "Death, are you up there?"

No response.

"I know you're there."

He leans over the opening, peering down at me and then disappears again.

"Can I come up?"

"No."

"Why can't I come up? It's my treehouse you know. What's wrong?"

"It's not in good enough shape to take both our weight."

"Okay, so are you going to come down then? I was going to make supper."

"You and your boyfriend can have supper together. I'll wait here to give you privacy."

"My boyfriend?" I ask, confused. What the hell is he talking about? "Wait, do you mean Matt?"

No answer.

"Matt is just a friend. Actually, he's Darrin's best friend. He's working at the grocery store in town but, he and his wife need something better. Their little boy is sick. Thomas told him I might be hiring. For the farm, you know?" I lean my hand against the tree trying to balance myself as I stare up into the dark hole.

"Oh," he says.

"Were you jealous?" I tease.

Again, no answer.

Death and I need to have a serious talk. I know a way to get him down. I've fallen into several of his traps, now it's time to set one of my own. I jog up to the house. There is a lot to do before it gets dark.

## Death

What a fool I am. I shouldn't have acted like a petty, jealous boyfriend. It's none of my business who she is friends or *lovers* with. But, I'm happy this Matt guy is only a friend. Really though, why does it matter? She wants to live and so, it's time for me to go.

"Brentley," the sweetest voice sings. My heart clenches. She used my name. My name. "I have a surprise for you," the siren below calls.

I lean over to peer down at her. "A surprise?"

"Yes." Her eyes twinkle as she smiles up at me, showing all of her perfect little pearly whites. This is a different smile than any other she has ever offered me. It's light, airy, dare I say happy?

"What is it?"

She shrugs and lifts her shoulders. "I guess you'll have to come down and find out." She winks and walks away.

I'm scrambling down the tree before my mind can even catch up with my heart. She has a surprise for me. For Brentley, not Death. For me.

When I get around the corner of the house she is sitting on a log in front of a green tent. A pile of wood sits beside her. She smirks when she sees me hurrying around the corner. I slow my stride and pull myself together. Trying my best to find my bored expression. "What's this?" I ask like I don't really care. But, I do. Oh, but I do.

"You said you wanted to learn how to build a fire. Let's see if it's a skill you can master."

"I master everything I do," I tell her taking a seat on the stump beside her.

She bites her lip and rolls her eyes. God, she is adorable. "So, do you want to learn or not?"

"Yes," I say without hesitation. I clap my hands together. I've learned many things in life, all through books. It's nice to have a teacher. Mia is a great teacher.

# Death and Daffodils

We get the fire going strong just as the sun is dipping past the horizon. It's nice and warm, cozy. The fire reflects in Mia's eyes. It's hypnotic. She notices my scrutiny, and her cheeks turn a shade pinker.

"Now, it's time for the best part." She giggles handing me a stick with a hot dog on it. I hate hotdogs but, if it means I get to sit here longer and witness the fire dancing over her beautiful face then I'm all in. I'll choke it down if I have to. She continues, "I hate, dogs but the trick is to burn them beyond recognition."

So, it seems we have something in common. I laugh. "I don't know if that sounds any more appetizing."

"It is, you'll see." She smiles and I think the fire may be melting my cold, hard, heart because I suddenly want to do everything in my power to make her smile like this every day.

"How is your head feeling," I ask as we both keep our eyes on the flames licking at our dinner.

"It's okay," she answers quietly. "Why did you run off?"

"I didn't run off." I shift nervously on my log.

"Brentley, I thought we were becoming friends. Friends talk to each other." She hands me a bun as she pulls her blackened hot dog out of the fire.

"Friends?"

"Yeah, friends."

I like the sound of that. I've never had a friend. But, it doesn't sound like enough. The way I feel here with her, well, I don't know how to describe it. "Death and Daffodil….friends," I smirk at the notion. Who would have guessed?

"No, not Death and not Daffodil. Brentley and Mia. I want to know you. Death isn't who you are, it's what you do. Big difference."

This hot dog isn't half bad. Perhaps Mia was right. My eyes roam up to hers to find she is staring at me, awaiting a response to her initial question. I groan. Showing weakness is not something I do. Ever. "Okay, I was a teeny, tiny bit jealous over you inviting Matt to dinner."

She giggles. "Is it bad that I like that?" She tips her head, covering her mouth after shoving a bite of hot dog in.

"I've never been jealous before. I didn't quite know what to do with myself."

"Being jealous isn't a good feeling I know. I'm sorry I made you feel that way." She tucks her hair behind her ear shyly.

"You did nothing wrong. Don't be sorry. You were trying to help a friend. My jealousy was unfounded." I drop my head. I want to tell her what else is bothering me, but I can't. *I don't want to leave you, Mia.*

"Yeah, he needs a better job and I guess I need to start thinking about the farm. I've seen so many family farms dry up like dust. Farmhouses neglected and then torn down. That's definitely not what I want for this place." She takes her stick and pokes at the fire, her eyes darting to mine nervously. Why is she nervous? She's going to tell me it's time for me to go…so she can move on. Who can blame her? I would be nothing but a constant reminder of her darkest days.

"This place is pretty incredible, Mia. You are lucky you grew up here." I focus on the sound of the crickets, the pop of the fire, the wind lightly blowing the leaves in the trees. I will miss this place. It quiets my mind. Maybe I should sell my house and buy a place in the country. As I churn the idea around in my head I realize it wouldn't be the same. It would be missing the one thing that makes this place so special…Daffodil.

"I have to ask you something." She's anxious. Her hands are in her lap strangling each other and her bottom lip is tucked between her teeth. Here it is. I sigh loudly as she blurts out her question.

*Wait.*

*What did she say?*

"Did you just ask me to stay?" I shake my head in disbelief.

"If…if you want to." Her eyes meet mine hesitantly.

"My presence won't be a constant reminder of how low you had fallen?"

"No, why would you say that? You've helped me pick myself up. You were right. Contacting you was the craziest thing I'd ever done. I was excited. God, I can't believe I'm admitting any of this to you but, you sparked a light inside of me. It's slowly grown over the past few weeks." She buries her face in her hands and continues to talk albeit mumbled now. "Oh, my god. Why did I even open my mouth? I'm so sorry."

My heart is beating wildly in my chest. She is opening up to me in a way I thought she never would. Is she ready to share her deepest darkest secrets with me? I want them. I want everything from her. Every. Thing. "I'll stay. How much are you paying me?"

Her head comes up abruptly. "You'll stay?"

"Well, you asked if I wanted to stay and work on the farm. I do but, money isn't really something I need. So, what you got to offer me?"

She rolls her eyes. "Seriously, umm, you owe me remember?"

"Technically, I owe your mom."

"Hmm." She taps her lip. "I have an idea."

"Oh, do tell." I slip over to sit beside her on her log.

"I'll pay Matt double, your share and his, while he teaches you everything you need to know about the farm. Then we will be even for what you owe *my mom*. It's a win, win. You can ease your guilt for taking my mom's money. Matt gets paid enough to help him get back on his feet and you get to learn all about the farm."

"Sounds fair. But, don't you think I should get something for all the hard, grueling labor I put in?" He bumps my knee with his.

"I'll feed and shelter you. How about that?" She laughs, throwing her head back. She knows what I'm hinting at.

"Okay, okay. Point proved. I'm getting a heck of a deal. Maybe, I should pay you." I lick my lips as I stare at hers.

She shyly looks away from me. "If, if you change your mind and want to go back to the city, promise me you'll let me know what you're thinking. Please don't just drop it in my lap."

I pull my head back. My heart beating even faster than it was. This is more than just the obvious attraction we have for each other. She is concerned for her heart. She really does want me to stay.

"And you'll do the same, should you want me to leave?"

She turns to face me and nods. Tears pool in her eyes. "I will, I promise. No secrets, from either of us," she says with such sincerity that the world stops. This is more than her needing help on the farm. This is more than her past. This is her letting me know she is ready to risk her heart again. Her heart is made of glass. I know this. Any more chips in it may cause it to shatter.

"I'll be careful with your heart, Mia. I promise."

She smiles. "We should toast our new friendship." She briskly wipes tears away as she pulls a thermos and two mugs out of her bag. She hands me one and pours white liquid in it.

"Milk?" I toss up an eyebrow.

"Yes, and Oreos." She taps her mug to mine. "To us."

"To us," I repeat.

Death and Daffodil or Mia and Brentley. Hopefully the latter.

# Chapter Seventeen

## Mia

He said yes! I don't know why I'm so excited. He said he would be careful with my heart. I sure hope so, the damn thing completely thawed out in front of this fire. For now, I'm just going to let things happen and see where it goes. I'm tired and maybe it's because I have been fighting for so long.

"What's the tent for?" he asks dragging me out of my head.

"I thought since you like the sounds at night that maybe you would want to sleep out here tonight." I start packing the mugs and cookies away in my bag. It's getting late and there is a lot to do tomorrow. I sit back suddenly. *Am I looking forward to a new day?*

"Sounds nice. Will you be sleeping with me?' he asks suggestively.

"Yep. There are two sleeping bags in there. I will sleep on one side and you can sleep on the far, far other side."

"Oh."

He sounds disappointed which makes me smile. He may be dark, but he is also a-door-able. "We could drag them out here and look at the stars for a while."

This perks him up. "I'll grab them." He dives into the tent as I finish cleaning up. I toss a few more pieces of wood into the flames. The smell of the fire brings back so many memories. Bonfires, barbeques, even the simple memory of my dad burning trash. I miss my parents so much. At least being home helps me feel closer to them.

Brentley lays each sleeping bag on the ground, scooting them together until they are touching. He plops down on one and pats the other for me to join him. I do. We both snuggle down inside, placing our hands behind our heads.

"Mia?"

"Yes?"

"Is this what you were talking about when you said it's always better to share an experience with someone? Because, this is nice. Way better than sitting at home, alone."

I roll my head to the side, studying his face. "Yeah, this is what I was talking about."

He rolls on his side and props himself up on an elbow, resting his chin in his palm. "So, you are enjoying me now."

"You are terrible." I roll my eyes at him and roll over. "Good night, Brentley."

"I'll take that as a yes. Sweet dreams, Mia."

I can feel him settling down in his sleeping bag since it's so close to mine. My eyes drift shut. I don't mind he is close. It's comforting. Tonight, I'm not as lonely but, I am tired. Still so tired. *Good night, Erelah. I love you baby girl.*

For the first time I sleep soundly enough for dreams to settle in my mind. Happy dreams of coming home from school to find my mom waiting for me, a bouquet of daffodils sitting on the table. The smell of fresh baked cookies wafting through the air. Timber comes running out of the kitchen, his nails clicking on the linoleum. He skids to a stop in front of me. "Hey, boy," I crouch down to greet him, swinging my bookbag off my shoulder. He laps at my face. "Timber, stop you are getting me all wet." Laughing I wipe at my face.

"Mia, Mia wake up. It's raining." My eyes slowly focus on the man leaning over me. A big rain drop hits me square on the forehead. I sit upright. "Shit!" I squeak.

He stands and pulls me to my feet. And then a cloud must break clean open above us because it is suddenly pouring buckets. "Holy, fuck!" he yells. The fire sizzles out, leaving gray smoke to billow out between the doused logs.

I start laughing, bending over to try and catch my breath. The rain is chilly, and we are soaked. Our sleeping bags drenched. Brentley's rich, chuckle joins mine and soon we are both laughing so hard we can't stop. "Okay, first lesson. We both need to start watching the weather. Good farmers pay attention to the weather," I tell him.

His starry eyes lock on mine. "So, you were serious. About me helping you with the farm?"

I nod and grab his hand running for the house. When we get to the porch he stops me. "We are going to get the floors all wet." He starts removing his clothing. Shit. What do I do? Well obviously, I stand there and stare at him. I shiver as he peels his shirt over his head. The shadow of his abs creates a sinfully, sexy air about him. He looks up at me through long, dark, wet eyelashes and my stomach clenches painfully. I keep my hands balled in fists at my side to keep from reaching out to brush the wet hair from his face.

"I'll go in first, so you can undress. Scouts honor, I'll go straight to my room...I won't peek."

I reach out and stop him. "It's okay. You can wait." I pull my shirt over my head then quickly kick my shoes off and peel my wet jeans down my thighs. He is paused on the threshold, eyes glued to me. "There are towels in the dryer." I point towards the house and he backs up a step to allow me to slide by him. As I pass his heat laps at my chilled skin.

Leaving puddles behind I make my way to the laundry room to grab the towels. When I right myself he is standing in the doorway. His wet boxes clinging to him and um...well evidently he isn't as chilled as me cause...well you know. I peel my eyes away and toss him a towel. I feel his eyes all over me as I dry off.

"I'll get the floor, toss me another one," he says. I grab another out of the dryer and throw it to him, keeping my eyes trained on the floor. When he steps out of the laundry room my breath shudders as his intensity leaves the room. Like oxygen being sucked out from a fire. Holy shit. Holy shit.

I'm taking an extraordinary amount of time drying off when Brentley finally reappears. He stalks over to me and swiftly turns me around. "Your locket," he whispers over my shoulder. "I don't want it to get ruined." He carefully unlatches it and dries it gently, as if it were the most precious thing in the world. And it is...to me. But, why does he care so much?

Once he is satisfied it is dry he reaches around me to clasp it. I turn to stare up into the stars of his eyes. The silver flecks suck me deep into the black hole. My subconscious mind prompts me to stand on my tiptoes and gently place a kiss to his lips. "Thank you, Brentley. For everything..."

He cups my cheek in his hand, and I lean into it. He is so warm. "I haven't done anything but, you're welcome, I guess." He shrugs and dips his head, kissing me again. Except this time, he pulls me close to him. His wet boxers press against my stomach and I feel him there. All man. This is something I never expected to happen in a million years. My only dreams for the past few years have been of leaving this place.

Brentley makes me want to stay. I had felt alone for so long. Sure, I had people around me. They tried to reach out to me. They saw my sadness but, nothing they said or did helped. I made them uncomfortable. But, him. He saw me. He saw through the sadness to what was going on inside. While I seemed sad on the outside, the inside was full of anger, fear, resentment and so much self-loathing that I was caught in a hurricane of emotions.

He saw that and it didn't make him uneasy. He didn't tip toe around it. He pushed me. Pushed me to talk about Erelah, to visit my family's graves, to leave the house, to trust him. But, more importantly he stayed by my side through it all. Unwaveringly, he stayed by my side.

When we part he takes my chin in his hand directing me to look at him. "We should get to bed. It's only two in the morning. You need to rest."

His eyes flirt away from mine to inspect the butterfly stiches on my forehead. "We can practice this kissing thing tomorrow."

I smile easily for him. Where once I would have been miffed by his remark, now I find I'm flattered. Flattered that he wants to kiss something as broken as me. I snuggle into his side and allow him to lead me through the house to my room. "Good night, Brentley."

"Sweet dreams, Mia. I'll see you in the morning." He walks away leaving my bedroom door open. A thump followed by a few curses echo down the hallway. I giggle, imagining him stubbing his toe on something. "I hear you laughing at me, Daffodil. Not nice."

"I never said I was nice," I holler back as I change out of my wet underwear.

A few more curses and then he must hit the bed. The sound of the rain pattering against the window makes me shiver. I'm still chilled from the rain. I could turn the heat on. My dad had certain periods of the year we weren't allowed to turn the heat on. He would say it's too soon or it's too late for that depending on the time of year. My mom and him would go rounds over it. Not seriously, it was all in jest. I wonder if he did it just to razz her. They were always giving each other a hard time. They made every little mundane thing they did together fun. Even arguing over the temperature.

After a few minutes of freezing under my sheets I decide to see if Brentley is cold. It wouldn't be very hospitable of me if I left a guest to freeze now would it? My feet pad softly down the hall like they did so many times when I was a child. Definitely not going to stub my toe. I know every nook and cranny in this house. When I get to the doorway of my parent's room I see him sitting on the edge of the bed facing the window. He turns towards me when he detects my presence.

145

"Is everything okay?" he asks.

Cautiously I take a few steps into the room. "Yeah, I was just wondering if you were cold? I'm freezing."

He swings his legs in bed and holds up the blanket in invitation to join him. "I'm warm blooded. Come here, I'll warm you up."

Lightning flashes, briefly giving me a view of him in the bed looking...I swallow hard...looking so damn sexy. The thunder that follows sends me skittering in next to him. He pulls me in close so that my head rests on his chest and he covers us both up. Shit, he was right he is warm. "I'm surprised you are awake." I mumble against his skin trying to still my shivers.

"I was enjoying the sound of the rain and I was thinking about you."

I look up at him. "Me?"

"Yeah." He sighs. "I've never met anyone like you."

"How is it in your thirty-six years you've never ran across a crazy person?" I snuggle in closer to him. Warm, warm, warm.

"You're not crazy, Mia."

"Pretty sure you're the only one who thinks that." My fingers get a mind of their own, lightly running over the hard muscles of his chest while his absentmindedly run across my back. It's almost as if our bodies have always known each other. No awkwardness exists. It's weird, he is a stranger. How can I feel more comfortable with him than I did my own husband?

"It's not productive to worry about what others think of you."

"I know," I whisper.

"But, if you must know I was thinking about how you make me feel. After my mom died I became obsessed with death. Her passing was strange to me. A bit anticlimactic for lack of a better word. One minute she was there and then she wasn't. It made me question the point of feelings and so I shut them off. I continued to live for her. But, I never allowed myself to feel anything for anyone or anything after that. I figured what was the point if we were all going to die anyway."

"I felt the same way after my accident. Everything seemed pointless."

He gives me a gentle squeeze. "You are making me feel again, Mia. I'm not sure what it is about you. It's just you. From the moment you emailed I felt it. First it was an excitement that grew the closer I got here. Since arriving at your front door, it has snowballed into a vast array of feelings. Tonight, made me question whether or not I have been living at all.

"Does it scare you?" His feelings mirror my own. I haven't been living, I've just been here like a bump on a log. Doing nothing. Feeling nothing. Until him. But, I'm terrified. I'm not sure I'm ready to risk the pain of it all again. Maybe it's better to remain a zombie.

"No, not in the way that you mean but I was scared when Matt told us you were in an accident."

"I'm scared of everything. Scared to allow myself to feel. Scared to live. Just plain scared." I swipe my hand over his chest wiping my stupid tears off him.

"You were handed a raw deal, Mia. I'd like to tell you that your heart will never be broken again but we both know it would be a lie. Life is unpredictable. But, you are strong, so strong and sweet and adorable and kind."

"Yeah, yeah. You can stop with the compliments now."

"No, I will never stop with the compliments. Maybe that prick of an ex-husband didn't give you the compliments you deserve, but I'm not him. So, forgive yourself for accepting less than you deserve but," he tugs my hair back harshly driving his point home, forcing me to look at him, "don't do it again."

He keeps his hold on my hair. Oh god. There is a connection between my scalp and my lady bits that I didn't know existed. *What the fuck? What the fuck?* Shit, he knows. I don't know how but he knows what he does to me. His confidence is commendable but unsettling. Is there anything that I will be able to hide from him? Do I want to hide?

He smiles slowly as he releases my hair. "There is no script for this, Mia. None. This, my dear, is going to be a journey of self-discovery...for both of us." He pushes my head back to his chest before placing a kiss against my hair. "Sleep tight, Mia."

No words come from my mouth. I just nod like an idiot, shifting beneath the sheets trying to ease the ache that has settled between my thighs.

I emailed Death for an ending.

Death is usually an ending right? A finality I understand better than most.

Is it possible that Death could be a new beginning?

My eyes fall shut as I draw in his scent, his warmth, him. But, as always my thoughts drift to my sweet baby before I find sleep and with it guilt for feeling anything other than pain.

# Death and Daffodils

*Good night, Erelah. I hope grandma and grandpa are keeping you warm tonight.*

# Chapter Eighteen

### Death

She slept in my bed all night. All night. In nothing but panties and a bra. It made me realize that I am a goddammed saint. A saint I tell you. I wanted to explore her. Inspect every square inch of her. I may be the one with no experience but, I'm getting the feeling that some of this is new for her too. When I pulled her hair, I saw what happened and I want to see it again.

Soon.

There is something about her. This morning when we walked to the graves of her family I swear I could hear her name whispered in the wind. Even now standing here in the garden the birds are singing a tribute song to her. Her. Her. Her. She's all I can think about. Each butterfly that flits by, reminds me of her delicacy. The clouds remind me of her soft breasts pressed against me last night. The sun reminds me of her bright smile.

Seriously, I do not know what is happening to me. If you asked someone to describe me before I came here to the country, they would have said I was cold, calculating even. If you asked my father he would have described me in one word. Psychopath. Until, meeting Mia I was inclined to agree with him. I've spent the better part of my life faking niceties with people. That could be why I see myself in Mia. She has done a lot of pretending too.

"Supper's ready," Mia says, bopping around the corner startling me. She laughs.

"You really aren't nice are you?" I tease. "Scaring an old man is just mean, Mia. Really."

"You're not old," she says rolling her eyes. "Come on, Matt is here. I want you to hear what Thomas has to say, so you know what you are getting in to. Farm life isn't easy."

"No, I don't imagine it is. But, the best things in life aren't easy." I wink as I make my way towards her. She blushes and backs up a step. "You aren't easy," I continue my spiel, walking straight towards her, "but, I'm certain you're worth it."

A tree halts her escape, and she sighs loudly. "You unsettle me," she says quietly, refusing to meet my eyes.

"Do I?" I brush a wisp of hair from her face tucking it behind her cute as a button ear.

"Yes, you do and I'm not sure what to do about it."

"Perhaps you should just let me unsettle you and see what happens." My hand leaves her ear and travels down her arm. I let my fingertips lightly trail against the side of her breast before gripping her wrist to pull her closer to me.

"I…I don't know if I can do that." Her eyes meet mine briefly before darting back to stare at my chest.

"Well, we can discuss that later. I guess we should get inside before Thomas sends out a search party."

She smiles and nods. When we open the door, I'm greeted to the most wonderful aroma.

"Oh man. Something smells good." Her smile brightens at my words.

"It's my mom's recipe. Spaghetti and meatballs."

Thomas and Matt both stand when we enter. We shake hands, discussing how much rain was received overnight while Mia sets the food on the table. "Mia, this looks delicious," Matt says.

Her only reply is a shy nod and a blush of pink on her cheeks. It's hard for her to accept a compliment. That really needs to change.

"She learned from the best. Her momma was an amazing cook." Thomas not being shy in the slightest digs right in. "This right here was one of my favorites."

Mia slides into the chair next to me. "It was always mine too. I don't know if I do it justice though."

"Oh, it's good," he mumbles with a mouthful. "If I wasn't afraid to be struck by lightning I might even say it's better than your moms," he praises.

She smiles at him, but it doesn't quite reach her eyes. Hmm.

Thomas relays his plans for the farm. First thing on his agenda is buying cattle for the pastures. Which includes fixing fences. After that, plans are made for planting corn and beans in the fields not currently being leased. I hadn't realized how big this farm is. Sounds like it goes on for miles and miles.

"Does that all sound good, Mia?" Thomas asks.

"Huh?" She looks at him a bit confused. Was she even listening?

"Does that sound like a good plan? If you have any ideas I want to hear them, Mia." His brows furrow in concern.

She sits up straight and smiles, visibly trying to ease his concerns. "It sounds great. I'm no farmer, Thomas. You know better than me. I'll stick to feeding you guys how about that?"

He shakes his head. "Mia, I want you to be a part of this. You are the farm now. It's yours not mine."

"I know. Your plan is fine." She stands and begins removing dishes, all the time smiling brightly. A little too brightly. "Matt, does this all sound good to you?"

"Yeah, Mia. It's a good start, especially since we are getting a late start on the season." He wipes his mouth on his napkin dropping it on his plate as she scoops it up. "I really appreciate you giving me a job."

"Would anyone like dessert?" she asks busying herself around the kitchen like a flurry of bees swarming a hive. Everyone nods as she pulls out a chocolate cake from the refrigerator. The smile never leaves her face. Why is she hiding? Is it because Matt is here? I suppose she is used to showing everyone a perfect persona. Maybe she is reverting back to the fakeness.

When she places a piece of cake in front of me I grab her wrist before she can pull away. "Could you both excuse us for a moment?"

Both men nod, giving us a curious look as I pull Mia from the room. I drag her upstairs. She tugs against my grip but is otherwise quiet. When I get inside her bedroom, I close the door behind us. "What is wrong?"

"Nothing's wrong," she says tensely.

"What's with the fake smile?"

"It's...it's not fake. Better question is what are *you* doing dragging me away from our guests?"

I like the sound of that. *Our* guests. Oh. Oh, she is good.

"Nice, distraction, Mia. But, I know something is wrong. What is it?"

"Nothing, I'm fine." She wraps her arms around her middle, hugging herself.

I pull her into my chest, resting my chin on her head. "Daffodil, something is wrong. Why are you pretending to be happy and content when you're not? You weren't listening to a thing Thomas was saying and it all was important stuff you should be aware of."

"H-how do you read me so well?" she whimpers.

154

"I pay attention, Mia. You're sad, scared, perhaps a bit of both?"

"This is all happening so fast. What if tomorrow I wake up and I don't want to be here. What will Matt do then? What if this isn't what my dad would've wanted. I didn't pay attention to what he did on the farm. He just did it."

"These are all things that you should be addressing with the people downstairs. It's okay to let them in, Mia."

"I've always just sucked it up and done what was expected. It's not polite to rant about your worries."

"It's not ranting. It's discussing things that are bothering you, with your friends, two people whom you seem to trust. It's okay for simply niceties with strangers but they are not strangers."

She peeks up at me with little tear drops clinging to her eyelashes like diamonds on a chandelier. "You've only known me for a few weeks, yet you seem to know me better than anyone. How is that?"

"Because I'm interested in every little bit of you, Mia. You can't hide from me. Your real smile is different from your fake one. The real one makes your eyes sparkle. The fake one doesn't even compare. You blush when you're feeling shy or embarrassed but, you blush a completely different shade when you're turned on." She smacks me lightly when I tell her this, but I continue. "You roll your eyes and squint when you are frustrated but when you roll them without squinting I know that you are secretly enjoying our banter. I could go on and on and on, Mia. I'm learning new things about every day."

Slowly she wraps her arms around my waist and hugs me tight. Everything is right in the world when I am with her. I'll never be able to let her go.

She is the only person that makes me feel anything. "Thank you, Brentley. If you hadn't shown up on my doorstep I don't know what I would be doing right now."

"Probably laying on the couch attracting flies."

She pushes away from me and crosses her arms over her chest, stomping her tiny foot. *There's my Mia.* "I'll remember that when you want to practice kissing later." She twirls around to head downstairs.

I follow right behind her. "You know I was only kidding right?"

## Mia

One-minute Brentley is sweet and the next infuriating. Attracting flies? Really? Was I really that bad? Yeah, I guess maybe I was. Matt and Thomas quiet when we enter the kitchen. Thomas turns towards me, concern etching the corner of his eyes. "Everything okay?"

My mouth opens to say everything is fine but, Brentley's touch at my back reminds me to be honest. "No," I say with a sigh, sitting down at the table. "Um, I wasn't really paying attention when you went over the plans for the farm. I got wrapped up in my head worrying."

Thomas reaches across the table to lay his hand on mine. "What are your worried about, darlin?"

"Everything. I don't know if I can do this. What if tomorrow I slip back into old patterns?" My eyes hesitantly shift to Matt's. He nervously averts his gaze to the table.

"One day at a time, Mia," Thomas says, softly squeezing my hand.

"I know. I'm sorry I wasn't listening. Could you go over it again with me?"

"Of course. I'm glad you told me." He looks over at Brentley giving him a nod of thanks.

"I'm trying. I really am but, sometimes my fears get the better of me."

"No worries. We'll get it all figured out."

After Thomas repeats the plan, *again,* I'm impressed with what he says. "It sounds perfect, Thomas. I think Dad would be happy with everything." My dad loved farming. He was a big city boy too. When my mom brought him home to meet her dad he didn't want to leave. So, they didn't. He learned everything from my grandfather he could and when pops passed away dad took over the running of the farm.

"I think so too, darlin." He stands and comes over to wrap his arms around my shoulders. "We'll make this work, Mia. We will." He kisses me on the head before heading for the door. "I got to get back to the bar. I'll see you boys Monday morning bright and early." Brently and Matt both nod in tandem.

Matt stands slowly. "I better be heading out too. Thanks for supper, Mia, it was good. Hey, I'm having a little get together tomorrow afternoon at my parent's cabin by the river. Why don't you and Brentley come? Potluck style. Soooo, if you want to bring those chocolate chip brownies that you're famous for I won't stop you."

I glance at Brentley and he shrugs letting me decide. "Yeah, sure. Thanks for the invite."

He shakes Brentley's hand. "See you tomorrow then." He pauses with his hand on the door. "Mia, you want to walk me out?"

Death shifts in his seat, the muscle in his jaw ticks slightly. "Of course." I get up and follow him out, pausing to look behind me. Death has transformed back to Brentley by the time I reach the door and I breathe a sigh of relief. I don't want him to be jealous. It's not a pleasant feeling. "I'll be right back," I tell him, and he gives me a genuine smile that makes my heart skip a beat.

I glance up at the sky on our way out. Looks like rain. Bummer. I was looking forward to another night of star gazing with Brentley. Matt stops before getting into his truck. "Mia, forgive me if I'm overstepping but, I'm getting the impression things have been a lot tougher for you than any of us thought."

It's not that I was unaware the statement's I've been making lately would lead him to this conclusion but, do I want to talk to him about it? I don't know. I toe a rock in the driveway avoiding his gaze.

"I'm sorry, shit, I shouldn't have said anything. Forget it. Thanks again for supper. I'll see you tomorrow." He opens his door.

"I have," I say quietly still kicking the rock, afraid to look up and see the judgement that is surely on his face.

Matt reaches out and gently lifts my face. "Mia, please come talk to me if you need anything. I can't imagine what the last few years have been like but, please, please don't feel like you're alone."

A tear meanders slowly down my cheek. "Matt, you have your own problems. I'll be fine, don't worry about me. Just worry about that little boy of yours."

"We all have problems. You are helping me with mine by giving me this job. It's okay to ask for help, Mia."

"I know. I've been feeling better lately." I turn to look back at the house. His eyes follow mine.

"So, are you two together?"

My eyes dart back to his. "Um, well, we are just friends." I shift nervously back and forth on my feet.

He gives me a knowing smile. "He is a little odd, but he seems nice. Darrin was a gigantic dick to you a lot of the time. He may be my best friend, but I never did think he treated you right. If this guy makes you happy then I'm all for it."

"Every day gets a little easier. Brentley is helping me and so is Thomas," I quickly add.

"Well, I hope you know you can count on me too. I should be going. I expect to see the both of you tomorrow afternoon." He pulls me close, gives me a squeeze and then hops in his truck.

"Is he going to be there?" I hurry to ask before he shuts the door.

He lifts his hat off his head and wipes at his brow with his forearm. "I'm not sure. But, if he is I promise I won't let him act like he did the other night. Okay?"

I nod and back away from the vehicle as he starts it. He waves, I wave back and then turn for the house. When I get inside I find Brentley going through the books on the bookshelf in the living room. He looks up as I enter the room. "Is it okay if I find something to read?"

"Yeah, of course. Do you like to read?" I perch on the arm of the chair watching his long fingers stroll over the binds.

"My whole life has been books. It's all I had." He turns offering me a sad smile.

"Well, take your pick. I'm going to go do the dishes." He nods, his attention back to the books. "Brentley?"

"Yes?" He is scanning the back of a novel he pulled out, not giving me his full attention. But, it doesn't matter, I need to reassure him.

"Matt just wanted to ask me how I was doing. The things I've been saying concerned him. That was all." I hurry to the kitchen. I hope that helps. Jealousy feels yucky and he admitted once that he was jealous over Matt. I want them to be friends.

He follows close behind setting the book down on the counter beside us. "Mia, you don't have to tell me your personal conversations. It's none of my business."

"I saw the look on your face when he asked me to walk him out."

Brentley grabs me by the shoulders and looks me dead in the eye. "I'll admit I want you all to myself, Daffodil. I've never had these kinds of feelings. Hell, I've never felt much at all. But, I will deal with it. Not you. You didn't do anything wrong. You had a conversation with a friend. I'm not going to let you feel guilty when you have nothing to be guilty for."

"Okay," I whisper. My mind is in overdrive. Brentley admitted being jealous but said it was his problem not mine. Darrin was jealous. Which is why when we moved to the big city, I didn't live in the dorms. He insisted we live together from day one. If I was five minutes late we played a game of twenty questions when I got home. I always lost. Always. Even if I had a valid excuse. I never went out with friends. Never bought anything without checking with him first. Actually, now that I think about it I don't know if I ever decided anything by myself.

160

"So, is this one any good?" He holds up the first book in the Little House on the Prairie series.

"Well, yes." I tell him giggling. "I'm sorry, I just didn't expect you to choose that one?"

"Why not?" He turns the book from front to back in his hands. "It's about the prairie and we are on the prairie. I thought it would give me some insight."

I nod still trying to stifle the giggles. "It will. Except the insight will be limited to a more historical one. Late 1800's, I believe. The series is geared towards children and young adults."

He shrugs his shoulders and takes a seat at the table, cracking the book open to the first page. "Well, I've never read it and it sounds interesting." He settles back in the kitchen chair.

"It's one of my all-time favorites. Enjoy," I tell him turning back to my dishes. I start to worry about tomorrow. Do I really want to go to the river? Not if Darrin is going to be there. No and no. I'll call Matt tomorrow and tell him I've come down with a cold. Shit, that won't work. He will be here Monday and then he will know I lied. Maybe I cou-

Brentley's rich voice permeates the room and I freeze. I close my eyes and take several deep breathes. He is reading out loud. Just like my dad used to do when my mom was busy in the kitchen. I always thought it was sweet and now…I swallow hard and slowly turn to look at him.

His eyes scan back and forth over the words. His long fingers grab the corner of the page to turn to the next. I swivel back to my task at hand…the dishes. This is all so familiar. So…so…comforting. Like a

161

warm blanket being draped across my shoulders. Or a cup of warm cider in autumn. Death is cold, but Brentley makes me warm.

I glance over my shoulder again, studying him for a moment. Or at least it felt like only a moment. Water runs over the edge of the sink. I shriek as it waterfalls down the front of my shirt and pants. Brentley jumps up to help. He grabs a towel and starts patting me down, down, down. When he reaches the top of my pants I pull away from him, tugging the towel from his hands. "I...I got it."

He laughs. "How did this happen?"

"I'm a scatter brain. That's how. Just keep reading will ya. I got it," I grumble. I don't know why I'm mad at him. I'm not. I'm mad at myself for...Jesus I don't even now. What is this man doing to me?

He goes back to reading...again aloud. His voice is doing things to me. Never has Little House on the Prairie sounded so good. So good. My eyes close again and my hips twitch on their own violation towards the counter. *Stop, Mia.* But, I can't.

Somehow by the grace of god I get the damn dishes done. The world outside is rumbling as a storm moves in. Brentley looks up from the book. "All done?" he asks.

"Yeah," I answer quietly. If he knows what his voice does to me he doesn't act like it.

"Want to continue in the living room? I'm anxious to see where this goes." He shakes the book in front of him.

I nod and follow him to the couch. He sits in the corner and pulls me in close to him, encircling me in his arms with the book in front of us. He kisses the top of my head and continues to read.

162

Oh, no. No.

I squirm in his arms. His voice vibrating against me, being trapped in his embrace is…is…I squeeze my eyes shut and try to ignore the tightness in my lower belly.

Squirm. Shift. Squirm. Shift. No matter how much I try I can't get the fire burning in my nether region to stop. Abruptly Brentley puts the book down. "Are you okay?" He pushes me back to study my face. My warm, flushed face.

I huff sending my hair fluttering away from my eyes. "I'm…I'm fine. Do you think it's a little warm in here?"

Whatever he sees on my face causes him to lick his lips and lean in close. His nose brushes against the side of my hair. He inhales deeply before speaking. "What's wrong, Mia?" he inquires on the exhale. His voice, his voice. Oh shit. He knows. He knows what is happening.

"I'm just warm that's all." I try to downplay, embarrassed that I can't seem to get ahold of myself. This is not like me. Not at all. "I'm…I'm just going to step outside and get some fresh air."

He pins me. Arms braced on either side of my hips. "It's raining out." His lips graze mine. Zing. Straight to the crotch. Fuck.

"I'll…I'll stay on the porch. It's fine." He doesn't move. Not. A. Muscle.

"I would like to explore your body, Mia. Would you allow me to do that?"

What?

Whaaaat?

Squeezing my legs together tightly I stare at him. The silver specks are twinkling. Fucking twinkling. He wants to explore my body. What exactly does that mean? I know he hasn't been with a woman but, the look in his eye makes me feel like he knows a hell of a lot more than I do.

"Mia?" he tilts his head to one side.

He is beautiful. Beautiful and dark. Dark and mysterious. Mysterious and sexy…*Mia stop*. I shake my head trying to clear my thoughts. The storm rumbles on outside right along with the storm in my head. Hell, in my whole body. Every cell is screaming *Mia, please, please let him explore*. But, my mind says no. If I let him do this it's a risk. A risk to my fragile heart. But, the rest of me wants his hands, his mouth, his whatever…to *explore*.

# Chapter Nineteen

**Brentley**

I stare into her beautiful blue eyes…waiting on bated breath.

A tiny nod of the head.

Fuck.

She said yes. She is going to let me touch her. See her. A shiver of delight runs up my spine.

*Slow down Brentley, she is fragile.*

This reminds me of the first time my mother took me to the playground. I meticulously went to each piece of equipment taking my time to explore everything. Learning which were my favorite. The swings? The slide? The monkey bars? The answer was everything. And, I have a feeling tonight is going to be much the same.

I have the entire night. Oh, yes. Yes. Yes. Yes. I'm going to explore every nook and cranny of the lovely creature before me. People have never interested me much. Especially women. But, this little flower, well…I want to see and feel every petal.

"Yes?" I dip my head catching her eyes.

She bites her bottom lip drawing my gaze there and nods in affirmation. I grab the blanket off the couch and lay it out carefully on the floor. She watches me with hooded eyes. Is she afraid? Excited? "Come here, Mia." Patting the blanket in front of me, I lower myself to my knees.

She slides off the couch and slowly crawls towards me. Oh hell. I can hear the thunder in my ears, beating in tandem with my heart. What is it about her? Why is she the one to suddenly make me feel? What power does she hold over me?

Once she settles in front of me she hugs her legs tightly to her. Her chest rises and falls. Rises and falls. I am enchanted. That must be it. A tremble runs through her and she squeezes her legs tighter. My eyes roam to her face and I see her lip quivering. "Are you frightened?" I ask, not moving from my position in front of her.

"No," she whispers. "I'm…I'm just a little nervous. Aren't you?"

"No." My arms reach out and gently push her back to the floor. She slowly releases the death grip on her legs and allows me to coax her back.

"But, I thought this was new for you?" She lifts her head, narrowing her eyes at me skeptically.

"It is. Now no more talking," I instruct. Mia is using words to distract herself from what is happening. I don't want her distracted. I want her focused on me. Only me. And, my exploration.

Oh, where to start? Top to bottom? Bottom to top? Somewhere in the middle. My eyes roam to her midsection. Her top has ridden up and a patch of pale skin has revealed itself to me. Middle it is. My thumb brushes over the exposed skin. A hiss leaves her lips and I'm not sure where to look. Her beautiful, lovely skin? My hand roams higher pushing the material of her cotton t-shirt higher. Or, should I look at her face? Hmm. So many choices.

I place my entire hand on her stomach lightly, watching it rise and fall. I look back to her face. Oh, her face tells a story. I pull my hand away letting my nails scratch casually over her creamy flesh. Oh, yes, her face is an open book. She may try to hide the secrets of her body from me but, her face will not lie. I make a mental note.

I grab the bottom of her t-shirt and tug it gently up her torso. She obediently lifts her shoulders from the floor and then her head, raising her hands above her to let me pull it off. Before she can lower her hands I grip her wrists and hold them hostage above her head, pressed to the floor. A little flash of fear dashes across her face but it's her hips I notice most. The way they lift in offering. *Oh, Mia.*

Sliding myself down beside her my nose grazes through her hair, seeking out her ear. "You can tell me to stop at any time, Mia," I whisper into it, letting my teeth nip at the cute little lobe.

"O…okay." She turns her head, her eyes meeting mine. "I want this, Brentley."

Hearing my name fall from her lips does wonderful things to me. I reach up with my free hand, allowing it to tickle along her skin beginning at her captive wrist and roaming all the way down until I reach the top of her shoulder. My hand pauses as I search her face for clues. Her lips have parted slightly, and her eyes search mine. Flicking back and forth searching, no not that, anticipating. Ah, she likes that she can't see what's coming next. I guess I'm feeling the same.

I lean in close to her, my hand sliding into her hair. My fist tightens around the silk strands at the nape of her neck holding her still. Her eyes drop closed, her breath is coming out in small little puffs. Her lips call to mine and I press them against hers softly at first. She makes a small noise from somewhere in the back of her throat that makes a beeline for my cock. More, I need more. I coax her mouth open with mine, exploring her, swallowing her groans of pleasure.

My hand releases her hair and roams down to her breasts. So soft. So perfect. Made for my hand. I reach under her to unclasp her bra and she rolls her body towards mine to oblige. She is in my arms, warm, alive. Thoughts of everything outside this room begin to break off in chunks floating away. Life exists of nothing but her and I. She rolls onto her back again and I toss the bra to the side. My hand hovers over her breast and I break away from our kiss. I need to see her.

I groan out loud at the sight of her pert breasts and the blush pink of her nipples. Oh, my god. My hand drops onto her warm skin, cupping her, squeezing. No wonder sex is such a big industry. I didn't get it. I simply didn't get it. Thought perhaps I was A-sexual, or it was the psychopath in me that kept my desires non-existent. But, no. Oh god, no. Daffodil has stirred the coals deep inside of me.

I want this always.

Letting go of her wrists so I can devote both hands to her beautiful tits, I kneel over her. She arches her back, leaning into my touch. Goosebumps have broken out over her skin making her tiny hair follicles stand on end. I didn't know my touch could affect someone like this. Like a drug. I want to be hers. I want her to be mine.

I must taste her. Every part of her. When my mouth wraps around one of her nipples she inhales sharply. My eyes travel up her body and see she is watching me intently. Her blue eyes drowning in desire. I begin placing kisses all over chest and stomach, studying each reaction carefully. In just a few minutes I learn so much. Where she is ticklish, which areas make her moan, which ones make her twitch. Once I've thoroughly explored her upper half it's time to move on.

As I move lower over her body I catch the scent of her arousal. Oh. Fuck. My own body sends out a surge of endorphins. I tug her jeans off of her and then lean over her cute, little pink panties breathing her in. Yes, she is a drug. A powerful one. I stare up the length of her. She looks nervous now and whatever she sees on my face has her clawing at the blanket, fisting it. I want her. She is mine. I tip my head slightly narrowing my eyes, gauging whether she wants me to continue my exploration and she whimpers. She fucking whimpers. Jesus Christ what that sound does to me. I'll take that as a yes.

I run my nose up her panties, finding them wet. Hmm, interesting. She is warm here in this sweet spot. I must taste. I look up at her again and her eyes are squeezed shut. "Can I take these off?" One thing I know is that a gentleman must always have permission.

"Yesss," she says hissing out the word. "I might die if you don't."

Well then. Continue on we shall. I grip the top of her panties tugging them down, feeling like a kid at Christmas. Saving the best present for last. I pull them all the way down her legs, slowly. Torturously so, it would seem by her reaction. She is writhing. Fucking writhing on the floor in front of me. I like this. I really like this. It…it makes me feel powerful. My writhing queen. I'll be dammed if anyone knocks her down again.

I've kept my eyes locked on hers but as her panties slide off her toes I allow my gaze to drop to the warm spot between her thighs. I close my eyes taking several deep breaths to control myself. My cock is pulsing painfully in my jeans. My hand runs over it willing it to behave. When I open my eyes, she is watching me. Her tongue snakes out to wet her lips. Oh, what would it be like to have her mouth on me there?

"You could…um…you could take your clothes off too," she suggests quietly.

The temptress taunts me with her hesitant words. I consider for a moment. It's tempting but, no. We don't have any protection and I don't know if I could control myself if I was undressed. Protection is not something I thought I would ever need to carry…until her. I will remedy that soon enough but, I will not have her worried about becoming pregnant. She is still too fragile for that. Tonight, is about me exploring her body. And I am one hundred percent okay with that. My cock will wait.

I shake my head no and she pouts. Her bottom lip puckers out. I seize the moment and quickly pounce on her and catch it between my teeth. Her hips roll up towards mine, grinding against the front of my jeans. "Please," she whispers, with her lip still caught between my teeth.

Reluctantly I release her and stare down into her blue eyes, brushing hair away from her face gently. "We don't have a condom, Daffodil." Her eyes widen as she realizes she had been so caught up in the moment she had thrown all thoughts of consequences to the wind. "It's okay. Tonight, is about you, Mia. Soon though, I promise."

She lifts her head and presses a kiss to my lips before pulling away. The expression on her face makes my heart swell. She trusts me. That asshole ex of hers must have done quite the number on her. The fact that I didn't take advantage of her surprises her. I would never hurt her. Never.

Now that is settled it's time to get back between her creamy, delectable thighs. I offer her one last flirty smirk before I settle back in the promise land. I inhale a bit exaggerated but, then again maybe not so much. Her musky scent brings out the most primal of urges in me. The tip of my tongue touches her sweet spot and she jolts like she's been electrocuted. My eyes lock onto hers, she is panting. Literally fucking panting.

Another lick, slow, circling and the pupils of her eyes roll back into her head. Hmm, much like a possession. I'll be her devil every day if she asks. It is a job I would take seriously. My fingers grip her tightly, dimpling the skin of her thighs. I push them towards the floor, giving me greater access to her. When I groan against her she begins to tremble, her need building and building. Can I make her climax? How? And, will I be able to tell when it happens?

My hand slides down seeking her warmth. I allow one finger to slide into her and she stills. Well, except for the increasing tremor skirting through her. I toy with her there, my tongue still dancing on her clit. "More," I hear her whisper. I smile against her slick skin. Oh, yes, Mia. I will give you more. Two and then three fingers enter her, and she cries out to God.

Exploring, watching, I go through every scenario. Cataloging every reaction until I have homed in on the things that make her writhe the most. She is shaking so fiercely now it almost has me concerned. Almost.

Just a bit more. A touch here, a push there, a flick of the tongue and then I curl my fingers inside her and suck her entire clit into my mouth and…

Holy fuck.

Maybe she is possessed.

Her eyes are rolled back in her head. Mouth open. Back arched clean off the floor. Hands fisted into the blanket, knuckles white. Muscles clenching, pulsing around my fingers. God, what I would give to feel that around my cock.

She screams my name. My name. I gave her this. Me. Un-fucking believable.

I must do this every day.

Every. Damn. Day.

Well, I guess that answers my questions. I can make her climax and I definitely saw it coming.

Damn.

It was the most beautiful thing I've ever seen.

### Mia

Jesus.

I lay limp, spent and grinning like a fucking idiot on the living room floor. What. In. The. Fuck. Was that?

172

Twice, I only came twice with Darrin. Most of the time he jumped on, jumped off. My pleasure wasn't his concern, only his. Most nights I went to bed disappointed or finished myself off in the shower. I hate to compare the two but how can I not?

This was…this was so different. I've never even made myself come like that. I was so wound before he even touched me there that I knew it wouldn't take much. It's been years. Years.

I was hyper focused on everywhere he touched. The way he watched. Oh my god, the dark, dirty looks he gave me alone was enough to bring me to the brink. Slow, then fast. Soft, then hard. And when he pressed on this spot inside me I didn't even know existed, I exploded. White stars broke out behind my eyes. I fucking felt it…everywhere. My body and my mind. How? Just how?

"Are you okay, Mia?" Brentley asks, hovering above me like a dark god.

I can't move, it's like he took the years of tension I had rat holed inside of me and set it free. Like a balloon that had swollen, swollen and then…pop. A smile and a nod are all I can muster. He smiles back and for the first time I open my heart to him. It scares the living fuck out of me.

How did this happen? Just, how?

"Did I do good?" He smirks.

Again, a nod.

"Speechless, that's a good sign." He glances between us, staring down my body.

Now that the cloud of lust has cleared my self-consciousness rears its ugly head. I move my arm to cover my scar. He looks up. His eyes searching mine.

"Don't hide from me, Mia." He lowers himself and places a kiss to my lips before sliding down my body and pushing my arm to my side. His lips graze over my C-section scar. He places gentle kisses all along it before looking up to meet my eyes. "This is where you birthed the most beautiful baby. Do not hide it from me. It is beautiful. And someday, when you are ready you will have life inside you again." His hand splays out over my stomach, creating a warm feeling in my chest.

Tears stream down the side of my face, pooling in my ears. How can this man who calls himself Death say such beautiful things? "Do you really believe that?" I ask.

"Someday, yes." I detect a sadness in his tone before he continues. "The man who gets to call you the mother of his child will be the luckiest bastard on the planet."

For years I have wanted nothing but death. And, now to think of bringing forth life. It's almost too much to comprehend. This man is healing me. In the most unconventional way. This is crazy. Just crazy. My fingers graze lightly over his. I grip them tightly and pull him back up to face me. Nose to nose we stare into each other's eyes. My hands sink into his hair, I pull him closer and kiss him. I kiss him like my life depends on it. And, maybe it does.

When I pull away his face says it all. Our souls have recognized each other. Long lost friends who searched through the span of time. Through the billions of people walking this earth. Through pain so excruciating it changed their very being. Against every obstacle they found each other.

I'm so afraid and yet I'm not.

Something about this simply feels right.

"Brentley?"

"Hmm?" he hums, lost in my eyes, his fingers running through my hair, his weight settled over me. It's all just so right.

"Do you think she brought us together?"

He lets his finger trail over my locket. The lamp light reflects in his eyes. Shit. Oh my god is he tearing up? His Adams apple bobs as he swallows. "I don't know if I am worthy of ever being part of Erelah's magic. She is your angel not mine."

He lays fully on top of me now. Resting his ear directly over my heart. I can tell how emotional he is. "I think you're wrong," I say softly. "You've given her more care than anyone. She would have loved you." My fingers run through his hair. No more words come from either of us. My heart aches for him the same as it does for her. What does that mean? Could it be? No, how could it? It's too soon. Too crazy. Too perfect.

# Chapter Twenty

## Mia

The mirror is mocking me. I decided on a dark blue, soft cotton t-shirt and a pair of jean shorts. Plain, simple, practical. My long dark hair is pulled back in a high ponytail. No makeup. It's what I like. What I want to wear. But, I know Rebecca will be dressed to the hilt. Full out. And pregnant with Darrin's baby. My heart sinks.

"Ready, Daffodil?" Brentley asks poking his head around the door frame. When I rise from my vanity he steps inside. "Wow, you look beautiful, Mia."

I look at myself in the mirror over my shoulder. "I don't know."

"I won't accept anything other than you being you. Is this you?" He points towards me.

Sighing I let my shoulders fall. "Yeah."

He grabs my waist pulling me roughly against his hip. "You are fucking sexy as hell. How am I supposed to keep my hands to myself all day? Now that they've taken a walk through the promise land that's all they can think of."

"Oh, your fingers have minds of their own do they?" I push against him, but he holds me tight. I give up and laugh, leaning my head against his chest.

"I know you are nervous about today but, you have me. I'm your secret weapon." He rocks us back and forth calming my fears. He smells so goddamn good today. He is in a pair of khaki shorts and a black tight fitted t-shirt which shows all his best assets.

"What kind of secret weapon?"

"The kind that can sense a damsel in distress. One that can whisk you away at a moment's notice."

"Wow, you make yourself sound like a superhero."

"A superhero of sorts, yes. Death at your service." He breaks away from me and leans over into an exaggerated bow.

"Well, come on superhero. Let's go." We stop in the kitchen to pick up the brownies I made for the potluck and head out.

Brentley drives, allowing me to get caught up in the beauty of the countryside. I've missed this. Nature. When we pull up the little path to the cabin a flood of memories come rushing at me. Matt's parents invited us out here all the time for barbeques. Most of the time we snuck out here for beer parties. Most nights I ended up leaving early, asking Matt to give me a ride home because Darrin would be so stinking drunk. Sober Darrin is tolerable, maybe. But, drunk Darrin is an a-number-one-a-hole.

I recognize Darrin's black Lexus in the driveway. Great. Fucking great. God help me. Brentley squeezes my hand. "You good?"

"He's here," I whisper, biting at my thumb nail.

"Just remember your secret weapon."

I smile at him. Okay, I can do this. I can. "Be myself and remember my secret weapon. Check."

Matt greets us at the door, invites us in and introduces his wife, Tina. Instantly we click. Her kind eyes ease my apprehension. Soon, we are following them out to the large deck out back. There are five other couples here all mingling about. Conversations halt as we exit the cabin.

Brentley wraps his arm around me, pulling me close. He chooses a bench seat opposite from Darrin and Rebecca. When I sit beside him he places his hand on the inside of my thigh. I smile at him and wrap my arm through his and rest my hand on his bicep. I notice all the women are staring at him like he is a slice of cake. But, then my eyes land on Darrin's.

Shit, he isn't happy. His jaw is clenched, working back and forth. He doesn't say anything though which surprises me. I assume Matt had a chat with him before we arrived. I rip my gaze from his and focus on the conversation at hand. Talk remains light and I begin to relax.

"Hey, Mia. Matt told me you had a run in with a buck. I got a garage in Davenport, bring ole' blue on down and I'll fix her up," Gage, an old friend of mine from high school tells me. He has always loved fixing up old cars. I used to hang out with him after school if my parents were going to be late picking me up. I would sit in the garage and watch he and his dad tinker under the hood of a clunker, eighties rock music playing in the background.

"Ah, that would be great. It's not too bad. Just a dented hood and a crack in the windshield," I answer.

He tips his beer at me. "Bring it over next week. I can pop that dent just like that." He snaps his fingers as he speaks.

Rebecca giggles and whispers to her bff, Candice, loudly enough for everyone to hear, "I think someone needs to take her license away from her. What's she going to hit next."

An awkward moment of silence ensues. Matt looks to Darrin and when he sees he isn't going to speak up, Matt does. "Rebecca, come on. Knock it off."

"What? Truth hurts, just sayin." She flips her hair and rolls her eyes.

Gage tries to steer the conversation, "I don't know about anyone else but I'm fucking starving."

Matt stands giving Darrin the side eye. "Yeah, I'll get the grill fired up."

The guys gather around the grill and Brentley joins them at Matt's request. Tina sits down beside me in his place. "Thank you for giving Matt a job. He's been so stressed and now he seems able to breathe again."

"He's the one helping me. I have no idea what I'm doing on the farm."

"It will all work out I'm sure," she says but our conversation ends there because the other women have all gathered around us. Talking resumes, all revolving around shopping and other random gossip.

This is the kind of stuff I haven't missed. Gossip is simply poison. It's like being in high school all over again. Candice goes on and on about a couple of girls in her younger sister's class who are trying to fundraise for their dance uniforms since they cannot afford them.

"It's not right. Like my parents have to pay for my sister's uniform. These girl's parents should figure it out on their own," she whines.

Good god. She has no idea what life is really like. She's had a silver spoon up her ass her entire life. I glance over at Brentley, he looks relaxed. Fuck, he is hot. I wish I was with the guys. I bet their conversation is better than this crap. My mind drifts to last night until I hear Rebecca talking about re-doing a room for her baby.

"I had to spend an entire day scraping stupid glow in the dark stars off the ceiling. Like how tacky. But, now the room is fab. Only the best for this one." She pats her stomach throwing a knowing smirk my way.

I…I can't breathe.

Erelah's stars. She took them down. Darrin let her take them down. He is replacing Erelah without a damn care.

You need to breathe, Mia. Breathe.

I need to get out of here.

Someone grabs my hand. "Mia, would you like to take a walk with me?" my secret weapon asks. I look up at him and he gives me the sexiest smile in world. My eyes dart around to the other women. All mouths are open, and eyes glued to the dark being standing in front of us.

"Yeah, sure," I say quietly forcing a smile to my face.

He pulls me to my feet and kisses me. No. He devours me and everything around us evaporates. He breaks away leaving me breathless and swaying on my feet. He turns his back to me and squats down low. He points to his back. "Hop on."

I don't have to force a smile. I'm giggling by the time I get on his back. My arms and legs wrap around him tightly. He tucks his arms under my legs, and we head down the steps towards the river. "Thank you," I whisper into his ear. He grunts in response.

We head past the dock that juts out over the river and follow the muddy river trail away from the cabin. Once we are out of sight he sets me on my feet and leads us to a log tucked back into the tree line. We sit and stare at the water traveling quietly by us. "You want to tell me what happened?"

I'm quiet for a few minutes, struggling to swallow the knot in my throat. He sits patiently beside me. "It's silly. I don't know why I got so upset," I tell him.

"What I saw on your face was pain, Mia. It wasn't silly. It hurt. Tell me." He places his hand on my knee and squeezes.

"They were just gossiping. Shit talking about some girls in the dance troupe who can't afford their uniforms." He patiently listens and tips his head when I stop there. He knows that is not all that was said. His gaze goes back to the water. Okay, maybe I can get the words out if he isn't looking at me. "She took Erelah's stars down. They are changing the nursery for their new baby." I bite my lip so hard I can taste blood. I don't want to cry here. I'll go back all splotchy and she will know she got to me.

Brentley raises his face to the sky. "Sounds like Darrin is getting what he deserves, a witch."

"It's fine. I don't know why I let it bother me."

He faces me. "Because you love her, and you miss her. Rebecca was purposefully trying to hurt you. She has an unnatural hate towards you. Why?"

I pull my foot up to the log and rest my hands and chin on my knee. I shrug. "They have always messed around together. I'm pretty sure he had been having an affair with her."

"Why did you stay with him, Mia?"

"It was always Darrin and Mia. I mean everyone just expected us to get married. Homecoming King and Queen. Star football player and cheer captain. It just was. I guess I never really thought about it being any other way."

"That's sad."

I nod slowly. "Yes, I guess it is. I did think he loved me. But, when he didn't come after the accident I knew he never did. I knew it was over. Life was over." I drop my foot to the ground with a thud. "Fuck, I'm so stupid."

"No. You weren't stupid you were a saint to put up with that crap. You settled." He grips my chin between his forefinger and thumb turning me to face him. "You're done settling. You, Mia are taking back your life and you are going to live it your way. You decide what happens from here on out. Fuck Darrin and fuck that awful woman."

"How do you always know the right thing to say?" Shyly I try to duck my head, but his grip only tightens.

"I don't. And when I say the wrong thing I want you to promise me you will call me out. Don't settle, even with me." He leans forward and presses his lips to mine. My hands land on his chest finding hard muscle and a flutter flares in my belly.

Our kiss evolves into hands roaming over each other's bodies. Seeking, searching, comforting. We stay by the river making out like teenagers for quite some time until we both realize we need to stop before clothes are shed. Laughing we pull ourselves together.

"So, should we stay or head home?" he asks.

Home. I like the sound of that. With him there it does feel like home even with the absence of my parents. "We should stay. For a while anyway. At least to eat. You have to try my brownies." I wrap my hand in his and we slowly start to walk back to the party.

"Oh, I do, do I? You seem pretty confident I will like them."

"I'm so confident I'll make a deal with you," I tease.

"Ooh, now I'm interested. You do know I love a good deal." He winks and I briefly think about going back to the log to finish what we started.

"How about if you don't like them, we go home, and I'll make you a dessert you do like."

One eyebrow raises at this. "And if I do like?"

"Then it's my turn to explore *you* tonight." I try my hardest to focus on the path ahead. Maybe that was too brazen? I don't know. Was it?

He stops abruptly, almost yanking my arm clean off. "Mia. Be very careful in the deals you make with me."

Placing my hands on my hips in feigned bravado I take a step towards him. "I'm only doing what you told me to do, Brentley."

"And what is that?"

"I'm doing what Mia wants. And Mia wants to win this bet." My eyebrows shoot up to my hairline in challenge.

He swallows hard and takes a step back. "Okay, I'm a bit nervous now."

"You should be." I leave him gawking after me but, I stop on the path to look at him over my shoulder. "Oh, and by the way. If you try to pretend you don't like them, I'll know." I point to my own eyes with two fingers and then point to him. "I'll be watching you."

He jogs behind me to catch up. "What if the brownies are gone by the time we get back? I mean if they're as good as you say they may be all gobbled up by now."

"There is a good chance they are. Don't worry, I made two batches. One is at home. Did I forget to mention they are Thomas's favorite too?"

"Daffodil. It's not like you to play dirty." He takes my hand in his bringing it up to kiss my knuckles.

"Help! Hurry someone help!" A voice yells in the distance.

Brentley and I slow to a halt listening through the trees. "Did you hear that?" I ask.

"Yeah," he pulls me farther along the path. More screams and yelling. Suddenly Matt is on the path heading towards us.

"Mia, come quick. It's Darrin." He grabs my hand tugging me to follow him. I dig my heels into the dirt. What is happening?

He senses my struggle and turns to look at me. "He needs you. Rebecca pushed him into the river. Gage pulled him out but he's not breathing, Mia. We need to hurry."

I allow him to pull me all the way down the path and out to the dock overlooking the swirling river. Everyone backs up and Matt shoos them away from the dock. I fall to my knees beside Darrin. He isn't moving.

I stare over him.

He...he didn't come for me. He is replacing our daughter. He...he...

"Daffodil," Brentley says quietly. I raise my eyes to see that he is crouched at Darrin's other side. "It doesn't matter what he did to you. You need to be who you are. And you need to do it now." He gently turns Darrin's head to the side allowing water to drain from his mouth and then he positions it back to center.

Shit. Shit!

I quickly begin CPR. It doesn't take long and Darrin gasps his eyes flying open. I swiftly turn his head to the side as he vomits. "You're okay," I say over and over, while helping him stay positioned on his side.

"The ambulance is on the way," Matt announces over me.

After a few minutes. Darrin regains some of his composure and I help him to sit up. He stares into my eyes and what I see there unnerves me. He's hasn't looked at me like this in a long time. Like...like he loves me. "Mia," he says coughing before continuing. "I...I should have given you a ride that night. It's all my fault. I'm so sorry, Mia. I'm so, so sorry," he cries, tears falling from his eyes.

Abruptly I release him, scrambling to get away. Sirens grow louder as I try to process what just happened. He almost died. He…he…god dammit!

He continues to apologize trying to scoot closer to me. "Mia, please listen to me. I'm sorry, you have to believe me. I didn't know what to do."

I stare at the wood grain on the dock, my head spinning. Booted feet of EMTs enter my vision. They surround Darrin. He fights them trying to get to me. Brentley crouches in front of my knees blocking what is happening. I reach out to him and wrap my arms around his neck. He picks me up. My face burrows into his neck.

I'm not sure what happens after that. All I know is I'm lost. I'm wandering through my thoughts trying to find a time when Darrin had looked at me like that. The movie playing in my mind keeps returning to the locker room in the hospital. *Please come get me.* Please come get me, I had asked. He was too busy. Too busy for me. Too busy for us.

A knock on the door makes me jerk to reality. Brentley is sitting beside me on the couch, worry creasing his forehead and the corners of his eyes. "I'll be right back," he says.

I strain to hear the conversation he is having with Matt at the door. "She's fine. A little shook up," Brentley says.

"Yeah, what a fucked-up day. Anyhow, I wanted to let you guys know he's going to be okay. They are keeping him overnight for observation." Matt continues to apologize for the events of the day but, Brentley reassures him that I'm good.

"We'll see you tomorrow, Matt. Go home and don't worry about us. Mia is strong. She can handle this. She can."

Matt's next words jab a knife right in my heart. "I…I just don't want her to hurt herself. You know?"

"She won't. I'll be with her all night, I promise."

"Okay, if you're sure."

"I am. She's good," Brentley reassures him.

Am I? Cause that little chant has begun in my head. *Please, take me. Please.* I take a deep breath. No, I can't go back to that. I just can't.

Fucking Darrin. My heart just let Brentley in. I allowed him to build a little fire beside it and it was slowly thawing. And then, fucking Darrin came in with a bucket of ice water and doused it. Goddamn him!

"Mia?"

My head bops up. My mask falls into place. He can't see my doubt. "Yeah?"

"Matt dropped off some food. You hungry?"

I nod and pull myself off the couch. When I enter the kitchen, he is standing by the table opening Tupperware containers. He peeks inside each one sniffing the contents. "Damn, these smell good."

Sliding into a chair I pull one to me and do the same. My stomach churns and I push it away.

"Matt says Darrin is going to be okay if you're worried about him."

187

"I'm not."

"Are you sure about that?" He grabs two plates out of the cupboard and starts filling them both from the containers.

"Positive."

His eyes slide to mine and then flit away again. "Do you want to talk about it?"

"What is there to talk about? He was drunk. He didn't know what he was saying."

"I think he did." He pushes my plate in front of me, pointing at it. "Eat," he orders.

"It doesn't matter if he did. Have you ever heard of a day late and a dollar short?" I poke at the pink fluffy sweet, salad that always seems to be a staple at every potluck.

He laughs. "Yeah, I have. But, seriously, Mia. He seemed pretty sincere to me. Maybe he is really sorry for how he handled everything."

"Stop."

"Stop what?" He takes a bite, his eyes locking on mine in challenge.

"Stop, trying to cover for him. Everyone does that. Not from you. I won't be able to handle it if you do it too."

"What did they cover for him, Mia?" His tone tells me he already knows my secret. He just wants to hear the words fall from my lips.

My arm swings across the table sending everything clattering to the floor. He doesn't flinch and he doesn't take his eyes from mine. "Tell me, Mia," he says calmly.

I pull my knees up to my chest and grip my hair in both hands, shaking my head furiously back and forth. "Don't make me do it, Death. Don't make me fucking do it."

"You have to, Daffodil. If you don't you will never be able to move on. You've been trapped for so long. It's sad that everyone looked away. Maybe they knew, maybe they didn't. Maybe they thought since you were pretending it was okay for them to do the same. I don't know. Losing Erelah, your parent's, killing that family, that might have been what drove you to the point of emailing me. But, you wanted out long before that didn't you?"

"He…" I shake my head, desperately trying to figure a way out of having to say it.

"He what, Mia?"

"He hit me." I pound my fist on the table. "He used to fucking *beat* me!" I scream.

It's deadly quiet in the kitchen. The scent of tobacco tickles at my senses. Oh no. No, no, no. When did he get here?

"What did you just say?" Thomas rasps.

My head darts up and he is standing, griping the doorknob so hard I think it's going to snap off. His jaw is locked shut.

I don't say anything. My eyes slide to Brentley. He too looks like he could kill someone. He closes his eyes and when they open again a look of

189

compassion replaces the murderous glint. Slowly he turns to face me. "I'm proud of you, Daffodil." He stands and offers his chair to Thomas.

Thomas shakes as he takes Brentley's vacant seat. "Mia, oh god, Mia. Why didn't you tell us?"

Tears stream down my face. So many times, I tried. I tried but I couldn't.

Darrin fed me venom filled words that paralyzed me.

*They love me Mia. They won't believe you. You're just being emotional. I'm sorry, Mia. I'm sorry. Why do you provoke me, Mia? It won't happen again. I promise. It will be different. If you would have just kept your mouth shut. I'll change for our baby. I've just been so stressed with football. With school. With work. Please don't leave me. We're perfect for each other. Please. Please. Please believe me, Mia. I'm sorry. You can't leave me. I'll find you. I'll find you, Mia. You wouldn't last a day without me. You're so stupid. You should kill yourself, Mia.*

I choke on pain and rush to the sink purging myself of all of the crap that he forced down my throat over the years. Brentley's warm hand rubs over my back. When there's nothing left in me I turn on the tap and rinse out my mouth.

Bracing my arms on the counter I fill my lungs and breathe out slowly. This may be the first real breath I've taken in…in years. The weight of a thousand stones have rolled off my back. I did it. I told someone.

My perfect life was never perfect. I lied to myself to keep going. After we graduate high school it will get better. After college. After we get married. After the baby comes. All lies.

Once the bubble broke and the perfect life slipped, he walked away. Let me go. Only he didn't. He's still had ahold of me. I've let him control my mind. Even without his presence I kept quiet. Today, scared me. Today I saw the look in his eye. He wants me back.

"It's...I'm okay. It was only a few times. It doesn't matter it's over." Only it's not over. I saw that it's not over. Who am I trying to kid?

"I'm going to kill him," Thomas grates, standing slowly from the table.

I rush towards him placing my hands on his chest. "No, Thomas please. Let it go. It's over. I'm not with him anymore."

"Mia, he can't get away with this." He grips my shoulders, gently trying to push me away from him so he can make his getaway. I glance behind me for help from Brentley. He is leaning against the counter running his hand over the stubble on his chin.

"Please," I beg.

He sighs and pulls me into his chest. "I don't want you anywhere near him. Ever. Again." I nod against his shirt. "Ah, Mia. If your dad would have known."

"I know. I'm sorry. In my mind I always thought it would get better," I say quietly.

"God, this explains so much. Why you didn't come home to visit. Why every time your mom and dad planned to visit you something always came up and you cancelled on them. Dammit, Mia."

I'm so ashamed. Thomas is disappointed in me. They would have been disappointed in me. I begin to sob uncontrollably. "I was so stupid."

"It's not your fault. It's his. You deserved so much better than that, darlin. It tears me up knowing you were alone."

Enough. I've had enough sadness and fear. I'm not with him anymore. I'm in charge of my life. Me. "I made your favorite brownies," I whisper.

Thomas chuckles. "Oh, Mia. I love you, girl."

"She plays dirty doesn't she?" Brentley says, pushing off the counter.

I smile into Thomas's shirt. Oh, yes. I haven't forgotten the bet and I will win.

## Brentley

I've known for a long time that Mia had been depressed if not suicidal before her accident. Today when Darrin started apologizing to her I saw the look of terror in her eye. It was obvious that his apologies were all too familiar to her. She scooted as far away from him as she could.

I didn't know if I should push but when she asked me not to make excuses for him it was the perfect window. Now, how to get rid of the fucker. There is more at stake than Mia. He is remarried with a baby on the way. Does he beat Rebecca too? More than likely the answer to that question is yes.

"I better skedaddle." Thomas leans back in his chair rubbing his belly. "I'll see the both of you tomorrow. Brentley, you and I are going to run in to town and get your damn license. We can't have you driving all over the country without one. Mia and Matt can start on the fence."

I nod in agreement.

"Fence, blah," Mia grumbles. "Sometimes I think you hate me, Thomas." She knows better though and gives him a shy smile. He pats her cheek before leaning over and giving her a peck.

She walks him out while I tidy up the kitchen. When she comes back in she stands with her hands on her hips. "Well?" she asks cocking an eyebrow at me.

"Well what?"

"Did you like them?"

"Eh." I flip my hand back and forth. "They were a little too sweet for my liking."

She narrows her eyes at me, frowning. "Oh, is that why you ate three of them?"

"Well, I had to be sure. I mean there is a lot at stake here." I drape the towel I was using to dry the dishes over the handle of the stove before turning to face her.

"I win," she states simply as she stalks past me to the living room.

"Uh, uh. No, you don't. I said they were too sweet."

She tosses me a look over her shoulder as she grabs a bath towel from the hallway closet. "Brentley, you ate three of them...three." The holds up three fingers, shoving them in my face.

"They were just too sweet. I'm sorry. Anyhow, that means I win. I get to pick my choice of dessert." I tap my finger on my chin as if deep in thought. "I choose you. You are my favorite sweet."

Her tongue darts out wetting her lips. "That's not fair."

"What's not fair?"

"It's my turn," she pouts.

Okay, I need to be honest here. I'm nervous. Why? Well, I don't know. Maybe it's the fear of giving up control. This woman already has me *feeling*. The last thing I need is to lose control of my body. And I will if she has unlimited access to it. I'm sure I'll embarrass myself somehow and I've, NEVER, been embarrassed. Sure, I put up a good front but, bottom line this *is* new for me.

"I'm showering, Brentley, and then I am going to explore your body. Just like you did mine last night. Besides, I need something to take my mind off things." She bats her eyelashes at me. Fucking bats them. Unashamedly, I might add. Right in my face.

I cross my arms across my chest. "Okay, I'll admit they were good."

"Just good?"

"Okay. They were amazing. Are you happy now?" I ask, my eyes narrowing in on her lips. Will she use them on me? Oh, shit. The image of her lips wrapped around…

She is snapping her fingers in front of my nose. "Earth to Brentley."

My gaze focuses on hers and I scowl.

She laughs, tosses her towel over her shoulder and saunters into the bathroom. "The showering alone rule has been lifted," she purrs. The door shuts behind her and I'm left standing in the hallway with my mouth hanging wide open.

I stare at the bathroom door and then the closet beside me. The water turns on and I quickly grab a towel from inside. Fuck it. I'm throwing embarrassment to the wind. If I come in two seconds, well then so be it.

I'm not passing up an opportunity to join her in the shower. Opportunities like this don't come around every day.

When I slip in behind her, I'm greeted by her cute, dimpled butt. Hmm, I should have explored more of her the other night. My hand glides over the swell of bottom. Damn. She flinches at my touch, the muscles at her hips tightening in response. A groan erupts from me. Mia finishes rinsing her hair before turning to look at me.

"I think I missed a few spots last night." My fingers trail along her spine and she shivers. She lays her cheek on my chest. I hold her against me for several minutes, enjoying her wet body against mine. She begins to tremble. Is she is crying? "Hey, shh. It's okay, Daffodil. We don't have to do this tonight."

She pulls her head back. "Did you see the way he looked at me?"

My hand comes up to cup her face. Slowly I stroke my thumb over her cheek. I did see it. He wants her. Thing is...Mia doesn't belong to him anymore. She doesn't really belong to me either but yet here she is, in my arms. "Do you want to work things out with him?"

This makes her angry. "No. How can you even ask me that? I'm here, naked, with you." Her eyes search mine.

"What do you want me to do, Mia?"

She takes a step back. Her gaze settles on me, her decision made. She drops to her knees in front of me. Her eyes trail leisurely up my frame not stopping till they land on mine. Her hands claw up my thighs. Her tongue peeks out from between her pink lips and then she licks me. Oh, fuck. My hips jerk away from her but, her hands wrap around to the back of my thighs pulling me close. Her breath blows on me purposefully and it is enough to make me lose all thought.

My hands brace against the wall in front of me and my head drops to watch her mouth fully engulf my cock. Oh. Jesus. Sweet, sweet Jesus. This is…

Her tongue snakes along me as she sucks down hard. "Mia," I rasp. When her hands grip at my ass, I almost fucking lose it.

She reads me like an open book. She keeps me on the edge for what feels like hours. Just as I am about to explode she eases, letting me catch my breath before pulling me back to the edge. Oh, god.

Not until the water cools does she decide to give me the relief I so desperately need. She shape shifts into a dark goddess before my eyes. Bowing at her god's feet she works me so hard I explode into another dimension. I explode right. Down. Her fucking. Throat. "Jeeeeesusssss," I cry out.

My vision clears, my eyes narrow and drop to find her still crouched in front of me. "Answer my question. What do you want me to do, Daffodil?"

"I want you to make me yours." She slides up my body and wraps her hands around my neck. She kisses me and I can taste myself on her lips. Oh, what that does to the raw, primal alpha in me.

"Soon, sweetheart. Soon."

Tomorrow I make her mine.

I don't know if that is the answer to getting Darrin to leave her alone. It's not like he has been seeking her out. Maybe we just need to stay here on the farm until he's gone. Surely he will leave soon. If he doesn't?

I can't think about that right now.

After drying off, Mia and I settle down for the night in her bed. She unconsciously mumbles words of love to their daughter as she lets sleep take her.

I want to do bad things to him.

If I do I will be forced to leave her behind. In order to do those things, I would have to flip the switch on my feelings to off. I just found the on position. Mia is my on switch. But, I can't have them turned off around her. For one she doesn't deserve it and two…I never want to hurt her. Having no feelings is, well, it's just that. It's nothing. I don't trust myself. Which is why I've never allowed myself to get close to anyone.

Death controlled me for so long. It buried me. Mia dug me out of that dark hole. A life with no feelings isn't one I want to return to but for her I will.

If I have to shut down and kill that bastard I will. So, help me god I will.

Even if it means losing her.

# Chapter Twenty-One

**Mia**

"Why is he even here?"

Matt takes his hat off swatting a bee that decided to join us in his pickup. "He put his old man in a nursing home. Want's to sell off the farm but, he's asking to damn much."

"You should buy it. It would be perfect for you and Tina. Doesn't it butt up against your mom and dad's place."

Matt laughs. "Shit, Mia. I ain't got the money or the credit for that. I'm drowning in medical bills right now."

"I thought his dad was doing good. I should go visit him."

"He was getting along okay. But you know Darrin. He doesn't want to spend any more time here than necessary, so he took him over to Davenport and left him there. He has no plans on staying, Mia. He hates this place. I know you want him gone. I don't blame you."

He rolls to a stop in the pasture and we set to work mending fence. After a few hours pass us by he brings the subject up again. "Why don't you buy it?"

I huff, rolling another new post out of the back of the truck. "I think I have enough on my plate with this place. To be honest I don't know if I can afford it either. Besides, some days it's all I can do to keep breathing."

He leans on the post hole digger. "Mia, shit."

"Stop, the last thing I want is for you to tip toe around me. It's fine." The sun is high, and my stomach begins to grumble. "Hey, how bout I run up to the house and grab us a couple sandwiches?"

He tosses his keys at me. "I'm starving, sounds good."

I catch them and toss them in my palm a few times. "Sure, you trust me to drive your truck?"

He frowns until he sees I'm only joking with him. "Funny."

"Be right back," I tell him. It only takes a few minutes and I'm back at the house.

I'm rummaging through the fridge looking for mayonnaise when I hear the crunch of gravel under tires in the driveaway. Are the guys back already? I straighten and lean my head back past the door of the fridge.

I slam the door shut. Crap. Crap. Crap.

I rush to meet him at the porch. "What are you doing here?"

He stops at the bottom step. "Well, hello to you too." He pulls his sunglasses off his face, hooking them over the top of his shirt. "I want to talk."

"I'm sorry, I don't see your attorney." I shield my eyes from the sun pretending to search the yard.

He chuckles. "I've missed your humor."

I'll let my silence speak for how much I've missed his.

"Can we go in?"

"No." I lean my back against the door. "I wasn't trying to be funny, Darrin. Anything you've wanted to tell me for the past two years has been done through your attorney. I don't see any reason for that to change. Besides there is nothing left to say."

He runs his hand through his hair, his eyes scanning the driveway. "Is Matt here?"

I nod towards the road. "He's waiting for me at the northeast pasture."

"So, you're alone?" His jaw ticks slightly.

This makes me stand tall and roll my shoulders back.

He puts his hands up in front of him in surrender. "I just want to talk. To clear the air between us. That's all, Mia. Please?"

"We can do that right here."

"I was stupid, Mia. I shouldn't have left you." He takes a step up and I press my back into the screen door, my hand gripping the handle.

"You should go."

"I'm not going anywhere until you hear me out."

Demands. Shit. I'm done. I pull the door open and swivel myself around the frame trying to pull it closed behind me. He takes the steps two at a time grabbing the door, ripping it from my grasp. "Go," I whisper harshly.

He pushes his way in and closes the door behind him. I fall into a chair. Dumbfounded that he is here. Here in my kitchen. Darrin is in my house. Fuck. The lock clicks and my eyes snap to his. "Don't be frightened, Mia. I just want to talk."

I sit perfectly still. My mind trying to remember where the kitchen knives are. Matt will come when I don't return to the field. Shit. He would, if he had a vehicle. Do I think Darrin will hurt me? No. Not here. Surely he won't hurt me here.

Darrin falls to his knees laying his head in my lap. What in the fuck?

"I'm sorry, Mia. You have to believe me. Seeing you again made me realize how much I love you. Please. Please forgive me."

"Darrin…I.." I'm holding my hands above my head not wanting to touch him.

He sits up, reclining on his heels. "Someone bought the farm today so I'm leaving. Go pack. Let's get out of here. You and me. Just like the old days. I'll take you anywhere you want to go."

"Darrin, you're married. You have a baby on the way." Unbelievable. He's lost his goddammed mind.

"None of that matters. I'll divorce her. They will be fine without me. I just want you, Mia. You." He wraps his arms around my waist.

That's it. He has to go. I try to stand but his grip only tightens. The chair slides out from behind me in my struggle, sending me to the floor. He crawls over the top of me. His lips find mine, so I turn my head forcing his wet lips to drag across my cheek.

"Stop!" I scream. My knee comes up and slams into his balls. He lets go of me and I crawl away from him. Cowering against the opposite wall.

He rocks back and forth on his knees holding his crotch. His eyes meet mine and what I see there scares me. "It's because of him. That guy. You think you can leave me for him?" he spits, angrily.

"I don't have to leave. We are divorced, Darrin. What the fuck is wrong with you? Stop this."

"Wrong with me?" he snarls. He crawls to me. Wrapping his hand around my throat, he pushes my head back against the wall. Oh fuck. My hands immediately fly up desperately trying to pry his fingers off of me. "Do you fancy yourself in love with him, Mia?" His hot breath blows over my face and I feel like I might be sick.

Why is he doing this? His grip loosens so I can answer him. He repeats his question. "Do you? Do you love him?"

"It's not your business who I love." I shouldn't argue with him, it's stupid. But, I can't lie to him either. "Please stop this," I plead. "Please just go."

"You don't love him." He lowers his face to mine. "Nobody can replace me, Mia."

Now I'm mad. No, furious. My hysterical laugh catches him off guard and he faulters back on his ass.

"Fuck you, Darrin. You replaced me. You replaced her." Slowly I rise to my feet, sliding up the wall. "He takes flowers to Erelah's grave every morning. Every. Morning."

He grips his chest. My words lancing his cold, hard heart. "Brentley listens to me. He takes care of me. He knows when I'm tired, when I'm scared, when I'm sad and when I'm turned on." Darrin scowls at this. I laugh, staring up at the ceiling before dropping my eyes back to him. "When was the last time you knew what I needed, what I was feeling?"

I keep talking as I inch to the drawer with the knives. He turns away from me for a moment to pull himself up by the table. "I don't know if I'm in love with him. But, what I do know is that I'm not in love with you."

He spins towards me at the same moment I pull the knife out of the drawer. It snags his shirt. He backs away few steps looking down at his torn shirt in shock. "Mia?"

"I told them what kind of love you gave me." His face turns to stone. He's mad. Mad I told someone our secret.

"You'll regret this, Mia." He stalks towards the door. "You think this guy is your knight in shining armor? Yeah? Well I hate to tell you they don't exist." He points at me with a shaky hand. "You'll take me back. You will. It's always been Darrin and Mia. It always will be."

The door crashes closed behind him and I slink to the floor my knuckles turning white, the knife still clutched in my hand.

## Brentley

Matt called Thomas and told him Mia is acting funny. He said she was in a good mood all morning until she went home to make them a bite to eat. When she returned she seemed unsettled and froze every time a car passed by them on the road.

I need to see her. To make sure she is okay.

Thomas and I got a lot accomplished today. We make a good team. We found a solution to our Darrin problem. He should be leaving town soon.

The puppy on my lap wiggles around, it's like he knows we are almost home.

"Maybe, she was just tired." Thomas says more to himself than to me.

"Could be. Is she going to be pissed at what we did?"

He chuckles with a cigarette hanging out of his mouth. He cracks the window, pulls the cig from his mouth and flicks the ash into the breeze. "It was your money. Naw, she won't be mad. Plus, you got that fluff ball on your side. No woman can resist one of those."

"I wondered what the dog dish was for in the kitchen. Maybe this will bring some life back into the house."

He looks at the dog and then back to the road. "Timber was a good dog. I hope this one is too. It'll take a bit of training but hopefully he turns out to be a decent cattle dog." The puppy acts like he knows we are talking about him. He crawls off me and bounces across the seat to plop himself in Thomas's lap. Thomas tosses his cigarette out the window and then rubs the dog's ears, smiling down at him.

# Death and Daffodils

When we get home, Mia is sitting on the front step staring off into space. When she notices us pulling in the driveway she drags herself upright. I sense her sadness before we even get out of the truck. The puppy jumps out as soon as Thomas opens his door. He makes a beeline right for her. Bouncing around her feet, begging her to pick him up.

She freezes, staring down at him. Then her eyes come up meeting mine. "What's this?" she rasps as we approach them.

"It's a puppy." I shake my head and chuckle.

She doesn't laugh.

She doesn't even smile.

She takes a step back, pushing him away from her gently with her foot. What the fuck? This is not how I envisioned this to go.

"Mia, what's wrong?" Thomas asks. "It's just a puppy."

"Take it back." She frantically looks between the two of us. "Take it back!" She yells louder than the first time.

"Mia?" Thomas takes a step towards her and she takes two quick ones back. The puppy jumps playfully around her, thinking it's a game.

She turns to me glaring. "Take it back," she says through clenched teeth.

"Why?" I ask, cautiously moving closer to her.

"Why are you doing this to me. Why?" Her eyes plead with me.

"Mia, I thought he would make you happy." I hold my hand out to her, but she looks at it distastefully.

"He…he will just die," she whimpers. "Take him back!" Panic begins to immerge over her features.

"Daffodil, everything dies. You can't hide from death but, you can't be so fearful of it that you don't connect with anything."

Tears fill her eyes. "It won't last, it never does. He will leave. You will leave." She shakes her head back and forth and balls her hands into fists at her side. "Why? Why are you trying to make me love it…to love you?" she screams.

The world stops, stutters and then starts again. So fast, it gives me whiplash.

She covers her mouth with both hands.

She runs. And fuck all, if she isn't fast. She is in her room with the door locked before I even get to the top step. I bang on the door. No matter what I say through the wood she refuses to answer.

Thomas comes to the top of the stairs after a few minutes. "Let's let her cool down, son. She will come out eventually."

We both pace around the kitchen for a few minutes. "I'm going to go take care of things outside." Plans still need to be followed through. This is just a little snag. I'll take the puppy with me. Let him run around before it's time to kennel him for the evening.

"Maybe, I should start looking for the key to that room," Thomas mumbles walking over to a drawer filled with junk. He begins sifting through the contents. "I'll shoot ya a text if she comes out."

As I work my mind swirls with her words. Does she love me? I'm pretty sure I love her. I've nothing to compare it to. There isn't anything I wouldn't do for her. If that's love then I've stepped in that shit with both feet. The puppy looks up at me like he is as confused as I am. "It's okay, boy. She'll come around."

She's scared. She should be. Loving me would be scary. I'm different. I know this. If I was a good guy I would walk away and let her go. I'm not a good guy. I think we've established that.

Anyhow, she can't get rid of me now. I'm her new neighbor. I paid the ridiculous asking price for Darrin's land and the buildings that were on it. Whatever. It's just money. No way will Mia and I be able to farm all of it even with Matt's help but it's mine now. That little pip squeak can fuck off all the way back to the big city.

I even called my attorney and had him put my home in the city on the market. For no other reason than to show her how serious I am about this. About staying. At first I thought the appeal of country life would fade. It didn't. Now I realize it wasn't the country as much as her. She is what I want. What I need.

"Okay, boy. Let's get back and see if your girl has come out of hibernation." I pat his head and make my way down the hill towards the house.

The puppy runs ahead of me. He stops under the treehouse and barks, his tail pointing straight out. He barks and barks. A plume of smoke wafts out the wooden window. I chuckle to myself as I make my way to him. "Good dog," I coo, patting his head.

"Hmph, maybe the local sheriff will take him," Mia snips above me. "He would make an excellent drug dog."

I send a quick text to Thomas, letting him know I found her outside and that she is okay. He replies to send a s.o.s . if I need help. He is going home and will see us tomorrow. Scooping up the little dog, I climb up into the treehouse. It's dark inside. The only light coming from the moon. It cuts beautifully across her face.

"I thought you said this wouldn't hold both of us," she states drily.

"It probably won't but at least we will go down together," I tease. I set the puppy down and he sniffs his way towards her. She allows him to curl up in her lap. Hesitantly, she lays her hand on his back. He tips his head giving her access to scratch under his chin. It's cute the way she gives in to his charm.

Her eyes slowly move across the space between us and eventually make their way to mine. "I'm sorry," she whispers.

"I get it, Mia. Really I do. No need to apologize." I relax my head against the window ledge, staring at her. God, she is beautiful.

"Do you get it? Because love equals pain, Brentley."

"Okay, maybe I don't get it. Feelings are new to me. But, what I do know is when you are hurting or sad, I get this ache in my chest," I confess to her.

Silence. Nothing but, silence for several long minutes.

"Everyone around me…"

"Stop." I scoot over to sit by her. "You will not wilt me, Daffodil. Please don't give up on whatever this is." I motion between the two of us.

"I haven't. I'm still here aren't I?" she lays her head on my shoulder.

208

Death and Daffodils

"Yes, but you need to do more than just survive. I want to see you live your best life. For years I thought I was living. I wasn't. I was existing. You, Mia. You've made me see that. Since, my first day here I've felt so alive. Truly alive. And, I don't want to do it alone anymore. I want to see where this takes us."

"I'm scared," she whispers.

"It's okay to be scared. I will be by your side, Mia." I place a kiss on the top of her head. She sits up and faces me.

"I think maybe I'm falling in love with you," she says quietly before leaning in and pressing her lips to mine.

My heart bursts inside my chest. "Can I show you something?" I ask once she pulls away. She nods giving me a shy smile.

I climb down, setting the puppy by feet. My hands lift to help Mia. She falls into my arms and I spin her around before placing her on her feet. She laughs. Truly laughs. "Come on." We jog down the path behind her house, puppy following on our heels.

Before we reach the hill I stop. "Okay, you have to close your eyes." She shifts from foot to foot nervously. "I won't let you fall. I promise."

Placing her trust in me she closes her eyes and lets me guide her the rest of the way. "I think I just felt a raindrop," she says fretfully.

"Yeah, I think you're right. But, this won't take long."

When we get to the top of the hill I tell her she can open her eyes. She immediately crouches down beside Erelah's headstone. Her fingers flitting over her name. The puppy curls into a little ball in front of the stone and yawns. Mia pats his head.

"Remember how you told me that you put the stars in Erelah's room so she could see them every night." I lower myself behind her, wrapping my arms around her.

She leans back into me sighing. "I can't believe Rebecca took them down," she says sadly.

"I know. But, it doesn't matter because Erelah isn't there. She is here. With us. And now she can see the stars every night. Even when it's cloudy." I reach around and tip her chin with my knuckle forcing her face to the sky above us. When she sees what I've done she jumps to her feet, spinning in a circle her hands held out. She is beautiful. I will remember this night forever.

"Brentley, it's perfect," she says choking on tears. "You. You are perfect," she jumps in my arms wrapping her arms and legs around me. She leans back and cradles my face in her hands. "I don't think I deserve you," she whispers.

"You don't." She narrows her eyes at me but, I continue. "You don't deserve me because I'm not good enough. I don't know any man who would be good enough. I'm not always going to do the right things, Mia. You must know this. I won't always be perfect, but I will try."

She places her forehead to mine. "Thank you for being so sweet to me...and to her."

# Chapter Twenty-Two

**Mia**

Brentley sets me back on my feet as I stare above us. He is amazing. The glow in the dark stars hang from almost every branch in the tree that hovers over her grave. There are so many. It's beautiful. They are bigger than the ones I had stuck on her ceiling. They are perfect, just like him.

Ever since Darrin asked me if I loved Brentley it's all I could think about. It scared me. I wasn't lying when I said love was pain. It is. It will be. But, maybe the pain is worth it. My love for Darrin wasn't worth the pain he caused. Brentley is different and I need to remember that.

Darrin never loved me. I see that now. But, Brentley does. And, he doesn't just say it, he shows it. In all the little things he does. Things like this. This had to have taken him hours. Hours I wasted sitting in the treehouse being scared to admit that my feelings for him are evolving. I do think I'm falling for him. I wasn't looking for it, but I think I may have found it. In the most unlikely of places. Could I have found love through death?

"I don't think you understand how happy these make me," I tell him.

"So, I'm forgiven for bringing home the fluff ball?" He dips his head to look me in the eye.

I roll my eyes at him and he smiles brightly. "I guess the fluff ball isn't so bad." Glancing over to said fluff ball I find him sleeping. "He can stay," I whisper, feeling bad for how I reacted to him. I mean he's just a puppy it's not his fault I'm messed up in the head.

He breathes an exaggerated sigh of relief. "That's good because I already told him he could stay." My eyes find his again and he winks.

We stare at the stars for a few more minutes but, when more raindrops begin to fall from the sky we decide to head up to the house. Brentley scoops up the puppy and we make our way back. "So, what's his name? It's not fluff ball is it?" I ask.

"Is fluff ball not a good enough name?" He ruffles the puppy's ears as the puppy tries to lick his face.

"If that's what you want, I guess," I say shrugging my shoulders.

When we get inside he sets the puppy on the floor and I notice there is already food and water in Timber's old dish. "We aren't replacing Timber, if that's what you are thinking." He tugs me into his arms and places his chin on my head. "Life has to go on, Mia."

How does he always seem to know what I'm thinking? "I know. I'll get used to it. Eventually."

"I have a confession to make." He drags us both to the floor so we can sit with fluff ball. The puppy is too excited to be back in the house though. He goes berserk, running to the living room only to return to our lap's moments later.

He is too cute. He is mostly grey except for his ears which are black. He also has one eye surrounded by a patch of black fur. After he makes a few more passes he gets tired and sits in front of us panting, looking happy. "I think he like it here," I laugh.

"That makes two of us," Brentley murmurs, nuzzling into my ear.

"Wait, you said you had a confession what is it?"

He smiles and leans back against the cabinets. "I've always wanted a pet. So, I selfishly bought the dog for myself." He tips his head and bites his lip looking guilty. "But, he's yours. I mean…ours?" He awkwardly stumbles over his words. I know what he is getting at.

"So, is *our* dog going to be stuck with fluff ball for a name?" I lean over and kiss him on the nose.

He laughs and rubs his nose. "I think we should call him Bandit."

I raise my eyebrows and nod. "You know I do kinda like that."

"Bandit, because he stole your heart. Just like you stole mine." He shifts in front of me bracing his arms on each side of my hips. "So, what do you say?"

"Actually, I'm going to agree with you on this one." He makes a face of mock surprise before a grin spreads across his handsome face.

"Bandit it is."

His smile. God, what his smile does to me. He holds out a hand to help me up but then stops, his eye catching something behind me. His eyebrows come together. He reaches behind me running his hand under the cabinet. When he sits back on his haunches he has the kitchen knife in his hand. Shit, did I leave that on the floor? Fuck.

"Why is this on the floor?" Death asks. Yes, Death has returned. I bang my head back into the cabinets.

"I must've dropped it and forgot to pick it up," I tell him, trying to get to my feet.

His hand lands on the center of my chest, fingers splayed, holding me where I'm at. "Daffodil?"

My eyes fall shut and I take a deep breath. It's not that I don't want Death to hurt Darrin because I do. But, Brentley is wanting to leave Death behind. I want him to leave his life of death behind. He wants a new way of life and so do I. If I let him hurt Darrin that will always be between us and I don't want that. That kind of guilt would eat me alive. "I told you I dropped it." The heat of his hand is searing right through my shirt. I'm sure his handprint will be branded on my skin.

"Once upon a time a girl asked a boy to stay with her. She asked him to be careful with her heart. He agreed. They made a promise to each other to always be truthful." My eyes open and I see the hurt I'm causing by keeping this from him. "Does that sound familiar?" His head tips and his jaw clenches. A deadly silence fills the air as I weigh my options.

If I tell him he will want to kill Darrin. That is fact. Can I trust him to adhere to my wishes and refrain from hurting him? Not for Darrin but for us. I think about the stars hanging over Erelah right now. Yes, I can trust him. I can. Brentley wants to share my life with me. He doesn't want me to carry the weight of everything by myself. My eyes fall closed again.

Trust. Trust. Trust.

"He was here today," I whisper.

I wait for the rage. When it doesn't come I open my eyes. He is staring at his hand still pressed to my chest. When his eyes roll up to mine there is an intensity in them that rocks me to my core. "You are mine, Mia," he growls.

Fuck. I shiver at the rumble of his voice. My head nods without thought. "I am yours." Oh god do I want to be his. The way he is looking at me is enough to melt my panties right the fuck off.

"I'm going to put Bandit in the kennel for tonight and lock up. Go upstairs and wait for me."

I swallow and clear my throat. "Um, aren't you hungry? We haven't had supper."

"Oh, I'm hungry. Go." He leans away from me and I quickly rise, skittering from the kitchen.

Fuck. Fuck. Fuck. I rush to the closet to grab a towel. Running to the bathroom I turn the water on in the shower and hop in. One hand rubs shampoo in my hair while the other clumsily drags a razor up my leg. "Shit!" I curse, cutting myself. He could have given me a bit of a heads up.

As I'm drying off I stare at my reflection. I'm nervous, excited, terrified, and, and, everything! This is it. He is going to take me tonight and if it's anything like the teaser he gave me the other night I better saddle the fuck up.

When I open the bathroom door I hear him talking to Bandit. "I know, I know boy, but I don't need an audience for this."

I quietly pad down to my room. Opening my underwear drawer, I sift through things at warp speed. Shit, I don't have anything sexy in here. I slam the drawer shut. The shower turns on down the hall. Okay, calm down I have time, he is showering too. Think Mia. Think.

Nothing. I'll wear nothing. I'm his. All of me is his. I run the brush through my hair, smooth the comforter out on the bed and wait. No, this still isn't right. I rummage through my drawer finding a candle and lighting it. I place it on the stand beside the bed. When the water shuts off I jump up, turn out the light and perch myself on the middle of the bed with just a sheet wrapped lightly around my waist.

Minutes pass and then my door slowly opens. Death steps inside quietly closing the door behind him. The candlelight flickers over his powerful, naked frame. My breath catches in my throat. I'm going to do this. I'm really going to do this. Sleep with someone other than Darrin. Something I had never even considered until Death knocked on my door. A man I very much want. Maybe, even need.

He walks to the edge of the bed. His dark eyes drink me in. A warm hand reaches out and cradles my cheek. My eyes drop closed and the mattress dips next to me as he crawls onto the bed beside me. His whiskers brush against the cheek not currently being caressed in his hand. He whispers into my ear. "You are mine, Mia." I nod and feel him smile against my neck.

# Death and Daffodils

When he pulls away I miss his warmth immediately and my body sways towards him, seeking more. More him. I open my eyes to see him sitting in front of me. Watching me. "Are you nervous?" I ask.

"No, I'm not, Mia. I'm happy. Happy that I finally get the chance to show you that you are mine. You've always been mine. I'm going to show you just how much I own your body."

A shiver races down my spine. His smile is evil. He is going to destroy me, and he knows it. The confidence this man exudes is terrifying sometimes. No first-time jitters from him. None. I sit frozen, waiting for his next move. The anticipation for his hands to be on me is killing me. His eyes move over my breasts and I swear I can feel them there. My nipples tighten into tight little buds and he grins wickedly. "You have beautiful tits, Mia." He palms them both as he speaks, and I groan. "Who do they belong to?"

"You," I rasp.

He leans in and kisses the spot where my shoulder and neck collide. The feel of his lips there, so soft, so warm make my thoughts scatter. My only focus is on his mouth, his hands. He is lulling me into a trance. My hands reach around to tug him to me, pulling him closer. He stills and pulls away. He backs off the bed. I want to cry. "I'll be right back," he says.

Where did he go? Did I do something wrong? He comes back with a box of condoms and his tie. Oh fuck. He sets the box on the bedside table and comes at me with the tie. He runs the silky material between his fingers. "Do you trust me, Daffodil?" He wants to tie me up. Death wants to tie me up!

"W-why?"

"Because if you touch me I will lose control. Tonight, I'm making you mine. I refuse to come like a goddammed school-boy. I *need* to be in control, Mia." His eyes are drowning me. He wants me to give him all the power. He wants me to trust him. "I promise I won't hurt you. But, I won't lie to you, Mia. You *will* beg me. You *will* believe you will die without my touch." The silver in his eyes catches the light from the candle. They are twinkling, pulling me into a dangerous, unknown galaxy. My body begins to tremble.

I place my wrists together and hold my hands out to him. I trusted him with my death, why wouldn't I trust him with my life? "Let the begging begin," I challenge.

He grins like a villain. The silk tie drapes over my wrists and he makes quick work of securing them together. My chest heaves with each breath I take. This is unlike anything I've ever experienced. Since he arrived at my doorstep with a vase of daffodils in hand my life has been anything but boring.

He pushes me back onto the bed with a finger to the chest. He kisses me…everywhere. From head to toe and then he flips me onto my stomach and it's the same. When he works his way up the back of my thighs his fingers grip my ass almost painfully and then he bites. He fucking bites me right on the ass cheek and before I can grasp what is happening he does it again to the other side. "Mine," he growls and fuck if I don't almost come. His growl is the sexiest thing my ears have ever had the pleasure of hearing. He grabs my hips pulling them off the mattress and his nose buries into my heat.

"Oh. *Oh*," I squeak. The pain of his bite morphs into something warm and inviting. His tongue delves and homes in on that wonderful bundle of nerves. "I'm…Brentley…I'm…" Two fingers thrust into me and I'm gone. Gone. Lost to him. To his hands, his tongue, his soul…he does *own* me.

I turn my head trying to catch my breath. His face is suddenly beside me, whiskers brushing over my cheek and I can feel the length of him rubbing between thighs as he presses me down into the mattress. My breasts ache delightfully against the sheets. I moan, long and drawn out. "You are so beautiful when you come," he whispers over my shoulder.

Suddenly, he flips me over raising my hands over my head. His mouth latches onto my nipple easing the ache there and then he slides over to worship the other. My hips embarrassingly rise and fall in the empty space above me. I want him there. Between my legs. I want him there so bad. "Please," I push my head back into the pillow as he nips at me, his teeth grazing lightly over my sensitive skin.

A deep chuckle erupts from his throat sending a buzz straight down my spine. My hips thrash harder. Something, I need something. I need him. His hand roams down, down, down. He presses on my pelvic bone, pushing me into the mattress, stilling me. "Don't move and maybe I'll let you come again," his eyes roll up to meet mine. I'm dying. He is right, I'm dying.

I still, trying so hard to hold every muscle motionless. But, I'm trembling, and I can't stop. I'm shaking like I'm caught in a blizzard, except I'm not cold. No, I'm not cold. I'm burning up. The devil has set me on fire and only he can put me out. His hand draws lower and when his finger drags across my clit I jump. I couldn't have stopped the bolt of electricity that coursed through me if I had tried.

Slowly, so torturously slow he teases me. My hips wiggle trying to position his hand where I need it. He clicks his tongue. "Mia. Mia. Mia," he purrs.

"You're not doing a very good job at holding still. You want to come don't you?"

Tears spring to my eyes in frustration. "Yes, yes, please let me come. Please," I whine, my eyes rolling back in my head as he slides a finger inside of me before slowly pulling it back out. He is like a drug that I'm quickly becoming addicted to. I need a fix. One fix. But, I know it will never be enough.

I lived my whole life not knowing how good this could be. So, good. I'm trying hard to hold still so he will let me come but I can't. My body is writhing over the sheets like a madwoman. If my hands were free I would grab him and force him to touch me where I need. "Please, please I need you. Please, Brentley, please take me. I'm…." My back arches off the mattress as his finger finds my entrance again. I grit my teeth, continuing to take whatever he decides to give me. "Please, please, I'm yours," I force the words out. I'm so close. "Christ," I scream in frustration.

All at once he is between my legs. He reaches over and plucks a shiny foil packet out of the box and through lust filled eyes I watch him tear it open with his teeth. I groan out loud, my eyes narrowing as he rolls the condom over his length. Oh, god. He looks like sin, kneeling between my legs. If this is what sin is then I never want to be good again.

He leans over me with his deadly weapon, it patiently awaits its target. My hips rise on their own accord. Encouraging the dangerous thing to come nearer. Yes, yes. He lowers himself over me bracing his forearms on either side of my head. He looks deep into my eyes as I feel the tip of him nudge at my entrance. "Yes," I hiss, and he smiles, that wicked, wicked grin.

"You're not going to keep things from me ever again, are you Mia?" His cock glides over me lazily. I'm so fucking sensitive I cry out, squirming under his hard body. "Hmm?" he hums, his lips lightly flirting over mine.

"Please," I beg and beg. Then he is there again, nudging his way inside of me. A sound I've never heard escapes me and I mumble dirty words into his mouth. He reaches up and quickly tugs at the tie around my wrists releasing my hands and instantly I have them on his ass pulling him closer to me. His thighs tense, keeping himself stilled with just the tip of him inside me.

"So impatient Mia. I want this moment to last. It is my first you know." He kisses me long and hard, his hips twitching slightly. His restrain is fucking amazing. He pulls back. "You are my first. My last. My only," he whispers and then he thrusts into me so forcefully I gasp. Oh fuck. Fuck. Fuck. Fuck.

I come so hard, my muscles clench around him. Mine. Mine. Mine.

He groans into my neck stilling when he bottoms out inside of me. He grits his teeth, sucking in a breath. "Christ, Mia you feel so good. So, good," he murmurs into my neck.

I'm barely coherent as he starts to rock his hips back and forth. In and out. "Oh, oh, god. Brentley, I'm...fuck...oh..." and again I'm lost in a black mist. I don't even get a chance to come down from my orgasm, I'm held there, suspended in the darkness. Again? Oh my god. "No, no, oh shhhhhhit!" I scream as the darkness swallows my words, my tears....me. It swallows me. My nails claw at his back.

I feel him getting harder, bigger, as he thrusts like he is punishing me, punishing himself. I'm trembling beneath him, spent. But, when my eyes lock onto his, an ember catches, and another orgasm taunts me. Again? You've got to be kidding me. My entire body tenses as he pounds into me. "Come for me, Mia," he groans, and I do. Oh, how I fucking do. It starts in my toes and creeps like a breathing, living beast through my body until I am screaming his name.

He stills and I feel him twitch deep inside me. He's hit me in a place that's never been touched by anyone but him. I'm his. From the moment he emailed me. I've always been his. This was always going to be the outcome. How do I know? Because I feel it deep in my bones. He is right, I've always been his. I feel it now. God. Do. I. Feel. It.

His body crushes me into the mattress and we both pant like we've just run a marathon. "Christ, Mia," he whispers, his face still buried into my neck. "That was…that was," he sucks in a deep breath before slowly releasing it, "life changing," he finishes.

It was. It really, really, was. He pushes up on his arms and stares down at me. His eyes flick between mine, he is searching for something. What? My hand comes up to brush the hair away from his face. "What's wrong," I ask gently.

"Did I…I mean…I didn't hurt you did I?" The concern in his eyes is enough to break me. Fucking break me. He could never hurt me. Never. The fact he is worried that he did makes my feelings for him grow and grow and grow until they spill out and run down my cheeks.

"No, Brentley, you didn't hurt me. You're healing me." And he is. With each moment that passes between us, I feel a piece of my soul mend.

It's odd. I've spent the last few years wanting to die. Afraid, to do anything that might feel even slightly good. Because I thought I didn't deserve it. And at the time, I certainly didn't want to feel good. But, Brentley is helping me see that if I let the good in, it only enhances my memories of them.

I'm still sad. But, I'm learning that I can hold on to them by breathing…by remembering. Brentley is helping me find a new way of living while keeping the past safely tucked away. Not in hiding, not like that. But, in a safe, cherished place in my heart. He allows me talk about them. He's not afraid to bring my memories to the surface for fear of upsetting me. He lets me feel the pain while keeping me grounded. Ensuring that my head remains above water while I grieve. Then he shows me that I am capable of feeling more than pain. He reminds me what it's like to enjoy life. He makes me *want* to live.

His stare is intense, he isn't satisfied. I smile up at him. "I'm good, you didn't hurt me."

The evil grin re-appears. "Well, it certainly sounded like I was."

I huff, slightly embarrassed. I suppose I was a little loud. He kisses my nose before rolling off of me. "Next time I'll be quieter, so you don't think you're hurting me." I roll my eyes.

He chuckles and tucks me against his chest, draping his leg over mine. "Oh, don't get me wrong. I love how vocal you are. I just wanted to make sure I wasn't actually hurting you. But, you are fooling yourself if you think you can be quiet with me. I'll only get better, Mia."

I shiver against him. Damn, I don't know if I can take much more than he gave. My limbs feel boneless the way it is.

"Is it too late to get supper? I'm a little famished after all that," he says, interrupting my naughty thoughts about next time. Next time, god I like the sound of that.

Laughing I push him onto his back and straddle him. "Did I not mention supper before we came up here?"

"You did, but nothing mattered in that moment except me making you mine."

Oh, yes, I forgot what led to this. Darrin showing up here today. Is it terrible of me to like how possessive Brentley is of me? "Come on," I say pulling him off the bed with me. "I better feed you, before you get all hangry on me."

He stays on the edge of the bed watching me pull a t-shirt over my head. "I'm selling my place in the city," he says quietly.

What? The candle flickers as we stare at each other. I don't know what to say. He caught me off guard. "Are you sure? I mean that's a big step."

He nods. "It is. I'm not trying to be presumptuous about us. But, I…well…I kinda bought a place down the road."

My eyes widen. "You, you kinda bought a place. How do you kinda buy a place?"

"He has no reason to stay now," he says. The murderous glint that passes over his face looks scary in the glow of the candle.

"Brentley," I whisper.

He holds up his hand to stop me. "I wanted to buy it. I want him gone, Mia."

"Brentley," I say again. "I can't let you sell your home in the city just to buy Darrin's farm so that he leaves. That's just too much for me to ask of you."

"I don't need to sell the place in the city. Money is not the issue. I want to sell it. You've made me want more than what I had there. I'm serious about us, Mia. I want to show you how serious I am."

I plop down beside him on the bed. My legs aren't wanting to keep me upright right now. This is big. This is him making a commitment. "Wow, I don't know what to say."

"Say, you're not mad at me." For the first time I see insecurity.

"I'm not mad. How can I be mad when everything you do is always with me in mind?" I lean in and place my forehead to his. "I want you to stay here, though, in this house. With me."

He presses his lips to mine and smiles. When he pulls back his grin widens. "I'm glad because I really didn't want to have to work up a custody arrangement for Bandit already."

"You are too much." I roll my eyes. "You and Thomas were very busy today. Did you even get your license or were you too wrapped up buying farms and puppies?"

"Of course, I got my license." He pulls me up and I follow him to my parent's room. I stand inside the door waiting for him to locate a pair of pants.

He bought Darrin's farm. When Darrin finds out he is going to flip. An uneasy feeling settles in the pit of my stomach. I replay his visit in my mind. Maybe he won't put two and two together. Shit. Of course, he will. It's a small town. People talk. He is going to be so angry. So angry.

Brentley leans against the door frame. "Why the frown?" His fingers brush down my arm to get my attention.

"W-what?"

"What has you worried? You were a hundred miles away just now."

I shake my head. "He is going to be angry."

"Thomas and I thought of that. I purchased it under Thomas's name. So, for now everything belongs to him." He grabs the back of my head and pulls me close, hugging me to his chest. "He won't know it was me."

My hands grip the top of his jeans, my forehead resting on his hard chest. I take a deep breath of his scent before I reveal my fears. "He told me someone bought the farm. He asked me to leave with him."

Brentley's muscles tense but he continues to keep me pressed to him. His fingers gently massaging the back of my head.

"I don't know why he thinks I would want him after everything that has happened. He was angry when he realized I wasn't going to go with him. Before, I knew what was happening I had the knife in my hand."

"Did he threaten you," he asks, deadly calm.

I push off his chest so that I can see him. "He tried to kiss me." His nostrils flare. He inhales so deeply his chest puffs out. "I stopped him. He was acting crazy. I thought he might…he wrapped his hand around my neck, and I thought…" Brentley's eyes shut as he exhales. "I didn't want to tell you because I don't want you to hurt him. I don't want him to come between us. He isn't worth it Brentley. Please tell me you won't do anything," I plead.

"The only thing I can promise you, Mia, is that I won't do anything without thinking it through. He can't get away with scaring you like that." He brushes a stray hair away from my forehead. "You are mine now, and I protect what is mine."

"Please, don't do anything that would take you away from me. I can't lose you too."

"I will never do anything to purposefully hurt you. Tomorrow we will go into town and talk to Thomas about this. I think we need to get a restraining order or something. You had a knife out, Mia. He scared you that much. That's not cool, not cool at all. He needs to stay away from you. Please trust me."

"Okay," I whisper. Trust isn't something that comes easy for me. But, he is right. Darrin needs to stay away. Doing nothing isn't an option anymore. It's time to do what I should have done a long time ago.

Time to make a stand.

# Chapter Twenty-Three

**Brentley**

Mia is quickly becoming my world. My everything. Making her mine was indescribable. Her body accepted me as if it were her own. Who knew coming together with another human being would be so…so…perfect?

I know why Darrin wants her back. Why he let her go in the first place is beyond me. But, she is mine now. Not Darrin, not even the devil himself could change that fact.

My feelings are all over the place. A bit hard to control but I will master them. I will. I must. We have a family now. Bandit, Mia and I. Family. I didn't think family was something I would ever have or friends for that matter. Now I have both. I'm not going to screw this up. Nope. So, calm, cool, collected. That is how I move forward.

# Death and Daffodils

We ate, showered…yes, together. In fact, I don't think I will ever shower alone again. Then we cuddled up and Mia drifted to sleep. I'm not a big sleeper. A few hours and I'm generally good but even a few hours are eluding me tonight. My mind is running through a million different scenarios. Mia is my responsibility and I need to keep her safe. The simplest way to do that is to kill Darrin. I could. Easily. No one would know…. except her. She would know. And, for some reason that bothers me.

No, we will go through the legal channels. That is what we should do. Mia has had enough death in her life. Lord knows I have. Which leads me to my next thought. I'm walking away from my profession. I don't feel bad about that. In fact, I'm excited to cut the string. But, I do feel bad for the hundreds of people who will seek my services only to find that I am no longer in business. But, I won't be him with her. No.

I will advocate for death and dignity, but that is where it will end for me. Few states have death with dignity laws. It is a shame that we treat our pets better at the end of their life than we do our people. I've never understood why humans have been made to suffer, for days, months, even years. Death with dignity. I will fight for it, but I will no longer be the deliverer of it.

Mia is life. My life. She is spunky, sweet, sassy, sexy. My eyes travel over her frame as she cuddles next to me. Yes, very sexy. For the first time ever, I'm feeling and it's all because of her. I'm not willing to let that go. She is like finding the pot of gold at the end of a rainbow. Something you dream of but never actually believe you will find. I found my pot of gold and I know better than to let it go. It won't happen again, it's a once in a lifetime chance. Mia is my chance for life and I'm not letting it go.

She wiggles her nose as the morning sun peeks in the window casting dust rays over the room. I'll let her sleep. I wore the poor thing out, it seems.

229

No help for that. I will do it again tonight. It will be fun seeing the heights I can take her. I slide out of bed and quickly dress to go to the hill. Today, I have much thanks to offer her parents. They should be proud of their daughter. She is so strong.

I don't spend long at the graves today. I'm anxious to get back to Mia. When I turn to walk away I see the asshole himself making his way towards me. Calm. Cool. Collected. The fact that he is on Mia's property makes me want to draw the edge of my knife over his throat. Calm. Cool. Collected. "Good morning," I say cheerfully, as my mask drops into place.

He doesn't say anything. He stares down at his daughter's grave. "Is Mia okay?" he asks without taking his eyes off his daughter's name.

"She is."

"I mean. I've heard that she's been suicidal since coming home." This time his eyes come up to meet mine.

*Keep fishing buddy. Not happening.*

When I don't say anything, he continues. "I feel bad she blames herself. She has always had mental health issues. I'm just worried that's all." He holds up his hands in front of him.

Again, no need for a response from me. I'm sure Mia did have mental health issues when she was being hit by her husband. Narcissistic bastard.

He notices the stars hanging from the tree and a scowl forms on his face. Ah, the true Darrin finally appears. I tip my head studying him intently. When he finally looks at me again I see the hatred there plain as day. I arch an eyebrow in challenge. I will eat him for breakfast and spit him out.

"She was always a sucker for the romance," he says pointing up at the tree.

My eyes bore into him. He shuffles nervously. My silence finally getting the better of him.

"How is it again that you two know each other?"

"Our mothers were college roommates," I state matter-of-factly.

"Funny, she never mentioned you."

I'm done playing his game. "I've encouraged Mia to get a restraining order against you."

He storms away from me and I follow. My eyes dart to the Mia's window. Please don't be awake. I don't want her to see him here. He stalks past the house and heads right for his car. Good, he is leaving. Before getting in his car he glares at me for a few minutes. "You know she will always be mine, right?"

I shrug my shoulders and laugh. "I thought you had a woman. Rebecca, right? Or, are you a collector of women? Because, I find that one woman is enough for me. Especially, a woman like Mia."

"She will never be yours. We have history." His eyes bulge with anger.

"Ah, yes, that is true. But, history is just that, history. A time that has passed. Don't worry, I won't be allowing Mia to repeat history. No. And, I can assure you that when I receive a call from her stating that she needs something. I. Will. Be. There." I accentuate each word nice and clear for the prick.

The door to the house swings open just as Darrin's fist connects with my nose. Fuck, that hurt.

"Darrin, what the fuck are you doing!" Mia screams rushing towards us.

"Stay, where you're at, Mia. Darrin was just leaving," I say, holding one hand over my nose and the other out to stop her from coming any closer.

"He's right, Mia. I'm leaving. Last chance to come with me, baby. Rebecca got on a plane this morning to go live with her friend in Florida. We're done. Please, Mia, come with me. Let's go home." He holds his hand out to encourage her to go to him.

"What you and Rebecca do is not my concern, Darrin. We are divorced. This is my home now."

"Please don't tell me that you and this…this man are living here together?" He takes a step towards her and I step in front of him. No way is he getting near her.

"Darrin, please don't do this."

"Tell me and I'll leave," he says through clenched teeth.

"Yes, Brentley is staying here with me. We are…we are together. He makes me happy, Darrin. I've never stepped in the way of your happiness. Please don't step in the way of mine," she pleads.

He stares at her for a moment, gives me a brief look of contempt and then gets in his car and drives away. As soon as he is out on the road. Mia runs up behind me wrapping her arms around my waist. I watch until I cannot see the little pricks car and then I turn to face her. She gasps at the site of the blood pouring out of my nose.

"It's fine," I tell her as she grabs the hand not catching blood and pulls me towards the house.

"I'm so sorry. God, Brentley. This is all my fault." She pushes me down on one of the kitchen chairs. Tires in the driveway have us both looking out the window. Thank fuck, it's just Thomas and Matt. I don't know how much more I can control myself around that fucker. I'm hoping he left for good.

Mia goes back to grabbing a towel and an ice pack from the freezer as Matt and Thomas step inside.

"What in the hell?" Thomas says coming over and tipping my head back so he can see the damage.

"Darrin paid us a surprise visit this morning," Mia says, pushing him out of the way with her hip. She gently holds a towel to my nose to get the bleeding to stop.

"He paid Mia a visit yesterday too," I add. She frowns at me. "Sorry, Mia, but we need to let as many people as possible know what he is up to. Abusers get away with the shit they do because everyone keeps it quiet. We are not doing that."

Matt sits down with a thud. "Christ, Mia. Did Darrin abuse you?"

She pulls the towel away satisfied that the bleeding has stopped. She begins to clean the dried blood on my face. "He...he hit me a few times. It's fine. It was a long time ago."

"Mia, look at Brentley's face. If he hit you it had to have been bad. You're so tiny," his voice cracks. "That's it. I'm done with him and his shit." He rises and storms out of the house.

"I'll get him," Thomas says, patting me on the shoulder.

Mia's eyebrows are drawn together as she works. "What are you thinking?" I ask, pulling her into my lap. She tosses the towel on the table.

"I hate that he hit you." She puts her hands over her face.

I tug them away from her face and lift her so that she is straddling me. "It's fine. I wanted him to hit me. When we go to get the restraining order, it will help our case. We need to do it today, Mia." I push her hair over her shoulder.

"I…I have pictures of what he did to me. Would that help?" she whispers so quietly it breaks my heart. A heart that never felt anything other than its own beat, until meeting her. Now, it hurts. Mia was right love does feel a lot like pain.

"Pictures will help, yes." I cup her cheek and she leans into my palm. "Have you shown them to anyone before?" I ask.

She shakes her head. "I uploaded them from my phone to a photo saving site. I had to keep them hidden. Darrin always went through my phone and my computer."

"Okay, Mia. It's okay." I hug her to me tightly. "Let's go find the photos and send them to print. Then we will go to town and file the order."

She nods into my shirt. I know she doesn't want to relive this. Doesn't Darrin understand what this girl has been through? Why doesn't he just leave her alone? I guess I know why. She is special. But, if you're going to call someone as special as she is yours, well, then you damn well better treat her as such.

Thomas and Matt decide they are going to work on getting the equipment up and running today. I think it's a way to stay close to the house. I'm glad. Mia needs to feel secure as much as possible.

Mia logs into the website she hid the photos on and stares at the screen for many minutes before finally turning it to show me. Oh my god. Oh my god. He is dead. He is literally dead. "Mia," I choke. I run my hand over my face. I'll never be able to erase the images from my brain. "How did no one know? How did you hide this?"

"I called in sick or you know, I'm really clumsy, so…" she looks at her hands in her lap. Her fingers are wringing the life out of each other. I place my hand over hers to stop her. "This, these," she points to the screen, "they were the worst times. The times I thought he might kill me. The times I wished he had."

I wrap my arm around her and pull her close. My lips rests on her head. No one should have to go through what this girl has. No one. How could he do this to her? How could he hurt her like this? "Let's go to town and get this done. We give ourselves today to deal with him and then tomorrow we get back to working on Mia and Brentley."

She pulls back and smiles at me. "Mia and Brentley do have a whole lot on their hands now that they have two farms to work."

"They do but I'm sure that they will still find time for themselves." I lean over and nip the air in front of her face, clicking my teeth together. She visibly shivers. Always so receptive. "Go get ready and I'll send these for printing."

She nods and hops up from the couch. She stops at the bottom of the stairs. "I was proud of you today, Brentley."

My eyes dart up to hers. "Proud?"

"You kept your cool today, Mr. Death."

"I always keep my cool, Daffodil."

"You do and I love you for it. I just wanted to let you know that it doesn't go unnoticed." She gives me a shy smile before heading up the stairs.

I rub my hand over my heart. I've always thought I kept my cool because I didn't have any feelings, they were turned off. But, now they are definitely not off. Who knew my cool would be the one attribute that would make Mia fall in love with me? Maybe my past had to go the way it did so that I could be the man she needs me to be. And maybe the hurt and suffering Mia went through made her into the woman I need her to be. The one who could bring my feelings back to life. She has taught me to feel again, to love again.

Have our lives been intertwined from the very beginning?

# Chapter Twenty-Four

### Mia

Weeks and weeks of work on the farm and I'm finally feeling like we are getting somewhere. Cattle have been moved to the proper pastures now that the fence is mended. Corn and beans are in. Equipment is up and running. Both farms are looking better than they have in a long time.

Matt and Thomas have done most of the planting and daily chores. Brentley and I have been focused on clean up and let me tell you it's never ending. Who knew cedar trees and noxious weeds could be such a pain in the ass? They are everywhere they shouldn't be. But, we are finally on the downhill slope of things.

Best of all. No sign of Darrin. Seems he went back to his life in the city. A restraining order was issued and that was that. I'm glad it's over. Every day is getting better. I'm not going to lie though. There are still moments I pray for my death. But, now I recognize when the chant starts in my head and I'm able to stop it, ground myself and continue on with my day. I want to live. I do. But, old ways of self-talk don't shut off overnight.

I wipe my brow watching the sun dip beneath the horizon. Purple and blues escort the day into night. Damn the sunsets here are amazing. Nothing to block the spectacular view.

"Guys, come quick I found some kittens." Brentley whisper yells from behind the pump house. Matt drops his shovel to follow me. When we make our way around the corner both Matt and I stop dead in our tracks, scrambling back quickly.

Matt starts laughing. Brentley crouches down trying to get one of the little buggers to come to him. "Should we tell him?" he snickers, and I smack him in the arm.

"Brentley, those aren't kittens," I whisper yell back to him. "Get away from them!" I bounce on the balls of my feet, encouraging him to follow me.

He looks up at me confused and then the mama skunk comes around the building and Brentley's eyes go wide. He slowly rises. Matt and I don't wait to see what happens next. We get the fuck out of dodge. We are laughing so hard we are having to hold each other up by the time we get back to Thomas who is waiting for us by the pickup.

"What the hell has got you two kids so giddy?" he drawls, his hands crossed over the pickup gate, a cigarette hanging from one.

"Brentley…" I laugh so hard I snort which only makes Matt and I double over again. Tears run down our faces.

# Death and Daffodils

We smell him before we see him. "Jesus Christ," Thomas grimaces.

Brentley comes into view. His eyes are watering, and he is gagging.

"Not nice you two," Thomas scolds Matt and me.

"What? We tried to warn him," I state for the record.

"God dammit, boy. You ain't ridding in my truck smelling like that. Hop in the back." Thomas shakes his head and Brentley hops in the back still gagging and drooling over the side.

Matt and I try to stifle our giggles, sliding into the seat beside Thomas. "You two ought to be ashamed of yourselves," he scolds again as we head back towards the house.

"He thought they were kittens," Matt howls causing me to snort again.

Thomas tries to hide a chuckle but isn't very successful at it. "Well, I wouldn't be laughing, Mia. You're the one who has to deal with his stinky ass."

Shit, I didn't think about that. My smile turns upside down and Thomas doesn't attempt to hide his amusement now that I've realized my predicament.

"Good luck with that, Mia." Matt jabs me in the ribs and I pretend to scratch my face, flipping him off.

"Do we need to go get some baking soda and peroxide?" Thomas asks.

"No, I'm pretty sure we have some. Good thing I know the trick. Timber was always getting himself sprayed by a skunk." I smile and turn to look at Brentley through the back window. I should feel bad for laughing but I don't. I haven't laughed that hard in a long time. I'll get him fixed up but, I'm going to have some fun with him first.

"Whoooweeee boy, you stink," Thomas whistles when we get back to the house.

Brentley grumbles and heads towards the house. "Where are you going?" I call after him.

"Inside to shower," he says without looking at me.

"Uh, water won't work I hate to tell you." He stops and stares at me.

I smile sweetly. "We'll have to put you in a cow tank full of tomato juice."

He hesitates, trying to decide whether or not to believe me. "That works?"

Matt holds his nose and walks to his truck. "Fuck, I got to get out of here, that shit stinks. We still meeting tomorrow night for burgers?"

"Yeah, if I can get the stink off him." I wave to him and then turn back to look at Brentley who is still staring at me, frozen in his spot.

Thomas gives me a bear hug from behind, picking me up off my feet and then hops back in his truck. "Good luck, see you kids tomorrow." He pulls out following Matt down the dusty road.

"So, tomato juice, huh?" Brentley grunts.

"I'm just kidding. I'm sorry I laughed, it's not funny," I say, but I can't wipe the smile off my face to save my life.

"I'm glad I bring so much joy to your life, Daffodil," he snarls. Oh, he is so cute when he gets all Death like on me.

"I'll go mix up my mom's secret skunk remedy while you toss your clothes in the burn barrel.

"But, these are my favorite Levi's," he pouts.

"No, I'm not trying to save them." I state and point to the barrel out by the barn.

"Fine," he mutters, kicking a rock in front of him. Bandit sniffs his pant leg but evidently he isn't fond of the smell either because he puts his tail between his legs and runs back to me. "Great, I even repel the dog," he grumbles throwing his hands up in the air.

I head inside and find everything I need mixing it up in a big bucket and then hauling it into the bathroom. When he doesn't come inside I go looking for him. I find him standing stark ass naked on the porch. My eyebrow twitches. Damn, farm life has enhanced his body. I peel my eyes away from his naked torso to meet his eyes. "Are you done ogling me now, Daffodil," he gripes.

I tap my finger over my lip. "I don't know. It's not every day I have an attractive, naked man standing on my porch." He lunges for me and I squeal. "Okay, okay. Go get in the shower."

Finally, he smiles. I love his smile. I follow behind holding my nose but admiring his ass. His tight, wonderful ass. Hmm, that's good stuff right there.

We scrub him down with my mom's secret skunk away mixture several times and soon the smell dissipates. "You sure you can't smell it on me," he asks pushing his shoulder into my nose. I inhale deeply.

"Nope, I only smell you."

"You're sure? Cause I swear I can still smell it," he sniffs around on his arm before thrusting it under my nose again.

"I'm sure, Brentley. Do you think I would lie to you?" I take my clothes off as he is smelling himself and join him in the shower.

This gets his attention. "Well, hello, beautiful," he murmurs, now sticking his nose into the crook of my neck making me giggle. "You see how this is supposed to work. I walked right into the shower without you having to drag me," he murmurs against my throat.

"What are you getting at?" I ask giving him a shove to the chest. It doesn't stop his exploration of my skin.

"When you stunk I had to drag you in here kicking and screaming," he teases. He sucks the skin on my neck into his mouth releasing it with a pop and then smiles at me.

"Oh, oh you just had to bring that up did you?" I cross my arms over my chest and turn away from him. "I came in her to apologize for teasing you about getting sprayed by a skunk, but I see how it is. I'll just shower and be on merry way." He is infuriating.

A deep chuckle erupts behind me. I ignore him. His hands glide around to my stomach and he pulls me back into his hard chest. "It's okay, no apologies necessary. Hearing you laugh today was worth it."

Well, hmm. It's hard to be mad at him when he says sweet things like that.

"In fact, I still owe you an apology for our first shower encounter." His hand drops down rubbing between my legs. My legs go wobbly on me, my hand shoots out to brace against the wall. "I'm sorry I scared you that day," he whispers into my ear. He presses his cheek next to mine, his whiskers brushing against my skin.

"It's...it's okay," I say huskily.

Suddenly, he pushes me flush against the shower wall. My cheek and breasts rest against the cold tile, a shiver runs up my spine. Yes, I like this side of Brentley. It feels wrong to like it but yet I do. So wrong but yet so, so incredibly right. His arm is trapped between the wall and my stomach as he continues to tease me with his fingers.

"It's not okay, Mia. I don't want you to fear me. Please don't ever fear me." The way he says it does something to my heart. He is a scary guy. He is, but he isn't. So hard to explain. But, I'm not afraid of him. I'm not. But, to be honest, I don't really know much about him. I guess I would be lying if there wasn't a niggle of fear. He assists people in their quest for death. That in itself is a bit scary. It takes a certain type of person to be able to do that. What kind of person? Well, someone like Death. Someone who can shut off their emotions. Does that make him dangerous?

His hand leaves me, and he takes a step back. Shit. Was he expecting a response? I hesitantly look over my shoulder at him. I see the pain in his eyes. He turns and steps out of the shower. "Wait, where are you going?" I push the shower curtain back, watching him dry off.

"I...I need to call my realtor. With the time difference I keep missing him." He doesn't look at me. Before, I have a chance to say anything he is out the door.

What the hell?

After I finish showering I find him out on the front porch. As I'm about to open the door I hear he is still on the phone. I hesitate a moment when his voice raises.

"I'm fine, Dad. I don't have to report to you every time I leave my house." I step back and press myself against the wall. This is a private conversation. I should give him some privacy. Should. But, don't. "Jesus Christ. I'm not going to answer that, Dad. Yes, I'm selling it. If you want it back, take it. I don't care." He pauses while his dad speaks. "You haven't contacted me in several years. Why now?" I peek around the corner watching as Brentley paces back and forth. "I wanted a change. You wouldn't believe me if I told you. I'm hanging up now. Goodbye, dad." Brently sits down on the porch swing clearly upset by the conversation with his father.

Maybe I should fix supper and give him some time alone.

As I'm putting supper on the table Brentley finally comes back inside. He steps behind me and wraps his arms around me.

"Are you hungry?" I ask turning my face to kiss his cheek

"I am. You know I'll never get used to this." He sighs and sits down in the chair beside me, patting my bottom lightly.

"Used to what?" I take the chair beside him.

"Having someone to share a meal with." I try to hide my smile behind my hair, but he leans over and pushes it behind my shoulder, tapping my chin. "No hiding, remember?"

"It is nice," I say, grinning at him shyly. "Did you get in touch with your realtor?"

He raps his knuckles on the table before picking up his fork. "Yeah, he has a young couple interested. Thinks they might put an offer in soon."

I watch as he chews. He said we would be honest with each other. Why doesn't he tell me he talked to his dad? I guess he could have talked to the realtor while I was still in the shower but it's weird he wouldn't mention talking to his dad too. Maybe he just needs some time, it sounded like a heated conversation.

We eat in silence for the most part. "Mia, that was good, thank you."

"You're welcome." I take his plate from him and begin clearing the table.

"Happen to have any of those brownies left?"

"Uh, the ones you think are too sweet?"

He gives me his wicked grin. "Yeah, that'd be the ones."

"Hmph, I don't." He frowns. "But, I do have cheesecake." He claps like a little kid. I pull it out of the fridge and dish him up a slice. He digs right in but when I don't leave his side he pauses to look up at me.

"I'm not afraid of you, Brentley."

He swallows hard, staring at me. Carefully he places his fork on the edge of his plate, pushing it aside. He pulls me into his lap. "Are you sure?"

I nod. "I'm sure. My hesitation wasn't because I'm afraid. It's because I want to know more about you."

"What do you want to know?" He tucks a stray hair behind my ear.

"Everything."

He grimaces. "You don't want to know everything."

I trap his face between my palms. "Yes, everything. I know it will take some time. Years, maybe."

Laughing he wraps his hands around mine. "Years sound nice."

"My parents got to where they repeated stories. Sometimes I would know my dad was retelling a story, but my mom would listen and smile at him like it was the first time she was hearing it. Other times they would finish the story for the other one and then laugh about it." Leaning in I place a kiss on his lips and then slowly pull back to meet his eyes. "I want that with you. The good, the bad, everything. I want to know you so well that when you tell me a story from your past it will feel like I was there with you."

We stare into each other's eyes for several minutes. So, long I begin to wonder if he is going to say anything.

"When my mother passed I felt like she took a piece of my soul with her. The part that allowed me to feel. I was living, going through the motions but I felt nothing. I learned to watch others, to see how they emotionally reacted to situations. I mimicked them, Mia. Until I met you. I felt it with your first email. Then when I met you. It's hard to explain. It was like being woke up after being in a coma for twenty-eight years. Everything rushed in at once. Color, sound, vibrations. It was as if the world had finally come alive. At first I didn't know if the world changed or if it was me. What had changed? Nothing and yet everything. Then I realized it was you, something about you opened a portal to my soul." He shakes his head, still in awe of what is happening between the two of us. I understand because I'm in awe too.

"I will tell you everything." He kisses me hard sending his point home. He pulls away for a breath. "Everything." And then he goes back in, devouring me as if he is afraid I will vanish at any moment.

When he breaks away my fingers flit to my swollen lips. A mischievous grin spreads across his beautiful face. "I think you are afraid of me, Mia."

My eyes snap to his.

"Admit it," his breath flutters over my temple as he pulls me close, grabbing my hips and grinding me over his growing erection.

"I'm not scared of you, Brentley," I moan.

"Oh, yeah? You should be. Because I'm going to take you upstairs and watch you fall apart at my hands."

"I'm not afraid of you or your hands," I giggle and try to squirm off his lap to run away.

"Oh, no, you're not going anywhere." He picks me up and tosses me over his shoulder.

I'm dangling over his shoulder, hands grabbing him tightly around his waist. Jesus, I hope he doesn't drop me. How caveman like. A warm, flutter grows in my belly.

I think I like this. I shouldn't like this, but….

He tosses me on the bed with a primal grunt that makes me clench my thighs together.

"Undress," he orders as he stalks around the bed, watching me like I might run away.

I should run away. This is the scary, Brentley. The one that takes what he wants. Scary Brentley does things to me. Things that I know I shouldn't want but, do.

247

Righting myself to my knees I pull my shirt slowly up and over my head. He studies me. Waiting, watching for the moment that he will go in for the kill. Rising up I unbutton my jean shorts and wiggle them along with my panties down my thighs.

When he sinks his teeth into his bottom lip I whimper.

I will never get enough of this man. Never.

He growls. Fucking growls. Ah, shit.

I'm completely naked, writhing on the bed from his gaze alone before he begins to undress. Slowly. And then he speaks. "The things you said to me tonight…" He runs his hand through his dark hair, tugging on it once before dropping his hand to shove his pants down. He shakes his head in disbelief before gripping his cock and stroking it from base to tip. "I want to make love to you, Mia."

I lift up on my elbows as he gets on the bed by my feet. Watching him crawl up my naked body with his cock in one hand is the most erotic thing I think I've ever seen.

"Will you let me make love to you, Daffodil?" his seductive voice whispers over my stomach as he continues maneuvering his way up my body.

This isn't sex. This is something different. It's why he is asking.

He is asking for permission to enter more than my body. He is seeking access to my soul.

Can I do it? Can I let him in? There will be no going back after this. Yes, we've been together but, this is different. This is more than two bodies seeking pleasure in each other. This is two souls melding into one.

When we are finally nose to nose, his forearms resting on each side of my head he asks again. His fingers run through my hair as he waits for my answer. I nod once. He closes his eyes and when he opens them again there is so much to see. We lay there, breathing each other in. His exhale is my inhale. His knee pushes my leg up as his thumb brushes over my bottom lip. "You are so beautiful, Mia."

His lips press against mine, firm and warm. He deepens the kiss as he settles more of his weight on me. I groan into his mouth as the head of his cock nudges against my entrance. He breaks our kiss so that he can watch emotions play over my face. Slowly, ever so deliciously slow he presses into me. Starry eyes envelope me, pulling me into a different dimension.

Over and over he buries himself inside of me. With each slow thrust he breaches another area of my soul. This time he lets me touch him. And, I love it. My hands are everywhere on him. In his hair, on his cheeks, his back, his ass. My fingertips skirt over his skin, memorizing every perfection, every flaw, loving them both the same.

We are emerging our stories into one. Everything before this was just the preface. This…this is the beginning of chapter one. Over the last month I had found myself wanting to be alive. Not every minute but enough to get by. Now, now I want to be more than alive. I want live. I want tomorrow and the next day and the next. Why? Because for the first time I don't feel alone. Brentley just laid the entire world at my feet.

Tears run down my face and Brentley licks and kisses them. He takes them and makes them his. He doesn't have to tell me he loves me. I feel it. It is the most unbelievable feeling. I'm hyperaware of him. His hand is on my hip holding me still, allowing me to savor every inch of him. I've never felt so completely owned, inside and out.

Suddenly, I have an overwhelming urge. I can't get enough of him, can't get close enough. "Brentley," I pant into his mouth.

"It's okay, Daffodil. I have you. Let go, baby."

And then…I die a little death.

I gasp for breath, sure that I have been starved for oxygen for some time.

"I love you," falls from my lips and lingers in the air, wrapping around him. My eyes flutter open just in time to see my words sink in. Magnificent. His eyes fall closed. He throws his head back, mouth open and the sexiest sound I've ever heard in my life comes from somewhere deep inside him.

I come again, from that sound alone.

Fuck.

That was…

Fuck.

He owns me, mind, body and now soul.

# Chapter Twenty-Five

**Brentley**

Never in my wildest dreams did I think I would love.

I love her.

I love her and I together.

Which leads me to something I never thought would happen. Loving myself. I can't love us without loving myself. She makes me want to be better. To do better. She looks at me like I'm her favorite person. And, I think I believe her. With every look she is quieting that voice inside my head. The one that says I'm Death.

For so long I thought I was a psychopath. Nothing more than the gatekeeper to the other side. Thought it was my calling. My gift. Until I met Daffodil. She sees me as so much more than that. She has the purest soul I've ever seen. Maybe that is why she was the one to breathe life back into me. Only the purest to penetrate the dark I was trapped in.

Someone who wanted my dark. She embraced it and hung on long enough to wonder if there was more. Then she did what no one else has ever done. She asked to see more. Can I give her more? I think so. She told me about Darrin. She told me, no one else. She gave me her dark and I swallowed it whole. Now, she wants my dark. Will it change the way she sees me? Probably. Most definitely.

Mia tips her head to look up at me. Her head is resting on my bicep, as she lays quietly beside me. "What are you thinking about?" she asks innocently, her doe like eyes kill me every time.

"How lucky I am to have found you," I answer truthfully. I may as well be honest. After what just happened between us I'm pretty sure she knows how I feel about her.

She giggles. "You didn't find me. I found you," she pokes me in the ribs making me grunt.

The door squeaks open a fraction and we both still, pulling the covers up to cover us. "What was that?" Mia whispers. We both jump as a tiny bundle of puppy attempts to jump up on the bed. His front paws scramble trying to hold on to the comforter. Mia laughs and sits up, giving him a nudge on his bottom to help him up. She lays back down as he bounds over her to jump on me.

"What's this, Bandit?" I rub under his chin. Crumbs fall onto my chest.

Mia laughs. "Bandit, did you eat Brentley's cheesecake?" she mockingly scolds him.

He slides off my chest, falling between us. Mia scratches behind his ear and kisses the top of his head. He gives us a big yawn and settles down, tucking his paws under him curling up for a nap. Mia looks from him to me. A tear slips down her cheek, plopping on his head but, he doesn't seem to mind. "I don't know how this all happened, but I'm glad it did," she whispers.

Something lodges in my throat, preventing me from speaking. I give her a squeeze, nod and push her head back down onto my chest before she sees me make a complete fool of myself. What is this girl doing to me?

Amazingly I fall asleep and sleep the entire night. A full eight hours.

When I wake up Mia is resting against the headboard with Bandit sitting on her chest licking her face. She is giggling soundlessly but her body is shaking. Again, something lodges in my throat. "What are you two doing?" I shove her leg and she bursts, giggles erupting everywhere.

Magical.

"I think he is trying to tell me he is hungry. He is eating my face off." She picks him up and sets him down near my head. Great now he is slobbering all over me. She laughs, tripping off the bed. "I have to pee." She giggles all the way down the hallway.

I scratch his ears. "Good, boy. You keep that up, you hear?" I make my way downstairs to start the coffee. I knock on the bathroom door as I pass by making Mia squeal on the other side. I laugh and pause by the door. "I'm heading down to start the coffee."

She mumbles a reply but, I'm already off. It's a beautiful day. I flip the switch on the coffee maker and open the door for Bandit to run out and do his business. Mia stumbles in, in my t-shirt from last night. Her hair is messy, sexy. She comes right to me and wraps her arms around my mid-section. She hums happily as we watch Bandit sniffing around the yard. Birds chirp angrily at him as he moves from tree to tree.

We spend the day outside. Who knew pulling weeds and mowing could be so much fun? Well, okay I wouldn't say fun but, definitely enjoyable to a certain degree. All because she was beside me. The garden looks great. Mia told me that the corn should be knee high by the fourth of July. Everything here comes in rhymes and old wives' tales. While I don't know if I believe them they are endearing. They are a way of linking this life to the previous, something that is hard to find these days.

"It will be nice to go out tonight. I'm glad Matt and Tina found a babysitter," Mia says walking in behind me as I'm brushing my teeth. I'm bent over so all I see are legs dropping into these cute little cowboy boots that make my dick go rock hard in two seconds flat. I stand and catch her eyes in the mirror. Innocence stares back.

I wipe my mouth off and turn, leaning against the counter. My eyes roam from the boots up, finding her in a cute little pair of jean shorts, a red and black checkered shirt tucked into them. The top several buttons are undone revealing the swell of her breasts. Nervously she waits for me to speak. I don't know if I can.

"I'm sorry. Too much, I'll change." She spins but I catch her wrist. Pausing she glances over her shoulder at me.

"I love it." I pull her into me. She settles between my legs and smiles at me. "Question is, do you love it?"

She nods shyly. "I do."

"So, this line dancing thing…" I nip at her bottom lip.

She tugs away from me, pinching her lip between her thumb and forefinger. "I'll teach you. I'm sure you'll master it in no time."

"My mom used to dance. Maybe I know more about it than you think?"

"Oh, do you? Show me," she whispers.

I stand, take her hand in mine and spin her away from me before quickly spinning her back, her back pressed to my chest. Our eyes meet in the mirror as she struggles for breath. I caught her off guard. "My parents loved to dance." I rest my chin on her shoulder starring at our reflection. We make a handsome couple.

"You don't talk about your dad much." She bites her lip, dropping her eyes to the floor.

"Yeah, not much to talk about. He thinks I'm a monster."

Her eyes dart up. "You're not a monster," she says defensively. It makes me smile. My little protector.

"He thinks I'm a psychopath, Mia. He called me yesterday. First time in years." It was strange that he called out of the blue, demanding to know where I was. He says he drove by and saw the for sale sign out front. I suppose it was a shock to find that I was away. I've never left. Never intended to leave…until Daffodil.

"What do *you* think?" she asks hesitantly.

I shrug and pull her closer to me. Rocking us back and forth in front of the mirror, we stand staring at each other. "I understand why he thinks that. I was the definition of one. No feelings. No remorse. Nothing. But, then I met you and now I think maybe he was wrong."

She turns in my arms and traces a finger along my jaw. Her eyes meet mine. "Maybe, you unconsciously buried your feelings after your mom passed. Humans have a way at self-preservation. Shutting your feelings off and burying them could have been yours."

"I don't know. Honestly, I don't care. I've never hurt anyone, Mia. Everything I've done was asked for by the parties involved. But, I'm not going to lie to you. I took their lives without feeling anything. It scared me, that I could be so cold. It's why I've always kept to myself."

"When I've been scared of you it wasn't in the sense you think. It was a scary, excited feeling. I know you will never hurt me, Brentley."

"A scary, excited feeling?" I dip my head trying to catch her eyes. She is flustered, her cheeks turning a lovely shade of pink.

"You know," she pushes against my chest.

My hand roams to her throat, my thumb pushes against her pulse. "Like this?" I squeeze lightly, cutting off a smidge of her oxygen.

Her tongue comes out and teases the top of her lip. She nods hesitantly. I release my grip before tightening it again, pulling her mouth to mine. "Just like that," she mumbles against my lips.

"I will never take you farther than you want to go." I force her to look at me, tipping her chin.

"I trust you, Brentley. I don't care what anyone else thinks of you or of me. As long as we know each other that's all that matters. And, I know you. You're not a monster."

My head tips back and I stare at the ceiling. Her pulse still beating beneath my hand. Mia makes me feel powerful. It's an intoxicating feeling. When our eyes connect again I see her determination. She will never let me bury my feelings again. She has me just like I have her. Apart we may be broken but together we are whole.

"Matt and Tina will be waiting for us," I whisper. She nods and pulls away giving me a smile that will forever be seared into my brain. Another impasse navigated successfully. I'm sure there will be more but together we can make it through anything. No, mountain is too big for us.

The rest of the evening goes great. The bar is full which seems to make Thomas happy. Matt and I have Tina and Mia rolling as they watch us perform the two-step together. "Awe, you guys make such a cute couple," Mia yells across the bar.

I throw her a wave and wink as we continue our shenanigans. She laughs and heads to the bathroom. I haven't had this much fun, ever. Who knew other people could be so enjoyable.

## Mia

I splash water on my face. God, Matt and Brentley are too much. Tonight, has been fun. The townspeople have seemed to have forgotten about my accident, or at least brushed it aside. And, they all seem to have welcomed Brentley into their fold. He is hard not to like. He is funny, carefree, genuine.

"Hey, Mia," a voice I haven't heard for many years says beside me. I look up blinking through wet lashes. She hands me a paper towel. "It's nice to see you out."

"Yeah, Thomas's burger night seems to be popular," I reply, looking at Mrs. Peters. She is the principal at the school. She was just starting her career my senior year. She was always kind to me. Sometimes I thought she saw through my false persona. Every now and then I would catch her looking at me with concern in her eye.

"No one misses burger night around here." She smiles at me warmly. "I've been meaning to stop by and thank you for the memorial you had set up in your daughter's name."

I toss the paper towel in the trash and spin to look at her. "Um, I'm not sure what memorial you're speaking of?"

"Oh, I thought you knew. Your friend came in and set it up. It was very generous. We were able to buy dance uniforms for the entire team. And, we will be able to buy uniforms for years to come. We are also going to be adding gymnastics and ballet to the program. A school the size of ours would never be able to do this without your donation. And then there is the scholarship he set up for graduates who want to go on and compete in college. It was very, very, generous, Mia."

I'm leaning against the wall my hand over my aching heart.

"I'm sorry about your daughter, about everything." She reaches for my hand giving it a squeeze. "But, she will never be forgotten, Mia. Brentley, helped the dance team come up with a memorial display inside the school." She let's go of my hand and rummages through her purse. She places a set of keys in my hand, wrapping my fingers around them. "Go this weekend and see for yourself. It's beautiful. Leave the keys here with Thomas and I'll pick them up Sunday evening.

I nod unable to speak. She gives me another smile and then heads out the door. After composing myself I stumble back out into the loud music and laughter. I pause in the hallway watching Brentley. He stops dancing long enough to take a long drink of water. Now that I think about it I haven't seen him drink any alcohol all night. He must sense my eyes on him because his begin to flit across the crowd, searching for me. When he finds his target he smiles, wide.

My knees go weak. Too much. He is too much. Something is going to go wrong. I just know it. Nothing good lasts. I spin and rush out the back door. And I run. I don't deserve this. I don't deserve him. Did he really listen that closely to what I had to say? He remembered the conversation our first night together. Remembered that I told him I thought Erelah would have been a gymnast or a ballerina. And even though she will never go to school here he made sure her peers would have those opportunities. Is this man even real? Maybe, I'm crazy and I've been imagining this whole thing.

Or maybe I've had too many margaritas and I don't know what I'm doing.

I stop in the middle of the street, leaning over to catch my breath. My run took me right to the school. I have to see. I have to see it right now. With shaky hands I unlock the door. It's dark but as soon as I step inside the lights blink on. One by one they turn on as I walk down the long hallway stopping outside the gym.

It is real. A glass case with a large photo of Erelah in the middle. She is sleeping on white silk, only she isn't sleeping. I choke on a sob. Slowly I creep towards the shrine to my daughter. There is a tiny dance uniform with her name embroidered on the vest, the school mascot placed below. I look at the other photos in the case. The current dance team and their coach. There's even an old picture of me and my dance team.

I study my face in the photo. A smile is plastered on it but, I know I wasn't happy that day. It was the day that Darrin said he would be there to watch. State championships. He didn't show. Even though I went to every game he had. Every. One. He couldn't make it to the biggest competition of my high school career. My parents were there. That should have been enough for me but, no I was so focused on Darrin I didn't even thank them for coming that day.

My knees crumble. I don't know how long I sit on the floor and cry but, when I open the door to leave Brentley is sitting on the steps waiting for me. I drop down beside him. "Thank you," I whisper.

He turns to look at me. "I was going to tell you. When you were ready. I'm sorry you found out this way."

"Brentley, don't be sorry for treating my daughter the way she deserves to be treated or remembered." I look up at the stars, they seem brighter tonight. I hope my parents and Erelah can see what this man has done. The good in his heart.

"My money has always felt dirty. It feels good to have it go to something good, something pure." He studies the dark sky with me. Could his thoughts be the same as mine? Is he hoping his mom is looking down?

"Matt told me that you paid off all of their medical bills and you offered to continue to pay them."

"It's nothing, Mia. Don't make me out to be a saint. I'm not." He lowers his head to stare at his shoes.

"I'm not saying that. But, you are making people's lives easier. I don't know if you understand how much stress you took off Matt's shoulders, Brentley."

I scoot closer to him on the step and wrap my arms around him. He gazes into my eyes for several seconds. "Daffodil?"

"Yes?" I squeeze him tighter, waiting with bated breath for his next words. The look on his face is so serious, whatever he is going to say he means.

# Death and Daffodils

"You are the light in my dark, Mia. The bright color on my dark pallet. The good to my bad. The warmth to my chill. The seed that found the tiny crack in my heart. You, Daffodil, you grew there, despite the desolate conditions that death left behind. That's strength, that's perseverance. You breathed life back into my dead soul. I will always be grateful to you for that. I'm going to spend the rest of my life showing you how grateful I am. So, no need to thank me." The corner of his mouth turns up in the sexiest smile I've ever seen. "I'm telling you, Mia, you will get tired of saying it."

This man.

"My mom used to talk to her flowers," I tell him. He chuckles at my abrupt change in conversation, or so he thinks. "She said it helped them grow. I thought she was crazy. She spent hours in her flower garden with quiet patience and an unwavering determination. And, she was always rewarded with a bloom." I scoot onto Brentley's lap and whisper over his lips. "If I grew in your heart it was only because you nurtured me. Talked to me, listened to me, loved me."

His Adams apple bobs, his jaw twitches and his cock grows hard against me. My stomach does a barrel roll and damn if I don't want to fuck him right here on the steps of my old stomping grounds. "Mia," he whispers into my ear. The rough scruff of his jaw brushes against the sensitive skin of my neck. "We need to get home. Now," he growls desperately.

"No, I can't wait. I need you now." I reach down frantically unbuttoning his jeans, rubbing my palm over his length at the same time.

His groan has me spiraling into a dark wormhole that tosses me into a galaxy where it's just him and I. Nothing else. He kisses me hard as his hands join the chaotic mix between us. He pushes my jean shorts and now wet panties aside. His finger glides into me.

A throaty moan erupts from me and he swallows it. Fuck, he is good. So. Fucking. Good. Finally, his cock springs out of his briefs, bouncing against his stomach. My hand slides from his navel, following the dark line of hair to the base of him. I grip him tightly and guide him to where his fingers are feverishly working in and out of me. He removes his finger and holds the material of my shorts to the side. We both watch as I lower myself onto him. My eyes fall closed as he bottoms out inside of me.

Sighing at the same time our eyes lock onto each other. He grips my waist as I slowly rock against him. Oh, fuck he feels so good. "Brentley," his name falls from my lips like a prayer.

"You drive me crazy, Mia. Fucking crazy," he rasps against my neck.

I continue to rock my pelvis against him. My breath hitches when his hand leaves my hip and wraps around my throat. He pushes me back slightly. "Don't look away," he orders and then he takes control. Grinding his hips upwards, he hits me at an angel that has me seeing stars and not the ones above us.

"Oh, god, Brentley. Don't stop, don't stop," I beg. His hand tightens around my throat, I struggle to keep looking at him, my eyes want to fall shut, so I can slip into the dark completely.

"Come for me, Mia. I want to feel you come on my cock." He thrusts, once, twice and I'm gone.

I fall apart, under the stars for all the world to see. On the god dammed steps of my old high school, where I spent my days pretending to be someone I wasn't. Pretending to be happy. Just as I'm about to close my eyes, his fingers release the hold on throat. I gasp for breath as I'm coming down from the highest I've ever been.

A deep guttural groan erupts from him. I bask in the thought that I drew that from him. Me.

He was right, this only gets better.

# Chapter Twenty-Six

**Brentley**

Walking into my home is, well, it's lonely. How did I live here for so many years by myself? How did I not know the world outside of these walls could be so vibrant? Life pre-Mia seems almost irrelevant now. Everything before laying eyes on her seems like a void. It's like I went to sleep at eight years old and didn't wake until meeting her. It's like sleeping beauty with the roles reversed. I was the one sleeping and it took the kiss of a princess to wake me.

My eyes dart around. So much to do before I can get back to her. My fingers dance across the screen of my phone.

**B: I made it. Miss you already.**

**M: Bandit and I miss you too.**

I smile. I love how she includes him. My little family.

It's late so I guess I'll get some sleep so I can get up and get a head start on the day. I'm spending two weeks tops here. Who am I kidding? I don't know if I can handle two days let alone two weeks. Maybe I should hire a moving company. Ugh, no I need to go through this stuff, take what I want and donate the rest. Two weeks…nothing longer.

I lay in my bed…for hours. Back to no sleeping. Great. My phone pings.

**M: You awake?**

**B: How did you know?**

**M: Did I ever tell you I moonlight as a psychic?**

**B: Funny.**

**M: Look in your bag.**

I get up and toss my bag on the bed. When I unzip it, I find a box I hadn't packed.

**B: What's in the box?**

**M: Really? You're asking? Why don't you just open it?**

**B: Nothing is going to jump out at me?**

**M: Again, really?**

I chuckle. When I open the box, I find two things. An iPod with headphones and a star projector. That damn knot forms in my throat. I set the projector on the nightstand, plug it in and turn it on.

Oh, Daffodil.

With the headphones in place, I lay back and press play. Suddenly I am back at the farm, listening to Mia's nature sounds of the evening with her beautiful stars above me. I'm never letting her go. Never.

**B: How did I ever live without you?**

I watch the little bubbles as she types her response. Then they disappear. A few seconds pass and then the bubbles re-appear. I wonder what she is thinking. This is her first night alone. I hope she is okay. I should be worried about her not the other way around.

**M: You haven't. I've always been yours, remember?**

Yes. Yes, you have, Mia.

**B: I haven't received a gift since my mother got sick.**

**M: You're breaking my heart. I need to hug you.**

I laugh.

**B: Don't be heartbroken, the wait has been worth it. My mother would have loved you, Mia.**

**M: I'm serious. Stop. Bandit is licking my tears as I type.**

The picture that forms in my mind warms my heart. That little fluff ball is definitely doing his job.

**B: Don't be sad, we are still under the same night sky. Thank you for sharing your world with me. Sweet dreams, Daffodil.**

**M: I hope you get some sleep. Good night.**

The little kissy face emoji she places at the end of her message makes me smile. I close my eyes, pretending I'm back at the farm. Back where I left my heart.

When I wake up in the morning I head to the cemetery to visit my mother. Some habits never die. As I approach I notice the vibrant yellow flowers in the concrete vase, and I stop. How? After glancing around hoping she will magically appear I conclude that she must have had them sent. The card tucked into the flower vase confirms it.

*Catherine,*

*Thank you for giving me the greatest man I've ever met.*

*Daffodil*

I fall to me knees. *Oh, Mia, you humble me.*

Never, never will I let her slip away from me.

"Mother, you won't believe what has happened to me. I do believe I've fallen in love, with the most amazing woman. She is sweet and spunky. Her name is Mia. Yes, your college roommate's daughter. What a small world, huh? So, maybe you could put in a good word for me with her parents…with her daughter. I know I'm not good enough for her. But, I promise I will do my best. Because now that I know she exists I'll never be able to live without her."

## Mia

While I'm picking weeds around my parent's headstone to keep my mind off Brentley, I chat with my parents. "Mom and Dad, you won't believe what's happened to be me. I've tripped head over heels in love with Death. Yes, I know. Small world, huh? Anyhow, could you put in a good word for me with the big guy? I'm so afraid this will be taken away from me. Please ask him not to do that. I'll do anything to keep Brentley in my life. Because now that I know he exists I'll never be able to live without him."

I wonder how long it will take him to clean out his place. This is torture, I miss him so much. It's only been one day and one night…one lonely, lonely night. I didn't ask to go with him. Selling his childhood home has to be hard. I can't imagine selling this place. He needs time alone to process, or at least that's what I told myself when he didn't ask me to go with him.

There is a lot to do here. I'm sure he knew I needed to be here. Yeah, I'm sure that's what he was thinking.

Fuck.

Who am I kidding? He probably needed a break from my crazy ass. Or did he change his mind? What if he's been lying to me this whole time? What if I wasn't his first? What if he has a girlfriend? Or a wife?

Stop.

I'm being ridiculous.

Or am I?

He's taking care of business. I'm sure he is.

My phone pings.

**B: My mom sent me a message from Heaven.**

268

I smile, swearing to myself that he has a sixth sense. He always seems to know what I need. Even from a thousand miles away.

**M: What's that?**

**B: She says I have to marry you.**

Wait. What?

I read the message over and over.

Should I?

**M: She sounds like a smart woman.**

I bite my thumbnail as I wait for his reply. Is this a text proposal? No. Well. Maybe. I mean it's not normal to propose via text. But, then again Brentley is different. No. He's not proposing. We barely know each other. Wasn't I just wondering if he had wife hidden away somewhere?

**B: Are you with your parents and Erelah?**

**M: Yep, you kinda got me stuck in this routine, you know?**

**B: I'm with my mother. Thank you for sending her flowers.**

**M: Repaying the sentiment. If not for you, I may have never gotten the courage to come here.**

**B: Are you sitting down?**

I laugh.

**M: Yes, directly under your stars.**

**B: Perfect.**

The text that follows changes my life forever.

**B: Will you marry me?**

My heart stops. Right along with the rest of the world. I blink a few times. Shaking my head to clear the thoughts bouncing around inside, I re-read all of our texts. Shit, this is a proposal.

**M: Brentley…are you being serious with me right now?**

**B: I've never been more serious, Mia.**

**M: If I say yes, I will need time. I want to know you completely before I become Mrs. Bennet. What would you say to that?**

**B: I would say that I am the luckiest man on the planet.**

My eyes dance over my family's headstones. I want to laugh, I want to dance, I want it all. I've never done what I wanted. I did what I thought everyone expected. But, this wasn't even expected by me. And, by god, I want it. With all my heart I want it.

"I'll be back soon," I whisper to my family.

I'm going to go get what I want. If I'm going to say yes to Brentley Barrett I'm going to say it to his face.

I head into town and by the time I get to the Tipsy Cow I am dead set on my decision. Thomas looks up from the bar as I step in the door. He quickly steps around, rushing towards me. "Mia? Is everything okay?"

Tears are falling from my eyes and I'm laughing. "I'm good."

He pulls his head back not believing me. "Tell me what's going on, darlin." He pushes me down to sit at the closest table.

"I need to ask you a favor," I say, wiping my eyes with a napkin.

"Anything." He rubs his hand over my arm. "I'd do anything for you, girl."

"Could you watch Bandit and look after the farm for a few days?"

He sighs. "Mia, you know I will but, I'm going to need you to tell me what's going on. I can't in good conscious let you leave without knowing where you're going and what's got you so worked up."

I laugh again. Brentley asked me to marry him. I'm still having a hard time believing it.

"Mia, you're not going anywhere till you spill it," he demands, crossing his arms over his chest, in a dad-like manner.

*Dad-like.*

"Thomas?"

He answers by lifting his eyebrows, letting me know he has about had his limit of bullshit for today.

I try to stifle my giggles with the back of my hand. "Thomas, would you walk me down the aisle?"

"Walk you down the aisle?" he repeats with a confused look on his face.

"Brentley asked me to marry him this morning."

Thomas sits back with a shocked look on his face. "What did you say?" he whispers.

"I didn't give him an answer yet."

He sits up and grabs my shoulders. "You are going to go give him your answer. Aren't you?"

I nod, quickly brushing tears from my cheeks.

"Okay," he says, slapping his hands on his knees. "Okay," he repeats as if he is slowly coming to terms with all of this.

"Do you think it's too soon? It's too soon isn't it?" I stand and start pacing around the bar.

Thomas follows me and pulls me into his arms. "Darlin, it's been over two years."

"Even so, we hardly know each other," I fret, grabbing him around the waist.

"Mia, you've thought with your head plenty. Why don't you think with heart this time around?" He gives me a quick squeeze before pushing me away from him. "Off with ya. Matt and I will take care of everything here. Just let me know when you land."

I hesitate for a moment and then head for the door. Before I walk out, I l glance over my shoulder. "About the aisle thing?"

"I would be most honored to walk you down the aisle," his voice cracks with emotion. He dips his head and quickly heads to the back.

Well, I guess the only thing that's left to do is catch a plane.

# Death and Daffodils

Deep breath.

Time to live life on my own terms.

# Chapter Twenty-Seven

**Mia**

God, maybe this was a mistake. To say I have cold feet is putting it mildly. "This is it," the cab driver states from the front seat. I look out the window at the quaint house beyond the glass. This is Death's world. One that I haven't been a part of. Will he be angry I'm here?

The cab driver sets my bags on the curb for me and then drives away. It's weird being back in the city. I never thought I would come back here. The day I left I had planned on being dead by the time the clock struck midnight.

He had been right here. Right under my nose. My time in the city was lonely. Every night I spent beside Darrin I was lonely. Funny how fate works. I'm not sure why I had to suffer the way I did. While I still feel terrible for all the tragedy my falling asleep behind the wheel caused, I know now this was the way it was supposed to be. I just hope Brentley sees it the same way.

I pick up my bags, straighten my shoulders and head up the steps. Moments go by at a snail's pace while I wait for him to answer the bell. He could be gone. What if all my fears were right and he lied to me? I pretty much have myself convinced that his wife is going to answer the door when it swings open wide. My eyes meet the darkest, stormy eyes I've ever seen.

Death's eyes.

He grabs me and pulls me through the door, ripping my bags from my hands. He kicks the door and shoves me up against the back of it harshly. My head is spinning. I'm not sure what the fuck is going on. He doesn't seem happy to see me.

Briskly he walks over to the windows, pulling the curtains back to peek out. His eyes scan left and right. Okay, maybe he does have a wife. I should have known. Oh my god. I've made such a mistake. Tears are on the verge of spilling out onto his shinny floors. Before that happens I turn, trying to open the fancy handle on his fucking front door. I need to get out of here.

"Take them off?"

"W-what?" I ask, trying to shove down my emotions, still fighting to get the door open.

"Your clothes. Take them off," he orders.

"I'm sorry, this was a mistake. I have to go."

"Mia, turn around and look at me."

"No."

Just as I get the damn door open he is behind me slamming it shut. He presses his front to my back, pushing me against the smooth wood grain. "Listen, my dad just left, and I didn't want him to see you."

"Y-you don't want me to meet your dad?" I choke on the question. Is he ashamed of me?

"He thinks I'm a monster, Mia. He wouldn't understand what has happened between us. I'm, well, I'm afraid he would try to talk you into walking away from me."

The air is forced out of my lungs. "Brentley, I would never walk away from you. You're not a monster."

"What were just trying to do then?" His lips trace over the shell of my ear. A shiver prickles over my skin.

"I…I thought you had a wife, or a girlfriend, or, or something like that. I'm sorry, my brain ran away from me."

He chuckles and the vibration against my back makes me instantly wet for him. Taking a few steps away, he repeats his original demand. "Clothes off. Now."

Peeking over my shoulder, I give him a shy smile. Okay, maybe I shouldn't have jumped to conclusions but damn this man is good. So good it doesn't seem possible that he was as inexperienced as he said he was.

"Now." He stalks toward me, turning me so that my back is against the door. He grabs the bottom of my shirt, slowly lifting it over my head. I can't tear my eyes from his. My knees begin to tremble. My mind is finally starting to catch up. My fingers make quick work of unbuttoning my skirt and shoving it along with my panties to the floor. A little kick sends them whisking across the shiny, marble floor.

He steps back. His eyes start at the tip of my head and rake sensuously down my body. The weight of his stare is heavy. Here I stand in nothing but a lacey bra and my fuck me high heels. Yeah, I dressed up, just in case there was some competition. I know, I know, I need to work on my trust issues.

His tongue darts along his bottom lip before his teeth sink into it. He smiles. Shit, did I just groan out loud?

"I've missed you, Mia." Did his voice get deeper?

"Umm, I missed you too." I shift on my feet, feeling slightly self-conscious since I'm the only one undressed at the moment. "I…I wanted to give you my answer in person. I…"

"Don't," he cuts me short. He steeples his fingers in front of his mouth before lowering them. "How long do I have you?"

"I fly back on Monday."

"Give me your answer Sunday evening. Until then, I just want to enjoy the fact that you are here with me. I'll admit I was worried when you didn't respond after my last text."

I grin, my cheeks heating. My eyes drop to the floor. "I hope it's okay that I'm here."

He steps towards me and tips my face to his with his knuckle. "It's more than okay. It's nothing short of amazing." His hand trails down my chest

277

and he flicks the clasp on my bra. My eyes fall closed when he palms my breasts in his warm hands.

And then it's like we've been starved for each other. Two addicts desperate to get their fix. I jump into his arms, kissing his face, all over. His hands grip my ass cheeks as my legs wrap around him. "I missed you so much," I whisper in between kisses.

He carries me past all the boxes stacked everywhere into a bedroom on the main floor. "I'm going to show you all of my favorite things while you're here. But, first I'm going to ravage your body. I want to hear your screams bounce off these walls."

I nod quickly in short jerky bouts. Yes, yes. I want him to make me scream. "What if your dad comes back. He might hear me scream and wonder what monstrous things you are doing to me."

He climbs on top of me and pushes my legs all the way back into my chest, holding them there. "I don't care if the devil himself, hears you. You are mine. Nobody is taking you from me." He shoves into me with one thrust and fuck if I don't scream. It feels good. So. Fucking. Good.

"That's scream number one." He smirks when I finally open my eyes to see why he isn't moving. He pulls out slowly before shoving himself back inside of me.

He fucks me slowly. The whole time never taking his eyes off of mine. I want to give him my answer right now. I'll never get enough of him. Never. There is only one answer. One. "Brentley," I moan.

"Don't. Not. Until. Sunday," he grunts out each word on a thrust.

Okay then. Sunday. Sunday. Sunday

Sunday, he will have my answer. He will have me. Forever.

## Brentley

Mia is here. In the city. In my house. In my bed. And, best of all…in my arms.

My fingers trail through her soft locks as she sleeps next to me. My theory has been proven. It's her that makes me feel. It has nothing to do with where I am. It's who I'm with. Her.

Her. Her. Her.

I had planned on taking her out last night, but we spent too long in bed. So, we ordered Chinese and then went right back to bed.

I'm such an idiot asking her to marry me via text. Who does that? Oh, yeah, this guy. I was so overwhelmed when I saw the flowers on my mother's grave. I just knew I wanted to marry this girl. She deserves more than a text though. She hasn't given me answer. I haven't let her. Why? Because, I'm going to give her the proposal she deserves. Nothing fancy. She's not like that. But, face to face. Yes. With a ring. Yes.

Thank god she arrived when she did. Five minutes earlier and she would have bumped into my father. Don't get me wrong. I love the man. I do. But, he doesn't understand me. Never has. He asked me over and over why I was moving and where I was moving to. He didn't get an answer.

If he would listen, I would tell him. I would shout from the rooftops my love for Mia. He wouldn't believe me. In fact, it was he who suggested I isolate myself. Which I did. For years. But, then I met Daffodil and everything changed. I've changed. My perspective of the world changed. It's a whole hell of a lot brighter. I'm not going to give him a chance to dim it.

"Mmm," Mia moans, as she stretches leisurely in my bed.

Okay, I really need to focus. Every little moan and grunt that comes from her makes my dick as hard as a block of cement. I can't keep her in bed the entire time she is here. My head knows this but, evidently my cock does not.

"Good morning, Mia," I whisper into her ear. She smiles even though her eyes remain closed.

"Mmm, morning." Fuck, she made that sound again.

"You really need to stop that or I'm going to tie you to my bed and keep you here all damn day," I tell her, lightly tapping her bottom.

She smiles again and opens one eye at me. "If that was meant to be a threat it wasn't a very good one. That sounds delightful." She pushes up on the mattress to rest on her forearms.

"I only have you for a few days. I don't want to spend the entire time in bed. Well, no, that's not true. I do want to spend it in bed but, I want to give you the chance while you're here to get to know me better."

She sits up and reaches her hand out to touch my cheek. "That sounds wonderful too."

I take her hand and place a kiss on the inside of her wrist before standing up. "So, what do you want to do today? Is there something you didn't get to do when you lived here before?"

She curls herself up in a little ball on my bed, hugging her knees to her chest. "I-I didn't do anything here. I mean I've been to a few restaurants, the mall, the grocery store. Most of my time was spent at home or at the hospital. Oh, and I can't forget the year I spent at the county jail." She shrugs her shoulders sadly.

"Mia." I sit back down on the bed, pulling her onto my lap. "How long were you here?"

"We moved here right after we graduated college. So, six years," she whispers.

"Hm, give me an hour or two and I'll see what I can do. I'll take you to all of my favorite places. Okay?" I dip my head to get her to look at me.

She nods and gives me a heart-warming smile. "Tell me what to pack and I'll do that while you're planning. Yes?" She taps my nose with her finger.

"You can pack my books. How about that. No better way to get to know someone than by seeing what they read." I push her off my lap. There is much to do. I'm excited. My mind is racing with all the experiences I can give her. She showed me a little country. Now, I'll show her a little city.

I hate Darrin more than I did yesterday. If that's possible. How could he drag her half-way across the country, away from her family and then not share with her what it has to offer? If she was mine. I would show her the world.

Wait.

She is mine.

Or, at least in my head she is.

I guess we will find out Sunday evening.

# Chapter Twenty-Eight

**Mia**

There was a time when I was not happy here or there. I was not happy anywhere. Sounds like a Dr. Seuss book. It was my truth. One I didn't face until Brentley made me face it.

Now, I feel like I could be happy anywhere as long as he is by my side. I'm not sure what it is about him. That's a lie. I know what it is. He simply lets me be myself. We've done nothing but site see, eat and laugh for the past few days. Not once did he criticize what I was wearing, what I ordered, what I laughed at. It was refreshing. Freeing.

I thought I hated the city. Come to find out I don't. It's amazing. I still prefer the quiet of the farm. That's where I want to live. But, this is a wonderful place to visit. "Brentley?"

# Death and Daffodils

"Hmm?" Brentley looks up from his menu.

"Are you sure you want to sell your home? I mean you said you didn't have to. Maybe you should keep it."

He folds the menu closed and sets it on the table. "Are you...are you saying I should keep it in case we don't work out?"

My eyes widen. "No, god no. I'm sorry that came out wrong. I was just thinking that being here with you has been amazing. If you keep it then we would always have a place to stay when we come back to visit."

He sighs loudly, dropping his shoulders. Shit, I scared him. Loosening his tie, he sits back against his seat. "To be honest I have thought about keeping it. But, I wanted you to know how serious I am about us. I didn't want you to question things at my sudden change of mind."

My foot taps his under the table until he looks at me. "I thought we were always going to be honest with each other."

He smiles. "You're right. I should have told you. But, I hadn't changed my mind until you got here. My home had been a very lonely place for me, Mia. Until you stepped over the threshold. You, you change everything."

"Is it too late?"

"No. Nothing has been signed. Do you really think I should keep it?" he asks, running his hand through his dark hair.

"Absolutely. I'm going to make you bring me back for more musicals. I loved them so much. It's been my favorite thing." I bounce in my chair, excited that he is keeping his place.

He shakes his finger at me. "I've created a monster."

I nod feverishly. Yes, he did. "I'm just sad I have to leave tomorrow."

"I'll be right behind you. Just give me a few days to ship some of my things to the farm and meet with the relator. Three days tops."

"Three, whole days," I pout.

He stands and scoots into the chair next to me. The waitress walks over to take our order, but he holds up his hand silently asking her for more time. She nods once and backs away.

He reaches into his jacket and pulls out a little black box. My heart stops. I know what it is. It isn't a surprise. He already asked but….

"Mia, will you marry me?" He cracks the box open and holds it out for me with one hand. His other slides to rest on the back of my chair.

Hesitantly I reach out and trail a finger over the beautiful ring. The band is rose gold with tiny diamonds set around the entire band. There is a large, square cut diamond raised in the center, with a rim of tiny diamonds surrounding it.

My eyes meet his anxious ones. "It's beautiful," my voice cracks and a tear slips down my cheek. He sets the ring on the table and whisks the tear away with his thumb. Leaning in he places a gentle kiss to my lips.

"Yes, a thousand times yes," I cry when he finally pulls away.

He smiles shyly, remaining quiet as he pulls the ring out of the box. Before, he slips it on my finger he pauses. "Towards the end of my mother's illness she couldn't speak due to her ventilator. She had a little white board she used to talk to us. The day she asked me…" He pauses and ducks his head

284

before continuing. "Well you know what she asked. When I told her that I would do it she responded by writing *my brave boy* on her board. Then she pulled this ring, her wedding ring, off her finger and placed it in my palm."

He slips the ring gently over my knuckle, settling it on my hand.

"She then wrote, *find love and you will find life*. Those were her last words to me. I didn't know what they meant at eight years old. This was her last gift to me," he taps the ring with a finger. "Those were her last words." A tear runs down his cheek. I reach over just like he done to me and brush it away.

"I don't place this ring on your finger lightly, Mia. Until, you I didn't understand what she meant. I thought I was living but, I wasn't. I surrounded myself with death thinking that would keep her close to me."

He smiles before continuing, "Maybe everything that has happened to you, to me, maybe it was all divine intervention. It was a dusty, dirty, bumpy road but it led me to you. I'd travel it a thousand times. I love you, Mia. More than the moon, the stars, more than anything. Finding love with you has given me life."

He kisses the ring before tucking my hands in his. I stare at him for a long moment. I could stare into his starry eyes for eternity. "Brentley, that was *thee* most beautiful thing anyone has ever said to me. Are you sure you don't moonlight as a poet too?"

He chuckles and leans back wiping at his eyes with the bottom of his palms. "Okay, enough sappy. Let's eat and then I'm taking my fiancé dancing before I take her home to make sweet, slow love to her." He waves the waitress back over.

Before she gets to us. I lean over and whisper to him. "Your love brought me back from the edge of death. I hope you know that."

He gives me a curt nod and swallows hard. "We walked each other back from that ledge."

"That we did." I smile at the waitress as she approaches.

# Chapter Twenty-Nine

**Mia**

I settle into my seat on the plane. Three days, until I get to see Brentley again. I'm so excited to tell everyone we are getting married. I have a lot to do when I get home. I'm going to clean out my parent's room and make it Brentley's and my room. Then I want to plan an engagement party at the bar. Nothing fancy, just a few friends.

The stewardess makes eye contact with me as she walks towards me. "Are you Mia Everett?"

"Yes," I reply wondering why she is asking.

"A Mr. Bennet says there is an emergency and has asked to speak with you. I must let you know that we are getting ready to pull away and you will not be permitted back on the plane if you get off."

"I have to go," I grab my bag from above and quickly scoot by her to exit the plane. Brentley wouldn't ask if it wasn't important. What could have happened in the time since we said our goodbyes less than thirty minutes ago?

When I get off I search for Brentley in a panic. I can't find him anywhere. I run towards the pickup doors and as soon as I burst through them there he is holding a car door open for me.

Only, it's not Brentley.

"Trust me. You'll want to hear what I have to say," Darrin says with a smirk on his face as he motions me to get into the car.

My eyes dart around. Brentley is nowhere to be seen. I should run.

"You wouldn't want your pretty boy to go to prison would you?" He points to the passenger seat once more. "Now, Mia."

He found out who Brentley is. He knows he is Death. Fuck. Fuck. Fuck. I have no choice. I'll go with him to find out what he knows and then I'll bail. Somehow I'll bail.

Slowly I inch towards him. The whole time my body screams to run, my head tells me to stay and find out what he knows and my heart...well, my heart simply weeps.

He takes my bags from me and puts them in the trunk while I slide into the seat. When he walks back to close my door for me he leans in. "Don't be scared, Mia. I'm only doing what is best for you." He runs a knuckle over the line of my jaw. I don't want to make him angry, so I nod and drop my eyes to my hands in my lap. This is the way he likes me, submissive. He shuts the door and makes his way around the car to get into the driver's seat.

# Death and Daffodils

When I look at my hands the sun catches my engagement ring sending rainbows everywhere. I quickly tug the ring off and stuff it in my pocket. No need to provoke the beast. I suck in two deep breaths as he gets in and starts the engine. Tears prickle behind my eyes. I knew my life with Brentley was too good to be true. I didn't deserve him.

"Where are we going?" I manage to ask. We aren't going to our house. I mean his house. His and Rebecca's. He passed that exit a long time ago.

"You need help, Mia. I'm taking you to get that help," he deadpans. Not one hint of emotion on his face.

"I'm not sure what you mean." What in the fuck does he have up his sleeve?

He doesn't answer me right away as he pulls into a parking lot of a small facility in the middle of nowhere. The sign in front says Riverside Behavioral Health. No. No, no. He cannot be serious. He places the car in park, shuts off the engine and then turns his whole body to face me.

"Mia. I know who that man is. Why he was at the farm. I'm not sure what is going on between the two of you now…" he pauses and then reaches out to brush a lock of hair behind my ear. "Why were you here in the city with him, Mia?"

"He…he's my friend. I told you." My voice shakes as I speak. I'm so afraid that he will cause Brentley trouble. Darrin is vindictive. Darrin is a high-powered attorney, used to getting what he wants.

"I think you need some time to think about things. You're suicidal and I cannot sit by and watch you continue like this without doing something to help you."

I shake my head back and forth. "I don't need help, Darrin. I'm not suicidal anymore. It was just the loss of Erelah and my parents. It was too much but I'm better. I promise."

He sighs and stares out the windshield at the building in front of us. "I want you to sign yourself in to this facility for thirty days. Give it thirty days. If you don't then I'm going to go to the authorities and report your *friend*," he says snarling out the last word in disgust.

"Darrin, please don't do this. I can't just up and leave the farm. Thomas will be worried about me."

"I will give you a few minutes to text anyone that will be worried, him included. Tell them you need some time to think and that you will be home once you've sorted out a few things in your head."

What?

"Phone, Mia," he demands. When I don't pull mine out he pulls his own from his pocket. "You leave me no choice."

"Wait," I screech as I dig through my purse quickly retrieving my phone. He watches as I type a group message to Thomas, Matt and Brentley telling them exactly what he told me to say. I feel terrible as I type because I know they will all be worried.

"They will take that once inside so power it down." He nods towards the cell in my hand.

Tears start and I can't stop them. I do as he asks, staring blankly as my phone goes dark. He pulls me into a hug. I try to fight him but it's no use. Darrin has the upper hand. I can't put Brentley at risk. I just can't. "Shh, don't cry, Mia. This is for the best. It's time to get the help you need. I'll come visit every Sunday. I'm here for you. Everything is going to be okay. You will see."

Finally, I break free of him. "Whatever you think about Brentley, it's not true. Please, please don't do this. I've never asked anything of you. Please let me go home."

"Your home is with me. I think we had both forgotten that. When we were at Matt's party on the river I remembered. You will too, with the help of these folks." He points to the door and then he gets out of the car. I watch in the side mirror as he unloads my bags. This cannot be happening. He cannot be serious. This is so fucked up.

I open my door. "What is it you think you have over him," I ask hugging my arms around myself.

He gives me a stern look. "You and I both know who he is, Mia. Don't play stupid. It doesn't look good on you."

I drop my head, focusing on the ground. Feeling twelve years old again at his reprimand. He stops in front of me dropping my bags to the ground. "This is a chance for you to get better. Erelah's death came between us but we can find our way back. We can." He kisses my forehead and then picks up my bags. "Come on, baby," he says jerking his head towards the entrance.

Inside we are greeted by a short, spunky woman with purple spikey hair. "Hey, you must be Mia. I'm Leslie," she says reaching out and shaking my hand and then Darrin's. "Let me get Fredrick and we can get started. Go ahead and have a seat." She leads us down the hall to a small room and motions to a loveseat in the room. It's opposite two chairs, a coffee table between them. "I'll take those." She points to my bags and he hands them to her before he sits down. I watch in horror as she takes my bags and shuts the door behind her.

My gaze falls to Darrin's. You would think that after all the years we have known each other that nothing would surprise me about him. Not the case. Surprise is putting it mildly. "Darrin…"

"Sit, Mia." He pats the spot next to him. My eyes glide back to the door of the room. Run. Run. Run. But, that's not what I do. Begrudgingly I take the seat next to him. His hand slides around my shoulders. I try to lean away from him, but he tugs me closer. He whispers in my ear, "You will do this. Thirty days, it's all I'm asking."

At least he didn't hurt me. He is being nice Darrin. Maybe he really thinks he is helping me. How can I explain Brentley and I to him? Thomas understands. Would Matt? Has he told Matt who Brentley is?

It's just thirty days. I did kill our daughter. This is probably the least I could do for him.

"I've spoken with the doctor here. He is the best in the field. His name is Dr. Giles. Will you please give him a chance to help?" Sincerity is in his eyes.

"Okay," I whisper.

"Yeah?"

"Yeah, I'll give it the thirty days."

He pats my knee. "You are always a good girl for me, Mia. Thank you."

# Death and Daffodils

I inwardly cringe at the term good girl. That's how he likes me. Good girl. It has nothing to do with being good. His definition of good girl is doing whatever the fuck he wants me to do.

I'm doing this for Brentley, not Darrin. Brentley.

There is one question burning a hole in brain. One question that I don't want to ask yet desperately need to. "What happens after thirty days?"

He smiles, leans in and kisses me.

Darrin's fucking lips are on my lips.

Nothing has ever felt so…

so wrong.

The door opens and a man in his mid-forties walks in just as Darrin pulls away, leaving my question unanswered…or was it.

"Mia." The man shakes my hand in a firm grip. "I'm, Fredrick, the man with the paperwork. Dr. Giles wanted to be here, but he was called away to an emergency. He said he will see you first thing tomorrow morning. I just need to go over the rules with you and there are a few places for you to sign. He sets the paperwork on the coffee table and slides it my way.

"Leslie is getting your room ready for you. She is going through your bags and writing down everything you brought with you. She will take out anything we feel you could use to hurt yourself. Those things will be kept locked in the office. If you need any of those items for any reason just let us know and we can discuss and decide then if they can be checked out to you. You will not be allowed to make phone calls. We feel it best that you focus on yourself during your stay here. As your husband has probably already told you, you will have family therapy sessions on Sundays with Dr. Giles."

My head spins. This is really happening. Everyone is going to worry about me. Brentley is going to lose his mind. I don't want to do this. But, what choice do I have?

None.

I'll just have to go along with this until I can figure something out.

# Chapter Thirty

## Mia

I didn't sleep at all last night. For one my mind could not wrap around the events of the day. I sat by the window staring out at the night sky, missing Brentley. One minute I'm sad, the next angry. Is Darrin doing this because he is really worried about me or is it because he's jealous? That is the question I keep asking myself over and over again.

A knock on the door interrupts my thoughts. Leslie bops her head in. "Dr. Giles is ready for you." She waves for me to follow her. I slip my engagement ring off my finger as I follow her down the hall and stuff it back in my pocket. It's the only thing helping me keep my grip on reality.

She opens the door. "Take a seat. He'll be right with you," she smiles and then closes it behind her.

A tall man with dark hair, peppered in grey walks in seconds later. "Mia," his voice is deep, rich and warm. "I'm glad to finally meet you. Your husband has told me a lot about you."

"My ex-husband," I correct, taking his offered hand in mine. He has a firm but gentle grip.

"Yes, he did say that you were divorced but he is hoping for a reunion."

"Not happening."

He sits down in the chair beside the couch I'm sitting on. "He is concerned about you."

"Yeah, well it's a little late for that."

"He explained to me what happened the night of your accident. It sounds like he feels responsible."

"It was my fault. No one was responsible except for me."

"Could circumstance be responsible."

My eyes dart to his, my mouth falling open.

"You seem shocked at my words," he says, looking at me intently with dark eyes.

"It's just someone else said that exact same thing to me."

"It's true. Sometimes things happen and no one is to blame." He scribbles something on his notepad and then his gaze falls back to me. "First thing I would like to know, Mia, is do you have a plan?"

"A plan?" I question wrapping my arms around myself.

He takes notice of my body language and jots something else down on his paper. "A plan on how to end your life?" He taps his pen over his lips waiting for my response.

"I don't want to kill myself. I mean I did, but not anymore. Darrin is overacting."

He nods and sets his pen down on his notebook. "He seems to think that you have hired someone to help you with this endeavor."

My eyes go wide. That motherfucker. He told this guy about Brentley. Well, fuck. Deny. Deny. Deny.

"No, I didn't hire anyone."

Dr. Giles sighs. "Mia, if this is going to work you need to be honest with me."

"I. Didn't. Hire. Anyone," I reply through gritted teeth. I'm getting angry. Fuck this guy. He doesn't know me, and he sure doesn't know Brentley.

"Tell me about him," he urges, cocking his head to one side.

Fuck no.

Not happening.

Kiss my ass.

Another long drawn out sigh comes from him. "Okay then. Anything you *do* want to talk about?"

"I'm here because Darrin thinks I need to be. We disagree on that. But, here I am. I'm not suicidal and I didn't hire anyone to do it for me. So…" I lay my head back against the couch and stare at the ceiling.

"So, you have nothing to say?"

"Nope," I say, accentuating the p with a pop.

"Okay." He tosses his hands up in the air. My eyes narrow on him. "I have someone I would like you to visit with this afternoon. He runs the group therapy sessions. He is a suicide survivor. His name is Johnathan. Would you like to attend the session?"

"Nope," I pop off again.

"Can I send him to your room for a one on one. Mia, please. We need to start somewhere. You can't hide in your room for thirty days. That's not how this works. I'm sure your hus..I mean your ex-husband would be happy to hear that you are at least trying."

"Fine. Are we done?" I scoot to the edge of the cushion.

"For today, yes."

Quickly I rise and head towards the door, anxious to get away from him. There is something about him. He doesn't make me uncomfortable. No. It's the opposite of that. He is the kind of man who gets what he wants. If I don't watch myself he will have me spilling my secrets by the end of the week.

"One more thing."

I pause half in his office, half in the hallway.

"I'm not your enemy here, Mia. I truly want nothing more than to help you."

He is right. This isn't his fault. The game is being played by Darrin and myself. Darrin is my enemy. Or, at least I think he is.

I nod once and then close the door behind me.

I'm doing this for Brentley, I remind myself. For us.

## Brentley

Where could she be? Thomas has searched at home. I have searched here. I'm so confused. She seemed fine when I left her at the airport. Happy. Did I push to soon? What an idiot I was to think she would want to marry me. Once she got on the plane did she change her mind? Get cold feet?

The ice is settling back in my chest. I need her. Maybe that's what scared her. My need for her.

I'm going to lose my mind. Thomas told me to stay here in case she returns to the city. He is staying at the farm, hoping that she comes home soon. We have all bases covered but, I'm not going to lie...we are scared.

I've even stalked Darrin. My mind ran rampant when I received her text. I thought for sure he was responsible but after watching him nothing seems off there. He went to work and then he and Rebecca left a few times together. Once to dinner and once to an Obstetrician's office.

The only thing keeping me from going off the deep end with worry is the playlist she made me of the sounds of the night and the stars from the projector. Laying in my bed, staring at the ceiling is all I can do until she returns or calls. I pull the blanket to my nose. I can still smell her.

I understand if she needs time. That's fine. Why didn't she just tell me? Why?

Oh god. What if she leaves me? The thought of living without her kills me.

So much unknown.

The one thing I do know.

Mia was right.

Love hurts.

*Please, Daffodil. Please come back to me.*

# Chapter Thirty-One

**Mia**

When I hear a knock on my door I slip the ring back in my pocket. I've been twirling it on my finger all day. It's my only connection to him and the only thing that keeps the ache in my chest at bay.

"Mia, Jonathan will meet you in the conference room. I'm heading out for the day. If you need anything please let one of the staff know. I'm only a phone call away if you decide you are ready to talk to me." Dr. Giles stands in my doorway. Tall, dark and at the moment brooding. Still there is something about him that comforts me while enticing me to challenge him at the same time.

"Sure, thanks," I mumble as I brush past him headed for the conference room.

He follows me down the hall and turns the light on for me. "Well, I'm sure he'll be along shortly. He has quite the story, Mia. Hopefully you'll feel comfortable talking with him."

I shrug my shoulders, cross my arms across my chest, lean my head back on the seat and close my eyes. Only when I hear him close the door do I open them again. My mother would scold me for my rudeness. That's not how we treat people where I'm from. Thing is, I don't want to be here. I feel trapped and Dr. Giles is top dog here, so he is getting the brunt of my irritation.

A quick tap on the door and Jonathan enters. When he closes the door behind him and turns to face me my stomach sinks.

Jonathan is a ghost.

"Oh my god," I gasp. I'm already headed towards the door when he grips me around the waist.

"Mia. Shit. Please calm down. I…I didn't know. Please, just sit down and let's talk," he says calmly. He is as shocked as I am, his face told me so.

He reaches around me and opens the door while holding me firmly around the waist with one arm. "Look, I'm opening the door. There is nothing to be scared of. We'll leave it open."

I'm trying to calm myself. It's a difficult thing to do when the man holding you is someone who threatened you while you tried to save his life. That night was like any other until I spotted him slumped over his steering wheel in the hospital parking lot. After that…everything changed.

*"If I live because of you, I will hunt you down and rest assured my next attempt at this will be successful and you will be coming along with me."*

# Death and Daffodils

He gently guides me to sit on the loveseat and sits with me, keeping an arm around my waist. "Breathe, Mia. Take some deep breaths for me."

Inhaling slowly, I try to listen to him but when I exhale a horrible sounding sob erupts. He rocks me back and forth as I cry. "I'm sorry I said those horrible things to you that night." He squeezes me tighter. "Christ, I never thought I would see you again. I've wanted to thank you and to apologize for what I said. Those words still haunt me. I didn't mean them. I didn't. That night I was so lost, I just wanted to die."

His last word is like a knife to my chest. "You, you cursed me," I cry.

"I'm so, so, sorry," he murmurs, pressing his lips to the top of my head.

"I wanted to kill myself and I couldn't. You cursed me," I whimper.

After the shock of seeing him slowly wears off and my tears dry up, I begin to get a grip. But, what astonishes me most of all is after all the time that has passed I'm meeting him here of all places.

"I didn't curse you. If you thinking I did prevented you from taking your life then I'm glad for it but it wasn't me, Mia. It was you. You were stronger than you thought. You stopped yourself from doing it. You stopped me from doing it."

After taking a deep breath I look at him. Really look at him. He smiles. "I'm Jonathan Landers," he says as he pulls his arm from around me to shake my hand. Hesitantly I take it in mine. He doesn't let go. "It's nice to finally meet you. My angel."

I blush and tear my gaze from his. "I'm no angel. I can assure you of that."

"That night you were." He releases my hand. "You saved my life."

303

I glance at him again. He's close to my age, handsome and most importantly…alive. "Hmm. I've often wondered what happened to you. If you had tried again," I say shyly, pulling my shoulder to my cheek.

He shakes his head. "No. That was my one and only attempt. While I was in the hospital recovering I decided that since I was getting a second chance perhaps I should give it a go. Test the waters and see if this time I could swim instead of sink."

Nodding, I offer him my first smile in this place. "I'm glad."

"Me too. I'm glad you're here," he says quietly.

"I'm not suicidal. My ex blackmailed me into coming here," I tell him sullenly.

"But, you were? Can I ask why? What changed?" He chuckles. "I'm sorry, I'm asking too much at once."

Should I tell him? I don't want him to blame himself for the events of that night. I've never blamed him. Not once. I was tired before I stopped to help him.

"The night I saved you I was very tired. I was overworked and pregnant." I pause and reach over to hold his hand. "That night I fell asleep at the wheel and wrecked my vehicle. I hit a family of three head on. They didn't make it. Neither did my baby."

He pulls his hand from mine and covers his mouth. "Oh god. Oh, god, Mia. If you hadn't…"

"Stop. It's not your fault. Two wise people have told me it was circumstance. Maybe it was. I don't know." He takes my hand again, so I continue. "I spent a year in jail for involuntary vehicular manslaughter.

Did my penance and when they released me I went back to my family home to die. Only I couldn't do it."

"I'm sorry." Johnathan pats my hand.

"It's okay, nothing for you to be sorry for. Slowly things have evolved. I'm happy now. I know it may not seem like it right now but I'm happy. Truly happy."

"So, this ex and his blackmailing you to come here, do you want to talk about that?"

I sigh loudly and pull my hands back into my lap.

"I'll take that as a no." He offers me a kind smile.

"Can I ask why you why you were in the parking lot that night?" I've wondered every day what caused him to take such drastic measures. It was a scary sight. So much blood. Too much blood.

"My father had just passed away in the very emergency room that ended up saving me." Johnathan stares at the wall across from us as if that night was playing out like a movie on the white paint. "He had a massive heart attack."

"Oh, I'm so sorry."

He laughs still staring at the wall. "See, now you're apologizing."

"You're right. It's a natural thing to do isn't it? To empathize with someone. To be sorry for them and their loss."

He takes a deep breath. "Yeah, it is. My father had a heart attack after I told him and my mother that I was gay."

My eyes widen with his brave admission.

He continues. "You know Dr. Giles told me that it wasn't my fault that it was circumstance." He laughs and turns to face me.

"So, you came here…for help?"

"Yep. Best decision of my life. Met my life partner here. You met Fredrick yesterday. He did your paperwork."

I grin. "I did meet him. He was nice and very handsome," I say bumping his shoulder to mine.

Johnathan pulls his billfold out of his back pocket and tugs out a photo. "This is us and our daughter. We adopted her two months ago. We named her Mia."

My eyes pop out of my head. "What?"

Chuckling loudly, he pats me on the back. "The hospital wouldn't give me your name. They said it was against policy but, I overheard a nurse telling someone that Mia had found me in the parking lot."

"This is all so unbelievable," I whisper.

"Dr. Giles always says everything happens for a reason. Sometimes we don't see it right away but, there is always a reason."

"Hmph, Dr. Giles." I roll my eyes.

He laughs. "You don't like him?"

I shrug. "I don't know. I guess I'm just grumpy I'm here. You know?"

"No, I don't know because you won't tell me but, I can tell you that Dr. Giles is a good guy." He stands and closes the door before sitting back down beside me. "I'm going to tell you something about Dr. Giles that will help you understand him better. I shouldn't because he confided this to me one night when I found him locked in his office in a drunken stupor but, I owe you for saving my life."

I make a motion to zip my lips. "His secret is safe with me."

"He does this work to counteract the actions of his son."

"I don't understand?" I blink, confused at what this means.

"His son assists people who want to commit suicide. Now don't get me wrong. These are people who are sick and dying already so that isn't the issue. It's that he thinks his son is a psychopath. He believes his son feeds his tendencies with these mercy killings. He says his son is incapable of feeling anything."

Oh.

*Oh.*

"Can you imagine losing a son that is alive? All your hopes and dreams dashed by a single diagnosis," Johnathan says sadly.

Blink. Breathe. Come on Mia.

"Um. Who diagnosed him? I mean did another doctor diagnose him or did Dr. Giles?"

He shrugs. "I'm assuming Dr. Giles. I doubt he took him to another doctor. He's spent his life trying to protect him. To keep him from

307

progressing further into the disorder. He was heartbroken the night I found him. He sobbed 'I love you son' over and over again."

My heart cracks clean the fuck open. I look up at the ceiling wishing I was outside. Wishing I was under the stars. I want to laugh. I want to cry. How did I not see the resemblance?

"I'm telling you this so that you know you can trust him. He will understand you, Mia. His child may still be alive, but he knows what it's like to lose a child. Whether you want to be here or not, you are. Let him help you."

Thomas told me there was something left for me to do in this world. Oh, how right he was.

I'm definitely going to use this time wisely. Except It won't be Dr. Giles helping me. I'm going to help him.

"Is Giles his last name?"

"No, his first. It's Dr. Giles Bennett," he says patting me on my knee. "So, you will talk to him? When he asked me to speak with you he was very concerned."

I nod slowly. "Yes, I'm sure he is concerned. I will talk to him. Thank you for sharing his story with me."

"I hope it helps you open up to him." He stands and gently pulls me to my feet. "How about you and I continue this over supper."

"That sounds great. Thank you."

My mind is running wild. Dr. Giles is Brentley's dad. I don't know how I'm going to do it but I'm going to make him see that he is wrong. Brentley is not a monster.

My child is gone but, Dr. Giles's child is not. He is alive and well. And not only that…he is the most amazing man I've ever met.

I'm going to make Dr. Giles Bennett see that.

I'm sure Darrin and Dr. Giles both agreed that I needed to be here. Darrin in hopes that I will come to my senses and leave Brentley. Dr. Giles in hopes of saving me from his monstrous son.

How sad.

I may not be able to save myself from Darrin but one thing I can do is bring a father and son together again. That way if Darrin forces me to walk away from Brentley at least he will have his dad to lean on.

The thought of leaving Brentley makes my heart hurt.

But, then again, I knew that falling in love with him would hurt.

Love always hurts.

# Chapter Thirty-Two

**Mia**

"Good morning, Mia," Dr. Giles says as he walks into his office. He takes his seat and smiles at me.

Now that I know he is Brentley's dad I can't take my eyes off him. The similarities are comforting but, they make me miss Brentley terribly. Absentmindedly I rub my hand over my heart.

"Are you okay?" he asks, leaning forward in his chair.

My hand drops. "Yes, sorry. I've been feeling a little under the weather. Probably just my nerves."

"The staff says that you have eaten little since your arrival. Would you like us to arrange for you to see a physician?" His eyes roam over me, his concern obvious.

"No, I'm fine. Like I said I think it's just nerves."

"Johnathan said you had a good visit yesterday. He was so excited he called me at home."

I smile at him. A genuine one and he visibly relaxes in his chair. "I never thought I would see him again. I'd always wondered what became of him."

"It's quite a connection you two share. He even named his daughter after you. Perhaps you will be lifelong friends."

"I'm sure we will. It's funny how things turn out isn't it?"

He chuckles. "It is. I've always said everything happens for a reason."

"I couldn't agree more." My eyes drift towards the window before turning back to him. "I'm ready to talk to you. I'm sure Darrin has told you about my accident and all of the deaths that followed."

"He did. Don't let that prevent you from telling me your perception of what happened."

"I'm fairly sure he portrayed those events accurately. Did he tell you about my parents as well?"

"Yes. Your story is one of the most tragic I've heard. I'm sorry for the loss you suffered."

"Since you know the why of what made me suicidal maybe we could begin with my attempts?" I question tipping my head.

"Mia, you can start wherever you want. I'm here to listen and give any guidance I can." He picks up his pen letting it hover over his notepad.

"When I was released from jail I couldn't wait to get home. My mind was set. I was going to end everything once I got home. I made several attempts but couldn't follow through with any of them. Something stopped me every time." I laugh as I remember sitting in the bathtub thinking I had been jinxed. "I even went as far as thinking that Jonathan had jinxed me."

He scribbles furiously over his pad, pausing to look up at me. "Why is that?"

"Let's just say he wasn't very happy when I saved him. I understand though. He thought he wanted to go. I can relate." He nods and goes back to writing on his pad.

"Do you like daffodils Dr. Giles?"

He stops writing at my sudden change of topic. His eyes shift to a photo on his desk. "Yes, my late wife had a friend who sent her daffodils every year for her birthday."

"My mother loved daffodils. After my attempts a friend of mine made me go weed my mother's flower garden. He thought I needed fresh air." I roll my eyes. "Anyway, while I was doing that I found an old coffee can buried under the yellow flowers. She hid her secrets among the beautiful blooms. In the can was the name of someone who assists with suicides."

Dr. Giles seems surprised that I so willing gave him this information. Quickly his mask falls back into place. "So, you did pay someone to help you?" he asks, a scornful glimmer in his eye.

"No. I didn't pay him. He came because he owed my mother. You see she had asked him to assist her and my father with their suicides. They had the accident before he was able to fulfill his end of the contract. My father had cancer. He was dying. My mother didn't want to live without him." As much as I try to contain my emotions I can't. I end up crying for a good ten minutes before I can speak again. Dr. Giles hands me a box of tissues.

"Are you okay to continue? Or would you like to call it a day?"

"No. I'm good. I'm sorry I just miss them so much." I dab at my eyes and cheeks.

"Whenever you're ready," he says kindly, resting his forearms on his knees.

"Anyhow, I did some digging on my mom's computer and found an email address for this person. He called himself Death."

Dr. Giles grimaces as he settles back into his chair.

"We emailed a few times and then I waited. Every morning I woke up hoping it would be my last sunrise. Hoping that Death would come. And then he did." I chuckle quietly. "I'll never forget seeing him standing on my porch with a bouquet of daffodils in hand."

Dr. Giles pulls his eyebrows together. "He brought you flowers?"

"Yes, you see I didn't sign my emails with my name. I signed each email with Daffodil." I smile. "Seems he's deemed it my nickname."

"So, you still communicate with this man?" He stabs his pen into his notepad a little too angrily.

Grinning I lean in and whisper, "He's kinda grown on me." I really enjoy the shocked look upon his face but, unfortunately the doctor is in for a whole lot more. "Do you want to know what he did after he showed up?"

He shakes his head yes.

Good, I've got him out of his professional mode.

"He locked me in a broom closet," I say, raising my eyebrows.

He leans in closer. "What? Why?"

"I had no idea at the time but, later he told me I had surprised him, and he didn't know what to do."

"You, you surprised him?" He looks as surprised as Brentley did that day.

"Yeah, I guess my reaction to him was unique. Not like his other clients, you know?"

"How did you react?"

"I was excited, and I hate to admit this but, I was a little turned on," I say quietly, heat rising to my cheeks. "I don't mean to sound cliché, but Death had never looked so good." I wiggle my eyebrows up and down.

My cheeks might be hot but, Dr. Giles is beat red. He clears his throat and pretends to be busy writing something important on his pad.

"Anyhow, he pulled me out of the closet, drug me outside and demanded to know what he was hearing." The doctor cocks an eyebrow. "Seems he had never been to the country. He was amazed he was hearing frogs and bugs. Can you believe he'd never seen the stars before? He's a city boy."

"You almost sound fond of this death person."

I sigh loudly and fold one leg under me. "I hated him at first. He was arrogant, bossy and downright infuriating. He insulted my stench and my mess. At the time that was what I needed. Someone not afraid to point out the obvious. Everyone had handled me with kid gloves. Anyway, I hadn't showered in weeks. His methods might have been a bit unconventional, but he got me to shower and to start taking care of myself again."

Dr. Giles stares at me so I continue. "I was furious when he said he wouldn't kill me. I begged him to do it…" my mind wanders to that first night when I cried on my knees in front of him. God I miss him.

"What are you thinking right now, Mia? I lost you there for a moment."

"I miss him," I whisper, blinking away tears.

"Mia, someone like this death person isn't someone you should get involved with. Are you telling me you are romantically involved with him?" I see sadness and pity etched in the worry lines of his face.

"Why?" I simply ask.

"Because someone like that is incapable of feeling. It will only lead to heartache."

"You are wrong. He feels." Dr. Giles tries to disagree with me, but I stop him by standing and walking to gaze out his window.

"He was the first person to say my daughter's name out loud."

"Mia," Dr. Giles shakes his head in total disbelief.

"No. It's true. Darrin never visited me once after my accident. Not. Once. My dad's best friend came to see me to tell me about my parents. He was the only one that came." I watch the clouds drifting lazily over the pale blue sky, wishing I was home instead of here. "The people that did talk to me never said her name. Never mentioned her. I don't blame anyone for that. Who wants to talk about dead babies?"

Dr. Giles doesn't have an answer for that. He is starting to look a bit defeated.

"That's how I knew he was different. I mean I knew he was different, obviously. But, when he asked me to talk about her and he used her name I knew he was special. He was someone who paid attention. So, I talked to him. And, you know what? I was right, he listened, really listened." I turn away from the window to study him. "Anyhow, that night he told me he wanted me to wait six months."

"So, you're still considering suicide as an option? That is why you are still in contact with him?" His hand is paused above his pad, waiting for my answer so he can record it in ink.

"No. I want to live. I'm still in contact with him because he lives with me."

He releases a long drawn out breath and raises his eyebrows. "This is all...I don't know, Mia. This is a lot to process even for me."

I walk back over to the couch and sit down again. "Each morning Death would get up and leave the house. One day I followed him. He went to my parent's and daughter's grave site. They're buried on a little hill a half a mile or so behind my home. I hadn't had the courage to visit them. I didn't even know my dad's friend had them buried there. When I saw Death lay a bouquet of daffodils on my mother's grave...." I pause and lean towards him looking him dead in the eye. "Well that's when I started to fall in love with him."

He pulls his head back. "You…you…what did you just say?"

"That's when I began to fall in love with him." I shrug easily. "I was surprised he chose daffodils. It was her favorite flower. Turns out he knew my mother and not just because of their contract." I study the doctor's face closely. "Our mothers had been college roommates."

I watch as he puts the puzzle together. When it clicks into place the color drains from his face.

"I'm sorry, Mia but I have another patient I need to meet with. Can we continue tomorrow?" He rushes to his desk, keeping his face turned away from me.

"Sure thing. I'll see you tomorrow then." I make my way slowly to the door.

Before I walk out I turn to him. "I'm glad you believe everything happens for a reason. Perhaps together we can figure out my reason for being here." As I shut the door I see him drop into his desk chair and put his head in his hands.

It takes ginormous effort to walk away. All I want to do is hug him. He is the father of the man I love after all. I owe him everything.

But, he needs time to digest everything I just laid at his feet. Darrin told him that I had hired his son to kill me but what he didn't tell him was that we were connected long before that.

### Brentley

317

When I open the door, Bandit comes running to me. "Hey, boy." I pat his head and glance around the empty kitchen.

God I miss her.

I had to come back. I couldn't feel her there. Here I see her everywhere. Standing at the kitchen sink washing dishes while I read to her. In the bedroom, in the shower, in the garden…she is everywhere.

If she needs time to think that is what she needs. It doesn't mean she is leaving me. It only means she needs time. She will return. I have faith.

At least I hope that is the case because if she is hurt…no, I can't think that way.

Anyhow, she would want me here, taking care of things. The garden and flower beds are in desperate need of weeding. There is irrigating to check on. Cattle to tend. Thomas and Matt shouldn't have to take care of everything by themselves. She would expect me to carry on.

When she gets back all will be in order. She will explain and everything will be okay.

It will. Everything will be fine.

At least I know I can still feel without her presence.

I feel all right. I feel so many things right now. But, most importantly I feel her love.

She loves me.

I hope she can feel mine.

Wherever she is.

# Chapter Thirty-Three

**Mia**

The next day Dr. Giles is ready for me. His mask firmly in place. Exactly what I was expecting. Doesn't matter. That was just the tip of the iceberg.

I plop down on the couch and lay my head back to stare at the ceiling.

"Fredrick told me you were not feeling well earlier this morning."

Sighing I tilt my head to look at him. "I've been thinking about what you said."

"Oh?" he tilts his head and my heart pitter-patters. It's as if Brentley is sitting across from me. They share the same mannerisms.

# Death and Daffodils

"About how someone like Death couldn't have feelings."

"I'm glad you thought about it, Mia. It's nice to see you taking your therapy seriously," he says picking up his pen ready to document his perceptions of my life.

I smile at him but remain silent.

"Would you like to tell me what your thoughts were?" he prompts.

"I thought about all the times I saw Death experience emotion. Or at least I thought he was but I'm not the expert. Could I tell you? Would you be able to tell me if he was well and truly feeling or if he was simply mimicking what he thought was an appropriate emotional response?"

"Without being there I couldn't say for certain, but I would like to hear some examples. Psychopaths are good at mimicking as you put it. They watch others to learn how the majority reacts to certain situations."

"Is that what you think he is?"

"I've never met him, Mia. I cannot be certain what he is, other than someone you asked to help end your life."

"I've seen him blush," I say, like it's a secret.

He smiles at this. "You have?"

I nod. "Surely that's a good sign."

Laughing he sets his pen and pad down on the table.

Halleluiah, he set the damn notebook down.

"It could be a good sign. Other than blushing why do you think he can feel?" He is leaning in towards me, on the edge of his seat. He is thirsty for information about his son.

"He gets excited over the smallest things. Like when our garden first sprouted and when I taught him to drive. I even took him to his first carnival which by the way is where he got his first kiss." I blush and dip my head, truly embarrassed. This isn't something you normally talk to your future father-in-law about but, I have to make him see. "I told him his first kiss would be special because he had waited so long for it. I didn't know that it would be me. But, when we were up on that Ferris wheel under a blanket off stars, I suddenly wanted it to be me. I wanted to be his first...his only."

He doesn't say anything. He blinks slowly. He is breaking.

"He is also humble, an emotion I wouldn't think a psychopath would be capable of. One night I told him I thought Erelah had brought us together and his response was that he didn't deserve her magic." Brentley's dad frowns. "I told him he was the person who had shown her the most care and that she would have loved him."

"He didn't believe me but it's true. She would have. The flowers he took to her grave everyday was just the beginning of the care he showed her. He taught me that I could keep her memory alive and to be honest that was what turned my death wish around. If I could keep her memory alive it was a reason to live. He saved me Dr. Giles." He hands me a tissue. I didn't even realize I had been crying.

I laugh, patting at my face. "He hung glow in the dark stars for her in a tree above her grave so that she can see them even when it's cloudy. He created a memorial fund for the dance program at the local high school in her name. Do you know why he choose the dance team? Because I had

322

once told him that I thought she would have been a gymnast or a ballerina. He had listened to me. A staff member told me about the memorial. He didn't do it for accolades. Would a psychopath do that?"

He blinks a few times. "I…Mia, I don't know. Without observing him I can't answer that."

"Could I show you? I mean I have a video and a few pictures on my phone. Would you like to see them?"

"Mia, we don't allow phones."

"I'm not going to call or message anyone. You can hold it the whole time. I won't even touch it. Promise." I draw an imaginary cross over my chest.

He sighs and runs his hand over his face. I'm sure he is fearful of what he will see. On one hand, if he sees the psychopath, his son is still lost to him. On the other, if he sees the Brentley he remembers before his wife's death then he will think he failed him.

"I…okay. Wait here, I'll go get it."

When he returns he sits down next to me on the couch. I smile at him like an idiot. I'm giddy sitting next to him. My soon to be father-in-law. That is if I can get away from Darrin.

He powers the phone on, and my phone does nothing but ding with messages for a few minutes. My heart aches. I know everyone is probably so worried about me. Dr. Giles looks at me with concern. "Did your friends and family not know you were coming here? You have a lot of messages."

I shake my head no, unable to speak or meet his eye. I recite my passcode and then help him find my photo app. "Start there."

He looks at me then slowly glances down at the image. It's a selfie of Brentley and I at the carnival. Our noses covered in powdered sugar from the funnel cake we had shared. We are both laughing, our eyes sparkling with reflections of the carnival lights. He swallows hard and begins swiping through the remaining photos. He stops on one I took of Brentley when he wasn't looking. He's lying in the grass cloud watching, one of our favorite past-times. Brentley has a smile on his face, and he looks peaceful.

"I know you are concerned that this man will hurt me. He won't. He has given up his profession." I continue in my defense of Brentley. "When he was a little boy he shut his feelings off to cope, to survive. I think he became Death to keep a connection to his mother."

"What changed? Why now?" he asks running his thumb over the phone screen not able to take his eyes away from the image of his smiling son.

"Me," I answer simply.

"You sound just like him," he says, laughing. When he realizes what he said he quickly looks away and scrolls to the next photo.

Before he gets to the last photo I have him click on a video.

*"Are you taping me, Daffodil," Brentley says stalking towards me.*

*"Nope," I tease, sidestepping him.*

*Brentley chases me. I drop the phone to my side and run from him laughing. When he catches me, the phone falls to the floor by the couch.*

Now the video only shows the ceiling but, it's not what Dr. Giles needs to see, it's what he needs to hear.

*Brentley is tickling me.*

*"Brentley stop I'll pee my pants," I say laughing so hard I'm breathless.*

*"What will you give me if I stop," he says panting from the effort of keeping me held down.*

*"I'll…ah…Brentley, this isn't fair. You're bigger than me," I cry.*

*"Come on, Daffodil. What will you give me?"*

*"I'll…shit…I'll tell you a secret," I scream.*

*"Oh, yes. I love secrets," Brentley says clapping. He climbs off of me and helps me sit up. "Spill it," he demands once I'm upright.*

*"Geez, let me catch my breath," I laugh.*

*"You're stalling," he accuses.*

*"No, I'm not."*

*He leans over to pin me again. "Okay, okay. I'll tell you." I pause and grab his cheeks in my hands. "I love you."*

*"Phst, that's no secret," he scoffs.*

*"It is. It's the first time I've said it to your face."*

*"You don't need to say it to me. I feel it," he says.*

*"I hope so," I whisper.*

*"I feel it all the way to my bones, Mia."*

Kissing noises follow. "Um, you might want to shut that off before…um, you know?"

Dr. Giles practically drops the phone in his hurry to shut the video off making me giggle.

He looks at me. Really looks at me. Not as a patient but as someone who loves his son as much as he does.

"There's one more photo. It's the most recent. It was taken the night before I came here."

As he is opening the photo app again I pull my ring out of my pocket and slide it on my finger. I lean over to look at the photo with him. The waitress took it for us right after he proposed to me. My hand is on Brentley's chest. The ring sparkling against the lights.

A tear slips from his eye and plops onto the screen.

"He asked me to marry him. It was the most beautiful moment of my entire life. His mother gave him her wedding ring the day she passed away. Her last gift to him. Her last words were 'find love and you'll find life'. Brentley and I found both," I say quietly. His eyes dart to mine at my mention of his son's real name.

Our tearful eyes mirror each other.

"I love your son, Dr. Giles. He is my life." I place my hand over his. He looks down at the ring on my finger. He grips my hand and rubs his thumb back and forth over it.

He breaks.

I pull him into my arms and hold him tightly. "Circumstance broke him as a boy. Circumstance made you do what you thought was best for him. Circumstance is to blame."

He sobs louder at my words. Once he quiets down. I pull away from him. "I know this is a lot to absorb. Tomorrow, same time?" I tease, offering him a genuine smile.

He nods and wipes his eyes on the sleeve of his dress shirt. "I didn't know, Mia."

"I know you didn't but, you do now." I give him a kiss on the cheek and then walk out of his office.

# Chapter Thirty-Four

**Mia**

The next day I wake up praying to the porcelain god. What the hell? I thought after coming clean yesterday I would feel better. Who am I kidding? I won't feel better until I'm back with Brentley. If I ever get back to him.

When I finally feel good enough to leave my bed I head down to Dr. Giles's office. He is sitting at his desk. He motions for me to take the chair across from him. Okay I guess we aren't doing the *therapy* thing today.

"How did he get you to come here?" he asks before my butt even hits the chair.

"Darrin?"

# Death and Daffodils

"Yes," he says tensely.

I'm afraid to tell him. Will he blame me for getting Brentley caught up in this mess with Darrin?

"Mia," he warns, so much like Brentley it's scary.

"He threatened to turn Brentley into the authorities."

He laughs.

Wait. Why is he laughing?

"You don't have to worry about that, Mia. Brentley is good at what he does. Darrin does not have anything on him." He leans back in his chair.

I on the other hand worry my bottom lip between my teeth. "You sound like him." He laughs again. "I don't think I can risk it. I won't risk it."

He cocks his head to one side and studies me intently. "I see why he loves you."

"I don't know why he loves me." I shake my head and put my face in my hands. "I miss him so much it hurts," I cry.

He stands and comes around the desk to kneel in front of me. "Listen, Mia. I've spent a lifetime trying to protect Brentley. Darrin. Has. Nothing. I'm certain of it."

I peek at him between my fingers. "You're sure?"

He pulls my hands away from my face. "I'm sure." His smile melts my heart. "When Darrin came to me he told me you had hired my son to assist in your suicide. I thought Brentley was escalating to the next level."

329

He swallows hard before continuing. "I only wanted to help you, Mia. I didn't know your ex-husband was blackmailing you. I also didn't know that you had fallen in love with my son."

"But, you knew he had changed?"

He nods. "I'm sorry, Mia. I'm going to make this right. How about we work on a plan to get you home?"

We spend the next hour talking about Darrin and honestly it feels good to get it all out. I tell him things I hadn't even been able to tell his son.

I'm still not feeling well so he sends me back to my room telling me not to worry. Our plan is to confront Darrin on Sunday when he comes to visit. He asked me to trust him and that's what I'm going to do.

I trust him because he loves his son. It's obvious. He won't do anything to jeopardize Brentley.

By the time Sunday rolls around I can't eat anything. Nothing stays down. I'm so nervous.

Giles hired an attorney who is with us in the room. He also informed me that there are two officers in street clothes in the lobby in case Darrin gets out of hand.

When Darrin comes in he heads right for me. Giles steps in front of him. "Why don't you have a chair over there." He points to a chair on the opposite side of the table.

Darrin sits down and throws me a questioning glance. I look away. The air ripples with the tension coming off him. "Mia?"

"Mr. Everett, I'm going to advise you to not speak to my client," the attorney tells him. "Let's get right to business. Mrs. Everett, has a restraining order against you and you have broken that order twice now."

"That's because she needs help. She *asked* for my help," Darrin says, so mad he is spitting.

My attorney pushes the pictures I took of my injuries all those years ago in front of Darrin. He fans them out like a deck of cards. Darrin's murderous gaze rises to meet mine. "Mrs. Everett does not want to see you. She's maintaining the restraining order against you."

Brentley's dad speaks up. "Mia told me you are an attorney yourself. I'm sure you understand the conditions of the order. I'm sure you also understand how these photos might look to your employer."

My attorney adds, "Mrs. Everett is being overly generous in my opinion by not turning these photos over to the police and filing charges against you. To be clear I have advised her to do just that. Seems she is willing to give you another chance for the sake of the child you have on the way."

Darrin shoves the papers away from him sending them flying off the table. "Go ahead, Mia. Marry the doctor's freak of a son. I hope you're happy."

He knew about the engagement. How long has he been watching me? When I don't respond he huffs and stands to leave.

"One more thing," Dr. Giles says. "I would take real good care of your wife and child. Mia will press charges if she catches even a hint that either are in danger or have been harmed."

Darrin stomps out and slams the door behind him.

I cover my hand over my mouth to stifle a sob. This was a long time coming. Something I should have done a long time ago. Thanks to Brentley and his father I finally had the courage to do it.

The attorney places all the paperwork back in his briefcase. "Mia, please call if you need anything else from me. He seems to have gotten the message loud and clear. Hopefully this is the end of it for you." He shakes my hand and then Dr. Giles's.

Brentley's dad pushes my chair away from the table and kneels in front of me. "Mia, let's get you home." He pulls two plane tickets from his back pocket.

"You're coming with me?" I ask on a hiccup.

"I think I need to apologize to my son for a few things. So, if it's okay with you, could I please accompany you home?" he asks shyly.

"I would like that."

# Chapter Thirty-Five

**Brentley**

Bandit is nipping at my nose and barking in my face. "What is it boy?" I roll over and look at my phone. "Who needs an alarm clock when I got you." I try to scratch his ears but that's not what he wants. He jumps off the bed and scratches at the door. "Are you in that big of a hurry to go out this morning?"

Just as I slide a pair of sweats up over my hips the door opens making me jump. "Shit, Mia, you scared me."

She sets her bags by her feet and stands in the doorway staring at me while Bandit bounces around her.

It's Mia.

She's here.

Relief washes over me in buckets and air fills my lungs.

She bends over and pats Bandit on the head, which seems to satisfy him. He rushes out the door past her. She chuckles. "Well he must not have missed me too much," she says, rising and closing the door behind her.

"He missed you terribly. We both did," I reply, finally finding my voice.

She drops her shoulders and lowers her eyes to the floor. "I'm glad you're here. I mean I was worried you would stay in the city and I know how much you like it here." She scratches her head. She's nervous.

"I figured you would want me here to help Matt and Thomas."

She nods, avoiding eye contact.

And then…

She is jumping in my arms, hugging me so tight I can hardly breathe. "I missed you so much," she cries.

"Hey, shhh. It's okay, Mia. It's okay." I run my hand down her hair, soothing her. I sit on the bed with her wrapped around me.

"Darrin tricked me," she whispers into my neck.

He. Is. A. Dead. Man.

"Did he hurt you?" I push her away from me so I can inspect every inch of her. She wipes at her face as I continue my inspection. No bruises. Thank god.

"He...he didn't." Her gaze locks on mine and all is right in the world again. Mia is in my arms.

She tucks herself back under my chin and she tells me everything that happened the past week.

I don't even know what to say.

That bastard. I thought she needed time to think about marrying me and this whole time she was locked up at my father's facility. They deceived my girl. "I'm so sorry, Mia. I didn't know. If I'd known I would have come for you."

"It's okay. I'm glad it happened. I think Darrin will leave us alone now. Your dad helped me, Brentley."

"I'm so angry at him," I whisper.

"Don't be. He loves you."

"That was a terrible thing to do to you." I hug her tightly. Thank god he didn't convince her to walk away from me.

"Your dad thought I was there willingly until he figured out who I was, and I explained to him how much I love you."

"You told him you loved me? How did that go?" I run my nose along her cheek, nuzzling it under her ear. She smells so good. I've missed her so damn much.

"I did. He was actually quite happy. Said he never dreamed he would have a daughter-in-law."

I stop nuzzling. "You told him we were engaged?" She nods. I pull away and look at her.

"Um, he's downstairs."

I blink at her. Did she say my father is here? In this house?

"Don't worry, Brentley. He knows he was wrong. I made him see you aren't the person he thought you were."

I stare at her ear and trace my finger over the shell of it. "What…what if you hadn't made him see? What if he had talked you into leaving me? I can't stand the thought of losing you."

"You didn't lose me. There is nothing that anyone could tell me that would make me walk away, Brentley. I love you. I know you and that's all that matters. I don't care what anyone else thinks of you or me. We're a team, nobody can change that."

I allow myself to look her in the eye. She is telling me the truth.

My mouth clashes against hers. I've missed her so much. So, fucking much. Our teeth click against each other. Our tongues battle for more. More. God, I've missed this. Missed her. Her. Her. Her.

"Wait," she says breathlessly pushing on my shoulders. "I…I've got something I need to talk to you about."

She climbs off my lap and grabs a grocery bag out of her luggage. She sits beside me on the bed and dumps the contents on the mattress between us.

It takes me a fat minute to figure out what I'm looking at. When my eyes meet hers, she is crying.

Shit.

One time.

On the school steps.

Shit.

I toss everything back in the bag, pull her to her feet and drag her down to the bathroom. I hear my dad talking to Bandit but, I ignore it. After closing the door behind us I pull her into my arms. "Whatever happens it will be okay. I'm not leaving you. We can do this, Mia. You can do this." She nods against my chest.

"I…I haven't been feeling well. At the airport I felt terrible. I thought to myself that I hadn't felt this bad since I was pregnant. Then it hit me, and I ran to the little store in the airport. I bought every test they had."

"Why didn't you do them there?"

She squeezes me tighter. "I needed you. I can't do this alone, Brentley," she mumbles into my chest.

"You don't have to do it alone. As long as I'm alive, Mia, I'll always be here for you." She takes a deep breath and takes a step out of my arms.

"Ready?" I ask her. She nods once.

We both busy ourselves taking all of the test kits out of their packaging and setting them on the counter. Neither of us speak as we work. When everything is laid out I hand her the cup. She takes it from me.

"I love you, Mia."

"I know. I love you too," she says. She quickly fills the cup and hands it back to me.

As I prep each test she flushes the toilet and then takes a seat on the edge of the tub behind me.

Now, all we have to do is wait.

I take a seat beside her and lock her hand in mine.

Two minutes never lasted so long.

When the timer on my phone goes off we both jump.

Before we stand I turn to her. "Mia, no matter what those show, Erelah will always be our first child. Always. We are not replacing her."

She nods, tears streaming down her face.

"Our children will know her. We…" I motion between us, "will keep her memory alive."

She hugs me tight. "I'm scared," she whispers.

"It's okay to be scared." I place a kiss to the top of her hair. We stand and take a few steps as if we are approaching the edge of a cliff. Our eyes lock in the mirror. "Count of three?"

She nods.

"One. Two. Three," I count out loud. We both jump, looking down at the same time.

A tsunami of feelings almost knocks me off my feet, stealing my breath away.

Love…love…love.

The words pound in my chest with each beat of my heart.

Mia lifts her eyes to mine and whispers, "What do you feel?"

"Everything. I feel everything, Daffodil."

She smiles.

I drop to my knees and turn her so that I can lay my head against her stomach. "I'm the luckiest man on the planet," I murmur to her and our unborn child.

Mia starts to laugh. I glance up at her. "Your dad was shocked to find out he was getting a daughter-in-law. What will he think about this?"

I rise to my feet and pick her up spinning her in a circle around the bathroom. "I don't care what anyone thinks. My god, Mia. We are having a baby. A baby. I thought planting a garden was exhilarating. This…this is…" I set her on her feet and turn to stare at the positive test strips, bracing my arms against the counter.

"Brentley?" Mia places her hand on my back. "What's wrong?"

I look over my shoulder. "I've only been Death. I never thought I would create life."

I hang my head between my arms. She hugs me from behind. "You'll be a great dad."

"I don't know the first thing about being a father, Mia."

"You do. You've already been one to Erelah."

How did I get so lucky? How?

"You'll tell me if I do something wrong?" I ask.

She giggles. "You know I will. But, something tells me you'll be a natural."

When I glance at her over my shoulder again, she smirks.

"You're right. What am I worried about?"

# Chapter Thirty-Six

**Mia**

Brentley had been excited to show his dad the farm. He was like a kid dragging him all over the place, chatting a mile a minute. What was exciting to me was seeing the expression on Giles's face. It was like he was seeing his son for the first time in years. Actually, since he was eight.

We didn't tell him about the baby that day. We haven't told anyone. It's been nice keeping it to ourselves. But, I'm four months along now and it's getting harder and harder to hide my belly. Plus, we are both bursting at the seams to tell someone.

Brentley opens the door of old blue for me. "Are you nervous?" he asks as I slide in.

"No. Are you?"

"Nope," he says grinning from ear to ear. He walks in front of the truck, knocking on the hood as he makes his way around.

I smile at him through the windshield.

Today is our wedding day.

Nothing fancy. Just a simple church wedding with our closest friends and family.

Brentley and I are anything but traditional. Him in his black dress slacks, blue shirt and no tie and me in a bright, blue sundress that matches my eyes.

I finger the heart locket hanging around my neck. Since, Brentley came into my life I can feel her. He made her real. I glance over at him and he gives me a toothy smile. I'm happy I didn't go through with my suicide. I would have missed all of this. Finding love. Getting married. Having another child. I was certain there was nothing left for me. How wrong I was.

When we pull up to the church Thomas and Giles are waiting outside on the steps for us. Brentley helps me out of the pickup.

"You kids excited to get this thing done?" Thomas asks.

"Yes," I squeal and rush to give him a big hug. "Wait, you don't smell like yourself." I pat his front pocket. No cigarettes.

"Yeah, darlin, I gave up smoking. Someone gave me a reason to quit."

I smile at him and kiss him on the cheek. "Well, I'm about to give you another reason."

He leans back. "What do you have up your sleeve now? I thought walking you up the aisle was a good enough reason. I had big shoes to fill. Your dad was a great man."

"You're a great man," I shove at his chest.

He chuckles and backs up so Brentley's dad can have his turn hugging me. "What's this big news you two couldn't wait to tell us. You got a whole church full of people waiting on us," Giles chides.

Brentley wraps his arms around me so that my back is pressed to his chest. "Go on, tell them," he whispers in my ear.

"You guys are both going to be grandpas," I blurt out.

God, that felt good. I've been dying to tell someone.

They both stand with their mouths hanging open. Once the shock wears off they begin hugging each other and then us.

Giles pulls me into an embrace and whispers to me, "Thank you, Mia. You've given this father the dreams for his son back. I've never wanted anything more than for Brentley to find someone to love him and more importantly for him to feel love for someone else. Thank you."

After many tears, hugs and smiles are passed, Brentley and his father disappear inside the church. Thomas and I wait a few minutes before following.

His hand reaches out to open the door, but I stop him. "You're not getting cold feet are you, darlin?" Thomas asks, a concerned frown on his face.

"No, I just never thanked you for making me pull the weeds in mom's flower garden. Thank you." I glance up to bright blue sky and say a quick thank you to my mom as well.

Thomas chuckles. "Nothing like fresh air and a hard day's work to get you out of a slump."

I roll my eyes but give him another peck on the cheek before he opens the doors wide.

Once inside my heart melts and I fall in love with Brentley all over again. He has outdone himself.

Each pew has a coffee can filled with daffodils tied to the end. As I pass each bright yellow display I replay the moments that brought Death and Daffodil together. Two souls who found each other despite the odds. When we reach the final pew, I see four empty spots reserved for our mothers, my father and Erelah.

Thomas gives me a gentle kiss on the cheek before handing me over to Brentley.

I stare into his eyes.

We are no longer Death and Daffodil, two lost souls.

We are simply Brentley and Mia, two souls who found love through death…and then, life through love.

*When we started this tale, I thought I was telling you the story of how my life would end.*

*I guess I was wrong.*

Death and Daffodils

*You never know what awaits on the next page.*

## The End

# Epilogue

## Mia

"Papa is makin brefast," Jaxon says as he crawls over Brentley to settle in bed between us.

"He is?" I say. Brentley grunts getting a four-year old knee in the stomach.

Jaxon nods as he snuggles down under our covers.

"What's he making?"

"Bread with an egg in the middle."

"Ohh, my favorite." Brentley rolls over and tickles Jaxon giving me a view of his tiny, white teeth as he giggles.

"I want to pop the balloons now," Jaxon tells us sitting up tall in our bed.

"We have to wait until our friends come so we can all be surprised together."

"But, I want to see the stars," Jaxon pouts.

"Stars? It's daytime, Jax, you can't see stars in the daytime. They only show their light at night." I tell him as I brush his baby soft hair away from his eyes. He is beautiful, just like his dad.

"I already know what the baby is…it's a secret," he cups his little hands around his mouth and whispers.

"How do you know? Mommy doesn't even know, and the baby is in her belly," Brentley teases while tickling him some more.

Jaxson scrambles back over Brentley and jumps off the bed, his arms spread wide. "Erelah told me and she is sending daytime stars," he squeals and then darts out the door.

Brentley and I stare at each other but neither of us comment. Jaxon has said strange things like this before. At Christmas last year he told us he knew he was getting a train because Erelah had told him he was. He was right, it was hiding in our closet. I thought maybe he had peeked.

Anyhow, we decided then that we would let him believe what he wanted. Whether it's true or not, we didn't see the harm in him believing that his sister was communicating with him. It doesn't happen a lot. Usually, it's times like this when something exciting is about to happen. Today is our baby's gender reveal party.

After breakfast we get busy setting up for the party. As our guests begin to arrive little Jaxon tells everyone that he already knows what the baby is but, he doesn't reveal his secret knowledge. I watch out the window as he cups his mouth and leans into my friend Johnathan's ear. I'm so glad he and Mia made it. Johnathan and I have gotten close over the years. He is always someone I can call on my bad days. Johnathan smiles kindly at my son, melting my heart.

"Whatcha thinking about, Daffodil," Brentley says, sneaking up behind me and wrapping his strong arms around me.

"How full of friends and family our yard is." I lean my head back against his chest and sigh. We watch quietly for a moment, chuckling when we see Thomas swat Dina on the behind. They are engaged. I guess she wasn't as much of a tease as he thought.

My eyes roam over to Matt, Tina and their son, James. I'm happy to report that James has been in remission for the past four years with no signs of his cancer returning. Jaxon runs over to James. Little Jax looks up to him like a big brother. James tosses a football at him, ruffling his hair.

Rebecca is even here. I sent her a letter before Brentley and I married, letting her know that if she ever needed a friend she knew where to find me. Unfortunately, she did. Brentley and I moved her into Darrin's old farmhouse, rent free. We put our differences aside and are slowly becoming friends. Her daughter, Hailee is Erelah's sister after all.

Needless to say, Rebecca was stronger than I had been. She turned Darrin in the first time he hit her. Between her and I we found the courage to report everything. He ran. We think he's in Mexico. Needless to say, I don't think we will see him ever again.

"Definitely lots of love out there." Brentley kisses my temple. "Remember, whatever the sex of the baby, Erelah will always be our first child, our first daughter. We are not replacing her."

I smile up at him. "You always know the right things to say to me."

"I say the truth, Mia. Not just what you want to hear," he reminds me.

I turn in his arms and place a kiss to his warm lips. "Even if it's that I stink," I tease.

"Even then," he says laughing. I love his laugh. Warm, rich and rumbly.

"Come on, they're all waiting," I say, pulling him behind me.

There are three big, black balloons floating just above our heads. One for each of us. "On the count of three," Brentley says to Jaxon and me. "One. Two. Three," he counts out loud.

Pop. Pop. Pop.

Jaxon squeals in delight. "Stars. I told you she was sending stars!" he exclaims.

Our friends all cheer.

Brentley and I stare at each other. Pink stars dust our hair and shoulders. Brentley huffs to blow one away that is caught in his eyelash.

"What in the…" he laughs, and I laugh too.

"It's a girl," I whisper in awe and throw myself into Brentley's arms, pinning Jaxon between us.

"Ugh, gross," Jaxon grumbles, squeezing his way out. "Time for cake," he yells as he runs over to the table with all of the food, Bandit hot on his heels.

Later that night after everyone has left the three of us decided to lay out on a blanket and star gaze.

Giles is quietly watching us from the porch. Swinging gently back and forth on the porch swing with Bandit sleeping by his feet. He moved in with us after he retired last year. It's been nice having him around. Jaxon loves having his grandpa here.

"Which one is Erelah's," Jaxon asks like he does every night we star gaze.

Brentley points up to the sky. "See the big one there surrounded by the three tiny ones?" Jaxon nods. "That's your sister's star," Brentley says, kissing Jaxon on the forehead.

On Erelah's first birthday Brentley had a star named after her. I'd like to say I've gotten used to the sweet gestures he does for my daughter...our daughter but I haven't. Every time he does something for her, I fall in love with him all over again.

"I'm going to go show papa," Jaxon says, hopping up and running over to Giles.

Brentley and I watch as he settles on his grandfather's lap and points to the night sky.

And, then I let my eyes wander over Brentley. My dark knight.

When he tears his gaze from his father and son he notices me staring at him.

"What are you feeling right now," I ask him.

"Everything...with you I feel everything, Mia." He tucks his arm under his head and stares up at the sky. "But, right now, my overwhelming feeling is happiness. I'm happy that I have you to share all this with."

I curl my big bellied self into his side and lay my head on his chest. "I told you it was always better to share things with someone. I'm glad you're my someone." He kisses the top of my head as I close my eyes, listening to the crickets' chirp. And, as always my mind drifts to my baby.

*Goodnight sweet Erelah*

**If you or someone you know is need of help please call the number below. You are not alone.**

**National Suicide Prevention Lifeline: 1-800-273-8255**

# About the Author

LM Terry is an upcoming romance novelist. She has spent her life in the Midwest, growing up near a public library which helped fuel her love of books. With most of her eight children grown and with the support of her husband, she decided to follow her heart and begin her writing journey. In searching for that happily ever after, her characters have been enticing her to share their sinfully dark, delectable tales. She knows the world is filled with shadows and dark truths and is happy to give these characters the platform they have been begging for. This is her fourth novel and definitely not her last.

Facebook: https://www.facebook.com/lmterryauthor/

Website: https://www.lmterryauthor

Made in the USA
Columbia, SC
05 February 2020